RIVER OF NIGHT

SHADOW KINGDOM
BOOK 1

NAOMI KUTTNER

Copyright © 2022 by Naomi Kuttner

All rights reserved.

No part of this book may be reproduced in any form or by any electronic or mechanical means, including information storage and retrieval systems, without written permission from the author, except for the use of brief quotations in a book review.

For my awesome beta readers

(you know who you are.)

Thanks a million.

1

This was the summer that divided Ivan's life cleanly in two.

He remembered it in a heady mix of bright colours shot through with shadows and darkness. Afterwards, everything changed.

The beginning, though, was simple. It started with a high school fight between Ivan and his best friend, Anders.

Ivan leaned his head back against the wall and felt the blood pool in his nose. His pulse slowly returned to normal, but the bitter swirl of emotions still churned his stomach.

"Pinch it. That'll stop the bleeding." His best friend Anders offered advice.

Ivan glared at him. "Go f-" he swallowed the abuse along with some blood from his nose and closed his eyes. He rested his head against the wall again and tried not to think about what had just gone down.

They were sitting on two chairs in the corridor outside the principal's office. It was Ivan's last day of high school. It was supposed to be fun. There was no more schoolwork to do and all the excitement of the summer holidays ahead.

Except Ivan had a secret—something he'd trusted only to Anders, his best friend. And Anders had betrayed his secret.

"Look, I'm sorry..." began Anders.

Ivan's fist clenched, and for a moment, he wondered whether it was worth finishing the fight right here, outside the principal's office. *Probably not.*

"Just shut up," he said. Slowly, he unclenched his fist.

It had happened like this. Ivan and Anders had been walking back to class after lunch, following Hamish and the rugby crowd.

The two friends were mock-arguing about their summer plans. Looking back, perhaps it hadn't felt that way to Anders.

"All I'm saying is, don't ditch your friends just because you're in looove." Ivan emphasised the last word, rolling his eyes.

Anders drew back, offended.

"What, you think I'm going to that Viking weekend with you instead?"

He said it loudly.

Hamish turned round, glee lighting up his face.

"Ivan's into Viking cosplay?" He smirked. "That lame as costumed nerd thing? What a freak."

Ivan stared at Anders, the blood rushing to his face. Anders looked horrified for a moment, then recovered. He squared his shoulders and grinned, trying to turn it into a joke. "Yeah, he's well into it. That's why I'll be hanging out with my girlfriend this summer."

Before he'd realised what he was doing, Ivan's fists were up, his heart pounding.

Anders raised his own hands instinctively.

"Oooh, Viking boy wants to fight," crowed Hamish. The slow chant of 'fight, fight, fight' started around the group of rugby heads, who quickly formed a tight circle around them.

"Hey, cool it, bro," said Anders, but Ivan was too angry to speak.

All his feelings came out in the uppercut that buried itself in Anders's gut. Anders doubled over, wheezing, and was pushed back towards Ivan by the boys behind him. He came back swinging, a roundhouse that Ivan barely blocked before a straight jab caught him in the nose.

Ivan stumbled back to a chorus of jeers from the crowd, and the fight was on.

They ended up in a clinch, each with an arm around the other's neck, pounding their free fists into each other's sides.

A hand caught Ivan's collar, yanking him backwards. The deputy principal and caretaker had arrived. The ring of onlookers abruptly dispersed, leaving Ivan and Anders facing each other, chests heaving.

Ivan's gaze burned, but he didn't take his eyes off Anders. Anders's blond curls were dishevelled, his usually cheerful face flushed, fists clenched. Ivan tasted blood as he bared his teeth at Anders.

What a great way to end the last day of high school.

Back outside the principal's office, Ivan opened his eyes and studied the ceiling. He couldn't bring himself to look at Anders. He had trusted him. He had thought Anders was his friend.

Not anymore, he isn't.

A crisp voice from inside the principal's office said, 'Enter.' Ivan trooped in behind Anders and slumped down in one of the two chairs facing the desk, angling himself away from Anders.

Their school principal was Ms Andrews, a thin lady in her fifties with hair neatly tied in a grey bun.

"Pinch your nose to stop the bleeding," she said, handing him a tissue. Ivan took the tissue and pinched.

Behind her desk, Ms Andrews regarded them both evenly.

"I would like to know, Ivan, why you ruined your excellent record at this school by fighting on the last day. With, I understand, your best friend."

Ivan didn't want to explain anything. That would just make it worse.

He'd been into Viking history for years. Then, last year, he'd found a forum on Viking historical reenactments. They had become his secret joy and his secret shame. He'd never meant for anyone in his home town find out. And now they had.

"Whenever you're ready, Ivan."

"I, uh—"

"It was my fault," said Anders. His blue eyes shone with honesty. "I betrayed a confidence and let Ivan down. I'm sorry, and I take full responsibility for what happened."

Ivan didn't look at Anders, but his whole face heated. *Now I feel like crap, and I have to forgive Anders for his big mouth.* A cold hard feeling settled in the region of his chest. *I don't care. I don't forgive him, and I'm never going to trust him again, ever. It's over.*

"Is that true, Ivan?" Ms Andrews turned steely eyes on Ivan.

He shrugged. "Yeah, sure. Whatever."

Anders, who had been looking hopeful, looked hurt, but Ivan didn't care. He was too busy feeling the cold, hard feeling take hold of his chest. Slowly he unclenched his hands and rubbed where his knuckles had lost some skin in the fight. *I'm going to leave this town behind if it's the last thing I do. This town, and these people.*

He tuned in again as Ms Andrews finished her lecture, gave them both detentions and said they had to shake hands before they left.

Ivan stood, scraping his chair back, and Anders did the same. They were almost the same height, but where Ivan was lean, with dark hair and a pale face, Anders was solidly built, with curly blonde hair, golden skin and clear blue eyes.

Ivan directed his gaze over Anders' left shoulder as he held out his hand and barely touched Anders's before letting go and stepping back.

Ms Andrews sighed. "Very well, boys. Any more fighting will earn a letter to your parents. And I do hope you'll get over whatever it was that started this."

Ivan ducked his head, ready to go, but Ms Andrews wasn't finished.

"One day, you'll see that the problems that seem so large and terrible now really aren't so bad. Hmm?"

"Sure," muttered Ivan and followed Anders out.

They stood in silence as the door clicked shut behind them, leaving them alone in the empty corridor.

"Ivan, I-" Anders began, but Ivan swung his school bag onto his back and headed back to class.

Hearing Anders's footsteps follow him, Ivan tried to ignore the thought that maybe Ms Andrews was right. *Maybe one day I'll see that this wasn't such a big deal. But that won't be for a long, long time.*

That evening, Ivan checked the conversation thread on his phone.

> Rager on the beach. Time 2 get lit mofos!!!

He sighed. Yesterday, he would have been already at Anders's place, preloading with liquor swiped from his dad's store. Now, however...

You have to go. You have to show them they don't even matter. Put on your game face and get out there.

The pep talk didn't help. Ivan paced his living room, the warm golden wood of the floor and kitchen cabinets giving no relief to his black mood.

The rest of the day had been a nightmare. Hamish and his friends cracked jokes all day about Ivan dressing up in tights and hats with horns on.

Ivan had set his face to unreadable and retreated to his inner world. It was like the days before he and Anders had been friends, when he'd always been the odd one out.

Now, the long summer day turned to twilight, and the evening he'd been looking forward to all year was ruined before it had even begun.

Ivan stalked out of the house and across the front lawn to the garage. A punching bag hung in one corner. In the other corner stood a different practice kit: his Viking sword and the target he used for throwing spears.

Ivan scowled at the gear. Even thinking about sword-fighting brought his black depression back. *Boxing it is, then.* His knuckles stung as he pulled on lightly padded gloves and began raining blows on the heavy boxing bag.

The hurt and anger gradually dulled as Ivan's arms grew tired, although sometimes the anger would flare again, and he'd picture Anders's or Hamish's face instead of the boxing bag.

C'mon Ivan. Get a grip. This isn't the end of the world.

The self-talk and aching muscles eventually calmed him. As the last of the day faded, Ivan got out of the shower determined to go to the beach party, stay cool, and face his enemies head-on.

He switched on the radio as he made coffee. An astronomer was telling a bored-sounding interviewer about a rare event tomorrow night. Five planets would be aligning with the moon.

"And that doesn't happen very often, does it?"

"The last time was about one hundred years ago."

Ivan lost the rest of the interview as the coffee machine foamed the milk. A mood, if not of optimism, then at least fatalistic determination, settled on him.

He would go to the party. He would ignore Hamish, Anders, and all their rugby head friends. He would hang out with the other people he knew, and he would drink beer. A lot of beer.

It would be fine. He could handle anything life threw at him. He had this under control.

An hour later, Ivan looked up from his computer. He was doing what he usually did when he wanted to avoid difficult things: chatting to people on his favourite Viking forums.

His chosen group, Vikon, was gearing up for their annual event.

This year they were having their main event here in Clarecross, his home town. And Ivan was split between excitement and a crippling fear of humiliation.

It's worse now that everyone at school knows I'm into Viking stuff. They'll be looking out for me. What if they see me in full costume? I'll be worried about it all weekend. Damn Anders.

He took an angry swig of beer and scanned down the conversation threads.

It was the usual stuff: people comparing gear and trash-talking.

He checked his phone. No messages from Anders. Ivan scowled at the beer bottle in his hand, then emptied it in one long swig and messaged his friend Galen.

> Hey, how's your combat training going? You ready for this?

A dancing dot showed Galen typing, and then his message popped up.

> We're going to send the Nostrund clan home in body bags. Check out my new score

A picture appeared, and Ivan whistled. It was a beautifully curved Viking axe.

Unlike some historical re-enactments, Vikon was a full-contact event. If you were in a pitched battle, you had better be kitted out in the best armour you could wrangle because you'd need it all when someone started whaling on you with a blunt steel axe.

> Dig it. Hey, gotta go man. Beach party

> Nice! You joining us for the big weekend?

Ivan hesitated. The icon wavered. Then he typed:

> Maybe. I'll see if I can sort it

> You better

A string of emojis followed, and Ivan grinned. He'd never actually met Galen, but he seemed like a cool guy.

Ivan sent an axe and wave emoji back, then shut his laptop. With a grimace, he pushed himself to his feet. He'd had the energy boost he'd needed, and now it was time to head down to the beach and face the music.

The bass amp thumped so loud Ivan could see it shake the sand it was bedded in. He swigged his beer and ignored Hamish and his friends standing across the bonfire, laughing and posing. Anders was seated to their left, snuggled up with his new girlfriend, Amelie.

"So, you getting out of here this summer?" His classmate Sophie yelled in his ear to be heard above the music.

"Yeah, that's the plan," Ivan yelled back. He stepped away from the bonfire, and the bass amp faded a little. "If I get into any universities."

"Heard you and Anders had a fight today," said Sophie.

"Yeah."

"What about?"

"Musical differences."

"I heard it was because you're into that," she mimed swinging a sword blade, "that historical remake thing. With Vikings and stuff."

Ivan's cheeks were hot, and it wasn't just the heat of the fire. "Where'd you hear that?"

"It's all around school. Clarice googled it. They're calling you Ivar the Boneless."

"Huh. Could be worse." Ivar was a historical figure, one of the great Viking raiders.

Sophie snorted. "It went downhill from there. Think of all the things you could do with 'boneless.'"

Ivan took a deep pull of his beer. *If my plan A for escaping this place fails, I have to sort a plan B.*

"Hey, Ivar," yelled Hamish from across the fire. "Boner! You going to try and fight me now? You brought your axe?"

His friends whooped and laughed, a chorus of catcalls and jeers echoing in Ivan's ears. He gritted his teeth.

"No, Hamish, I came here to drink beer and forget idiots like you exist."

There was a chorus of 'ooh's' from the other side of the fire. "Viking boy wants a fight," said one of Hamish's friends.

Adrenaline surged through Ivan as Hamish squared his shoulders in the classic 'you want a piece of me' stance and started towards Ivan. Anders got to his feet, shedding blankets, and put a hand on Hamish's shoulder.

"Hey mate, leave it." Anders shot a look over at Ivan. "And you, be cool."

"Butt out, Anders," said Ivan.

"That's right," said Hamish. "Your freak friend wants to start something? Let him."

Ivan clasped his beer bottle, feeling the smooth curve of it in his hand as the last of the beer spattered down into the sand.

"I don't want to start anything, Hamish. But if you come a step closer to me, I'll break this bottle over your head and then shove the broken glass into your face." He said it without inflexion, coldly.

Silence spread around the fire. Ivan could feel the tension rise as people edged away from him, shocked by this threat of violence.

"You're such a freak Ivan," spat Hamish. "No wonder you've got no friends. Loser."

The tension eased as Hamish turned back to his friends.

Anders shook his head. "You always take things too far."

Ivan swallowed down the bitter taste in his mouth. *If I'm to fight my battles alone, then I have to go all in. Taking the middle path means you get trampled on.*

No one wanted to talk to Ivan after that. He spent an uncomfortable few minutes standing by himself, staring into the flames, and then decided it was time to go.

The night air cleared his head as Ivan headed down to the craggy rocks at the end of the beach. He climbed them to sit looking out over the midnight waters. The wind off the sea brushed his face, and the moonlight painted the tops of every wavelet silver.

So, last night of high school. Damn. I can't wait to get out of this town.

The earth swayed as Ivan nearly fell off the rock he'd climbed. *I am drunk. Very.*

Things went hazy after that, but Ivan's homing instinct kicked in.

Time for a new beginning. Time to stop hiding in the shadows. Ivan's last coherent thought guttered out as he collapsed on the couch into alcohol-laced darkness.

2

Ivan groaned and covered his eyes, reaching blindly for the bottle of water on the ground beside him. He was stretched out on the wooden schooner chair in his back garden, wishing the clear English summer sky wasn't so bright. Or that there was any sunlight at all.

His stomach churned, and he wished he was still passed out.

Lucky Mum and Greg are away on their anniversary holiday. First time they leave me home alone, and look how well I do.

As he dozed and tried to tame his fierce headache, the morning sun turned into midday sun, and Ivan started to feel the burn. It drove him back inside, sipping his water bottle in a vain attempt to settle his stomach and feel like life was worth living again.

The kitchen was dark and cool compared to the brilliant day outside. With a grimace, he cleared away last night's pre-party dinner, the greasy chips wrapper smelling of stale dreams.

And the next day of the rest of my life begins. Hurray.

Wincing slightly, he went out to the letterbox and collected the post - a few bills, a postcard from his mum and stepdad, and an envelope with a university crest on the outside.

Coming back, Ivan caught a reflection of himself in the hallway mirror. Dark blue eyes, high cheekbones, thick, unruly black hair, and pale skin that did nothing to hide the fresh bruises from his fight yesterday. He'd finally reached six feet this year, but his build remained slender, unlike Anders. *That git.*

As he ripped open the letter with the university crest, Ivan was disgusted at himself for feeling a tremor of anticipation.

"To Ivan Luca,

We regret to inform you..."

He threw the letter in the wastepaper basket without reading more. On the pinboard above the kitchen bench was a list of university names. Ivan crossed 'University of Bristol' off it. Blowing out a long breath, he glowered at the list. Only a few names were left. *What if I don't get in anywhere?*

Ivan's hangover headache returned with a vengeance. *I'll stay here, get some dead-end job and turn into a useless waster like my dad was.*

Over on the couch, where he'd abandoned it last night, Ivan's phone beeped.

He ignored it. *Maybe food will help me feel better?* His stomach lurched. *Maybe not.*

His phone beeped again. Then started to ring. With a huff, he stalked over and picked it up. The screen displayed 'Anders Calling.'

For a moment, he considered chucking the phone down on the couch and going back to sleep for the rest of the day.

I don't want to talk to him. Anyway, I bet he's just calling because he wants something.

Ivan hesitated. Then with a curl of his lip, he swiped across the screen to accept the call.

"Ivan." Anders sounded breathless like he'd been running. "Shit, I'm glad you picked up, bro. I need your help. Something bad has happened."

Ivan slumped down on the couch, tilting his head back and closing his eyes. His head thumped like someone was compressing it in a vice.

"Define bad."

"It's Amelie. She didn't get home from the thing last night. I've searched everywhere. No one knows where she is. I swear something's happened to her. Can you help me find her?"

Ivan's heart did a complicated lurch. "Why me? Why not ask your best mate Hamish?"

"Please, Ivan, don't be still salty. I said I'm sorry, and I am. Look, I really need your help."

There was silence on the end of the line. Then Ivan gave a drawn-out, gusty sigh. "Fine. I'll help you look for her. Since you seem so upset and all."

"Thanks, mate," the relief in Anders's voice made Ivan feel even worse. "I'll be at yours in five."

"Whatever," said Ivan and hung up.

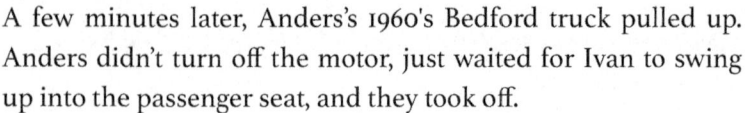

A few minutes later, Anders's 1960's Bedford truck pulled up. Anders didn't turn off the motor, just waited for Ivan to swing up into the passenger seat, and they took off.

"So, you reckon your girlfriend's gone missing," said Ivan. He turned sideways to study Anders. Usually easygoing, his friend's face was strained. "Explain."

Anders hauled the wheel of the truck around a small country lane corner and changed gears with a grate and a shudder of the engine.

"Here." He thrust his phone at Ivan.

On the screen, a small dot was pulsing in place. Ivan recognised the location, a small glade in the woods out the back of their seaside village.

"You have your girlfriend under surveillance? How romantic."

Anders flushed. "Don't be an asshole. We both have the app so we can keep track of each other. Anyway, Amelie walked home from the party last night, then this morning when I called her...well, she didn't pick up. So I checked the app and went to where it said she was. And her phone was just lying there in the grass."

A chill crept down Ivan's neck. "She probably dropped it while drunk. I bet she's still asleep at one of her friend's houses."

"I checked her place, messaged all her friends. Ivan, none of them have seen her."

"What about her family?"

Anders gripped the steering wheel. "They live in London. Amelie would have told me if she'd gone all the way there."

"You left the phone where you found it?"

"Yeah, because…"

Because you'd be the number one suspect if anything happened to Amelie. Ivan had watched enough true crime docu-dramas to know how the police viewed this kind of case.

"So, why do you need my help? You want me to give you an alibi when we go to the police and report Amelie missing?"

Silence. Anders hunched his shoulders. Ivan knew that stance. Anders was about to give him news he knew Ivan wouldn't like.

"On the way back from finding Amelie's phone, I ran into Karl."

Ivan's face went stony. It was what his mum called his 'resting scowlface,' the expression that let no one in and nothing out.

"Karl." The word came out flat above the roar of the truck.

Anders pulled into the little port of their fishing town and juddered the truck into a lower gear, then into neutral as they coasted up to park behind some warehouses.

The silence in the truck was heavy as Anders cut the engine.

'Yeah, Karl." Anders's fingers tensed on the steering wheel again. "He was acting really strange," his fingers gripped tighter, "like he knew something and wanted to tell me without giving anything away. So after I threatened him with, well, threats, he told me a crazy story. It sounded too crazy to be true, but after…well, you know…I think maybe it's true."

Ivan shoved a hand through his thick black hair, pushing it out of his eyes. He wanted to punch something, preferably Anders, but kept his voice level.

"What did Karl say?"

A few minutes later, Ivan stood on the dock next to Anders, looking down at his family's small sailboat. He still couldn't believe he was going along with this.

If I didn't know how batshit crazy Karl's family is, I'd be looking for hidden cameras.

"What I don't get," he said slowly, "is why you think this is a good plan. The whole thing is mad. Is this just some elaborate setup you've dreamed up with your rugby mates to make me look like more of a tosser?"

"No way," said Anders. "I would never do that. Truth."

Ivan jammed his hands into his pockets. He was playing for time. *I know what I'm going to do in the end. But it just sounds too weird. Even for this town.*

"So Karl told you his dad's kidnapped Amelie and a group of them have gone out to the island to murder her in some weird ritual. Anders, you know how crazy this sounds? Actually, it is crazy. Like I keep saying, we should call the police."

It was the third time Ivan had said this in the last ten minutes, but Anders wasn't listening. Anders grabbed his arm as Ivan went to take his phone out of his pocket.

"I told you we can't!"

"But why?"

"Karl said...some of our local coppers are in on it too."

"This gang has a policeman on their payroll?" Ivan rolled his eyes. "Gimme a break."

Anders was gulping air and clenching his fists. "We have to go get Amelie back, Ivan. If we don't, she'll die, and they'll pin it on me." That last bit came out in a whisper, as if Anders was ashamed to admit that was even a thing he was worried about.

Seeing him like this made Ivan pause. Anders's eyes were wide and scared, quite unlike his usual confident, sunny self. His broad shoulders were hunched, and he kept clenching and unclenching his jaw.

Ivan scowled down at his boat. "I said I'd help," he said slowly, "but if we go out there, and Karl's story is true, we're sure to be outnumbered. Why don't we talk to the coast guard? Or the police outside of Clarecross?"

"Because there's no time!" Anders was practically jumping in place on the dock now, his face twisted with worry. "And no one will believe me except you. Like you said, it sounds mental. But you know better. Look, I'm sorry about...about yesterday. I don't know how many times I have to say it, but I am. I really need you to help me. We have to get there before something bad happens to Amelie. And...you're the one."

"The what?"

"The guy I trust to go all the way. When it really counts, you don't back down."

Slowly Ivan blew out a breath.

Back when I needed it most, Anders was there for me. I owe him.

"Fine," he said, and Anders relaxed a fraction. "We'll go to the island and check it out. But if it's a stupid hoax, we're going straight to the police. Don't worry. I'll cover you with an alibi. You'll be ok."

"Thanks, bro," said Anders. "I owe you."

They both paused then and looked out to the island. It sat about three miles offshore, a squat and rocky shadow crouched against the blue. Here in town, the day was bright and sunny, but dark clouds were gathering above the island.

Ivan swallowed, unease blossoming in his stomach. While Anders disappeared to the dockyard toilet, Ivan unlocked his family's boatshed and slipped inside.

It was time to collect an item he'd had for years, ever since he'd joined the local pistol club in his search for tools to face a hostile world. It was an item he'd acquired in secret and had kept secret, partly based on the belief that he'd never actually use it.

The interior of the boatshed was dark and cool. Ivan crossed to the bank of shelves at the far wall and unlocked one. Inside the drawer was a case, and inside the case, a pistol gleamed darkly. He opened the cardboard box of ammunition and removed sixteen bullets. One by one, he slid the bullets into the magazine where they nestled, each one a pocket of potential violence.

Ivan felt oddly calm as he shoved the loaded pistol in his backpack and left the shed. The boat bobbed gently as he climbed on board and stowed his backpack in the forward compartment.

Looking up, the clouds over the island had doubled in volume. *That was fast.* They were now an inky blue-black and stretched high up into the sky. *Those are thunderhead clouds. Bad weather's coming. But there's no storm warning for today.*

Despite the warm sun on his back, goosebumps rose on Ivan's forearms. He bent down to pick up the oars and, seeing the island out of the corner of his eye, started in surprise.

For a moment, one of the billowing clouds looked exactly like a wolf, muzzle raised to howl. Ivan turned to look at it straight on, and the wolf shape became just another stormcloud, dark with pent-up energy.

Anders reappeared, shaking his hands dry.

"All set?" Now they were taking action, he seemed almost cheerful.

Ivan scowled. Anders always thought things would turn out alright. *He's never had to face betrayal and nearly dying.*

"I have a bad feeling about this," he said.

The boat rocked as Anders hopped in and began undoing the ties around the mainsail.

"You always have a bad feeling. We're about to head to an island everyone says is cursed to stop a madman who's kidnapped my girlfriend. What could possibly go wrong?"

3

Ivan braced against the soaked timber of the boat, knuckles white as he fought the tiller against the pounding ocean. He was stiff with cold, pumped with adrenaline, and focused on one thing: survival.

The smudge of shadow up ahead was all they could see of the island through the storm, and it didn't seem to be getting any closer. The sailboat timbers creaked and groaned as wave after wave crashed over the sides of the boat, and Anders doggedly bailed out water, but never quite as fast as they shipped it.

"Bear windward," Anders yelled, pointing at the rain-drenched island ahead, "Or we'll miss the bay!"

Ivan pulled the tiller a little tighter towards him. The sail cracked like a whip, and the boat shuddered as it headed further into the wind.

How the hell did this storm come up so fast? It doesn't seem...natural.

Even if they'd wanted to head back to the safety of their village harbour, they couldn't now. The storm had them. Ivan pulled the tiller closer, squinting against the rain and seaspray.

"Get ready with the oars," he yelled at Anders. The island was close now, the gathering gloom masking how fast they were coming up to the small rocky beach.

This was the only place on the island to land a boat. Ivan would have liked to see more beach, but the tide was full, and grey breakers were foaming and running high up on the pebbled shore.

"As soon as we lose the wind, you'll need to row like a madman," shouted Ivan. "We need to come in behind a wave, or we'll be rolled."

Anders nodded and fitted the oars into the rowlocks. As another swell passed under them, Ivan looked back over his shoulder.

There was a wave coming. He saw it almost too late. It was twice the size of the others, and foam was already gathering at its peak.

"Change of plan," Ivan shouted. "We're riding this one in."

Anders swore and shook his head.

"I hate your plan!" he yelled.

"And I hate your stupid rescue mission! Just help me keep us straight on, or we're screwed."

Anders drew in a deep breath, then hoisted both oars, tension clear in the set of his shoulders.

Ivan swore at the storm in general and Anders in particular. Now the wave was almost upon them.

"Sonnova*bitch!*" said Ivan as a mad grin spread across his face. He braced himself against the boat timbers, waiting for the wave to hit.

With a roar, the wave engulfed them. The foam surged over the stern, threatening to sink them before the boat shot forward.

Ivan's numb fingers gripped the tiller tighter, holding their line as the boat slewed and swerved under the rush of the wave. If they swung to the left or the right, the wave would flip them easily. Their voyage would end with them rolling through the rocky shallows in a mess of splintering timbers and coiling ropes.

With a surge, the boat shot out into the clear, just ahead of the wave. The shoreline loomed. There was a grating crunch as the boat ran up the rocky beach, and then they stopped.

The boat settled to one side, and Ivan slowly relaxed. He had to consciously unclench his frozen fingers from the tiller. In front of him, Anders slumped, letting out a deep breath, and stowed the oars with a clatter. The wild wind was quieter here in the lee of the island, and their sails hung limply, soaked with rain. The waves still dumped on the beach, rattling the rocks around, but the full fury of the storm was muted.

Ivan looked at Anders, seeing relief and underlying tension mirrored in his friend's face.

"Is the tide going in or out?" asked Ivan.

"Out," said Anders. "We should be okay." He clambered out of the boat and tried to stamp some warmth into his legs.

Ivan surveyed how far the freak wave had pushed them up the beach. Then he took the bow line anyway, climbed out of the boat, and tied them to a rock further up.

"So, we're here," said Ivan. *Yeesh...what a trip. Now what?* "If this gang is here too, where's their boat?"

"Karl says there's a sea cave," said Anders. "Their boat'll be hidden in there."

"It'll be wrecked in the storm then," said Ivan. He rolled his aching shoulders and tried to get some feeling back into his hands.

Anders shook his head. "He said it's a big cave. They can pull the boat up from the sea."

"This just gets better and better. Anders, there's no way we can get into the cave in a storm like this. We should never have come."

"Karl said there's another entrance to the cave. Near the centre of the island. There's a tree split by lightning, and the entrance is under that."

Ivan rubbed salt out of his eyes and shook water out of his thick black hair, trying to stop it from trickling down his neck and under his rain jacket. It didn't help.

"You trust Karl?"

Anders grinned. His curly blond hair was wet with spray and hung over his eyes, making him look like a sheepdog. "No, he's a lying little snake. But I dangled him over the weir. You know he can't swim. He was way too freaked out to think of any lies to tell me."

"Right. So, we find this cave, then run in there and demand they let Amelie go or—"

"Ivan. You know what Karl's family is like. We'll figure something out when we get there. Please." Anders took a deep breath as if he was about to say more, then didn't.

"Fine!" Ivan hunched his shoulders defensively. "Ok," he said more calmly. The dark gathered in around them as the light fled the sky, chased away by the storm. "This is going to be just lovely." Ivan tried to ignore the fear coiling in the pit of his stomach. *We're going to do what we have to. Whatever that means.*

They dropped the sails, and Ivan opened the small waterproof lockbox in the bow. He took out two head torches and, after a second's hesitation, two hunting knives. Then, when Anders turned to get something in the boat's stern, Ivan quickly opened the other compartment in the lockbox. There in his backpack, shining darkly, was his pistol. He checked the safety and slipped it under his rain jacket into the waistband of his trousers, at the back, like they do in gangster movies. It felt cold against his skin.

They walked up a narrow path to the top of the island. The wind found its way over the crest of the hill and gathered force until they were leaning against the storm with every step.

The tree, when they came to it, was dead, with a blackened split to its core from a lightning strike years ago. A little way below was a huge rock overhang and a dark hole. Ivan looked at Anders, who pursed his lips, frowning.

"I guess that's it."

Ivan let out a long breath and stared into the darkness. Then he cracked his neck, first to one side, then the other. "Let's do this thing then."

What the hell are we doing? Answer: I have no fucking idea.

4

They shone torches down the hole. It had a small opening, just enough to allow someone slim and determined to enter.

"You could go first?" said Anders. "In case I don't fit."

Ivan rolled his eyes. "In your dreams. You're not that buff." *However, I am the one with a gun.*

Ivan lowered himself into the hole. His feet touched rock about four feet down, and he let go. Cautiously, he shone his torch down further. Steep steps disappeared into darkness.

He made space for Anders, who had a bit of trouble getting his shoulders through the gap. As the light was cut off by Anders's bulk, Ivan had a sense of oppression, of something alive in the darkness below them. He focused on keeping his breathing steady as Anders kicked and wormed his way down to join him.

They stripped off their soaked oilskins, leaving them in a pile on the first stair. Then they picked their way down the steps, trying not to make any noise.

The darkness, almost a physical presence, pressed close around Ivan. He stifled the urge to brush it away from his face.

He wanted to ask if Anders could feel the same pressure, but the words died in his mouth. Anders was probably only thinking of their rescue mission.

The stairs ended in a tunnel that wound away before them. It was high enough for Ivan to stand up in but narrow. Black rock arched over their heads, glistening in the torchlight.

Ivan stopped, and Anders nearly ran into the back of him. Anders waited a few seconds, then leaned over to whisper hoarsely in Ivan's ear.

"We need to hurry!"

Ivan took a deep breath. His heart was pounding. *Think, Ivan!*

"We need a plan," said Ivan. "Tell me again how many men Karl thought there'd be."

Anders counted on his fingers. "Karl's dad Magnus, Michals, Gundersen...there's at least three of them."

"And there's just two of us," said Ivan.

"We have knives."

"They'll have knives."

Anders swallowed.

"They have Amelie!" said Anders. "We have to go."

"Just...we can't just go rushing in! We'll end up dead. *She'll* end up dead."

Anders let out a small explosive puff of breath. "You have a better plan?"

When Ivan didn't answer, Anders pushed past him and started on down the tunnel.

Ivan gritted his teeth and clenched his fists. Frustration was good. Anger was good. It distracted him from the sick hollow feeling in the pit of his stomach. *Why the hell did I agree to this...*

He caught up with Anders and whispered to him. "Screw you too, then. Just go carefully. Surprise is pretty much our only advantage, so let's not blow it."

Anders turned his torch down to its lowest setting, barely a glimmer, and Ivan switched his torch off. The pistol stuck in his waistband had warmed up to skin temperature. He could still feel its hard, unyielding shape pushing into the small of his back.

As they crept along, Ivan slowly became aware of something unusual. The earth had a pulse down here. His head had started throbbing in time with it. *Is this part of the storm above, or just nerves?*

Ivan tried not to squelch his wet shoes on the cool rock as they went down the tunnel. The strange pulse was still there, and it seemed to be quickening. With each pulse, small coloured lights strobed in the corner of Ivan's vision. *What the hell is going on?*

Up ahead, a light was growing. Anders switched off his torch completely, and they inched forward. The light wasn't the steady glow of electric torches but the flickering light of a living flame. Now they heard the low humming of male voices in a chant that made the hairs rise on the backs of Ivan's forearms.

The notes of the chant held a strong discord that whined and twisted unpleasantly. Ivan couldn't recognise any of the words. It sounded like another language, guttural and harsh.

At the last turn in the tunnel, they hugged the wall, moving very slowly along the rock face, determined not to give away their presence. Ivan felt the tension in the air around his friend. Anders was ready to fight.

But something about the drone of the voices was hypnotising Ivan. The pressure squeezed on his head like a vice.

He pressed his face up against the coolness of the rock wall. The pulse was so strong now the edges of his vision shimmered with it, like a heatwave. *This is too weird. Am I having some sort of stroke?*

Anders dropped down to peer around the corner at knee height, and Ivan edged his head to look into the lit cavern with one eye.

The tunnel opened into a wide cave where six men dressed in black robes stood in a semi-circle around a raised plinth. *Six? That's way too many...*

There were candles lit around the cave, thick, yellow and sooty with use. Rivers of wax dripped and dribbled in frozen stalactites down the rock.

Anders's sharp intake of breath mirrored Ivan's shock. The stone plinth in the centre of the room was the length and breadth of a person. And on it lay Amelie.

She wore an old-fashioned white dress, which contrasted oddly with her Nike trainers.

She was just lying there. For a second, Ivan's stomach turned over, thinking she was dead. Then he saw her chest moving as she breathed. *She's alive. But unconscious? Drugged?*

Ivan clenched his hands hard. *We should have told people we were coming here. This is so stupid. But Anders was right - what the actual fuck! How the hell are we going to rescue Amelie and get out of this alive?*

There was a sudden rage of thunder from outside, audible even down there. The storm must be right overhead.

As if that were a signal, the chanting stopped. To Ivan's horror, the lead chanter looked up, right where he and Anders crouched in the shadows.

His hood tipped back from his head, and he smiled, teeth glinting in the candlelight. Ivan recognised him, and a sick feeling coiled in his stomach.

It was Magnus Hagen, Karl's father, the man who'd taught Ivan to hunt and sail. When Ivan was a kid, before things had gone wrong, he'd looked up to Magnus more than anyone else.

Ivan shoved his panic down before it clawed away his control. He deliberately slowed his breathing. *Ivan. You're not that kid anymore. You can do this. You can face him. You have to.*

Magnus spread his arms wide and reeled off a string of words in a language Ivan didn't know.

As the robed men responded, Ivan realised maybe Magnus hadn't seen them. They were in deep shadow, after all. And he was sure they hadn't been heard above the chanting.

The strange pressure pulsed in his head again, and Ivan struggled to see straight.

Magnus let his arms fall by his side. In a sheath on his belt was the polished handle of his hunting knife. Unlike the robes and candles, the knife looked new. Knowing Magnus, its blade would be wickedly sharp.

Ivan let his awareness widen, recording where each robed man was standing and where the candles were. *If Anders and I could somehow douse the candles, we could pull Amelie out of there and back up the tunnel. Could we do it in time to get away in the confusion?*

He reached down to draw Anders back into the tunnel and tell him his plan when he noticed Anders was gone from his side.

Helplessly, Ivan watched in disbelief as Anders walked forward, straight into the cave.

Ivan felt cold with fright, then hot with anger. *IDIOT! I'm going to kill him! I'm actually going to kill him before anyone else does.*

Anders looked at Magnus, his face pale but determined.

"It's over, Magnus. You can't do this." Ignoring the robed men ranged in an arc around him, he knelt beside Amelie, cradling her head, trying to rouse her. Ivan drew back into the shadows as Magnus smiled.

"Anders Berg. How unsurprising. What a hero. How inconvenient of you to show up at this crucial moment."

Ivan watched as hooded men moved to surround Anders, blocking the passage where Ivan crouched. They hadn't seen Ivan yet, but this was going bad very quickly.

Ivan! Do something!

Ivan tried to shake off the sluggishness that seeped through his limbs, but it was as if a frosted pane of glass stood between him and the world. *Like one of those bad dreams where you can only move in slow motion.*

The chanting sounded like a prayer or invocation, and Ivan shuddered, that pulse thrumming through his whole body now, so strong he could hardly think.

Magnus said something to the robed man on his left. Ivan couldn't quite catch the words, but the man nodded and stepped towards Anders. Anders was trying to lift Amelie off the stone plinth, but she was a dead weight, slippery and unresponsive.

Why does Anders always have to be a bloody hero? And why does it feel like I'm already too late to stop what's going to happen?

The pistol dug into Ivan's back. Slowly, he pulled it out of the waistband of his trousers. It was inevitable. He'd known it from the moment he stowed the pistol in his boat. *At least I've taken a gun to a knife fight,* he thought. And: *We're all going to die.*

Anders had one arm under Amelie's shoulders and was hefting her up, but two robed men were closing in on him now.

"Anders Berg," said Magnus, and it was chilling how calm he sounded, how normal. "There's nothing you can do now. Her sacrifice will fuel a greater plan, a greater good. You cannot save her. And I'm afraid you've seen too much." Magnus's smile was benevolent as he gestured for the two robed men to seize Anders.

They grabbed Anders high up on his arms, forcing him to let go of Amelie. She slid back down onto the plinth, her head hanging at an awkward angle. Anders struggled violently against their grip, but a third man buried his fist hard into Anders's stomach, and he doubled over, wheezing.

Which is when Magnus looked directly at where Ivan was crouching. His heart raced, thudding in his chest. *He sees me!*

"Welcome, Ivan," said Magnus calmly.

Seeing no other option, Ivan stepped out into the flickering candlelight. He kept the gun behind his back and tried to gaze coolly up at Magnus.

The cult leader appeared confident, in control, but Ivan sensed an underlying tension in him. It was the thrum of anticipation, even fear. The small hairs on the back of Ivan's neck bristled at the pressure building in the air.

"It's time for us to go, Magnus," said Ivan. Magnus raised his eyebrows, mocking. His meaning was clear. *There are six of us and two of you. The one you're trying to rescue is unconscious, you don't have a chance.*

Ivan drew his pistol and levelled it straight at Magnus. He hated how he felt right now, stupid, embarrassed. *Like a kid with a toy gun.*

He tried to channel every action movie he'd seen and deliberately unchecked the safety. The click sounded clear in the silence. Ivan stared straight into Magnus's dark eyes, willing him to break, to show some sign of backing down.

Instead, Magnus's eyes gleamed with malice. "Boy," he said softly. "We both know you're bluffing. You haven't got what it takes to pull the trigger. You're a blank, a nobody, an empty vessel. You're a follower, not a leader. Always were, always will be."

Fuck you, Magnus, Ivan thought. But the words weighed inside him with a growing feeling of weakness. *I feel like an empty vessel.* Deliberately, Ivan blocked the thought. His finger was slick against the trigger. *Squeeze, don't pull. Shit...am I really going to do this?*

On his left, one of the robed men inched along the cave wall to get behind him. Anders, still hunched over and held by two men, tensed his shoulders, ready to make a move.

There were nine candles in the room, and sixteen bullets in his pistol, and Ivan's heart was beating so hard it blurred inside his chest, and the pulse in the air had sped up to match it. Ivan felt like a diver before the plunge.

The candle flame reflected off the surface of Magnus's eye. Ivan heard the rustle of robes on stone as the man behind him prepared to attack. The shadows each of them cast flickered dark on the cavern wall.

And then everything happened at once.

The man behind him sprang, and Ivan ducked to get under him, hitting the man low, so he rolled over Ivan and landed with a crunch against the stone plinth. Anders yanked one man holding his arm towards him, and all three men went down in a flurry of fists, knees and elbows.

Ivan raised his gun again to point at Magnus, whose hand was on his knife hilt. His own finger rested on the trigger of the pistol, ready to pull. *Can I do this?*

Before he had a chance to find out, another man grabbed Ivan from the side in a crushing bear hug, trying to wrestle the gun out of his hands.

There was a rumble of thunder from the storm above, and at the edge of his awareness, Ivan found something he could use. It came out of the shadows, filling the emptiness inside Ivan, and gave him strength. *Time to take the fight to them.*

As the man holding him shifted his grip, Ivan stamped down hard on the man's foot. With a cry, the man's hold loosened, and Ivan jerked his head backwards. There was a satisfying crunch as the back of Ivan's head flattened the man's nose, and the man let go of Ivan altogether.

Ivan staggered forwards, his pistol pointing at Magnus. *If I could just get Magnus to* listen*, for once.*

"Stop now, damn you!" Ivan's cry was cut short as the man he'd just headbutted grabbed him again, hands wrenching at his gun.

There was a loud bang.

The man loosened his hold on Ivan and slumped to the ground.

Ivan stared wide-eyed at the fallen man. His hood had been pushed back in the struggle. It was Michals. The last time Ivan had seen him, Michals had been behind the counter of the greengrocers, serving customers.

His pistol gripped in shaking hands, Ivan backed away. Anders's mouth hung open in disbelief, then he surged towards the plinth, picking up Amelie and staggering backwards towards the cave exit.

Ivan couldn't take his eyes away from Michals. He was lying very still, and his eyes were closed like he was sleeping.

It was an accident, a voice in Ivan's head kept saying. And: *He can't be dead. But I shot him.*

A strange rattling sound came from Michals's chest, and his jaw opened slackly. Something was streaming out of his mouth, a blue ribbon of smoke lit up bright. It looked like a cheesy special effect from an 80s movie and impossible, but Ivan knew Magnus saw it too because the older man started in surprise.

The shock was replaced by a look of triumph on Magnus's face that Ivan didn't like. Raising his arms, Magnus shouted out a string of words.

Ivan couldn't understand the words, but as he heard them, his knees slowly buckled and jolted as they hit the rock floor.

Now's not the time to — and the thought was swallowed up by a rushing sound in his ears. *I'm fainting...shit. This is not the time to* —

Ivan struggled to stay conscious, but it was no use. Darkness issued from every corner of the cave, overwhelming him. There was a blast of air, and all the candles went out.

What the —

For a moment when Ivan saw nothing but pure black, and then he was both in the cave and outside in the storm above. His eyes saw one reality, and his mind's eye saw another.

In his mind's eye, Ivan was standing in the open on top of the tall rock at the centre of the island. Above him, lightning forked down from the sky in fractured instants. In those fragmented moments, Ivan could read the lightning like it was a language he'd always known but somehow forgotten.

Everything is alive. Everything is awake, and listening, and speaking. Holy shit.

The rain hung motionless, and each suspended droplet shone blue with the lightning as, achingly slowly, it inched down from the sky.

Ivan realised the lightning bolt was coming exactly to him. They were going to meet, Ivan and the lightning, on top of the island, and in that moment, he couldn't tell the difference between the two. His focus contracted to the lightning, only inches away now, glittering fierce and blue, more alive than anything he'd ever seen.

Ivan had a moment to brace himself, and then the lightning arced forward, and struck him right in the chest.

There was a huge 'Crack BOOM,' and Ivan was back in the cavern, being pulled away by Anders. It seemed only a few seconds had passed in the real world.

Lit in jagged flashes by Anders' torch, Magnus and the robed men gathered at the other side of the cave, ready to rush them and finish what they'd started.

But now came a roar so loud it hurt his ears, and the same lightning that had arced down from the sky came on through the roof of the cave. There was a crashing of rock as the ceiling fell, then silence and total darkness.

5

Ivan's panicked breathing was loud in the dark. He reached his hands down, and when he touched rock, his arms buckled, and he kept going until his head rested on the cave floor. It was cool.

A minute or so later, a lucid thought came into the blankness of his mind. *I'm still holding the pistol.* He flicked the safety on, tucked it back into his waistband, and then pulled his torch out of his pocket.

Amazingly, it still worked when he flicked the switch. *What a great advert for MagLite torches. Has fight, shoots man, survives rockfall, light still works.* Then, as his ribs ached painfully, Ivan corrected himself. *Kills man. Shit.*

He shone the light in front of him. Where the cavern had been was a solid wall of tumbled rock. Ivan listened hard but heard nothing from the other side.

"Let's get the hell out of here," he said. Behind him, Anders drew in a shaky breath.

Ivan shone his light straight in Anders's face. His friend was rumpled, with dust streaked through his hair and a rapidly swelling lump on his cheekbone where someone had hit him. He had Amelie cradled in his arms, her bleached pixie hair turned grey with dust. *Bloody hero.*

Ivan shook his head to clear it. The harmonics humming through his head since they arrived had gone. *It was probably just the storm overhead, and now it's moved on.* He felt relieved there wasn't something wrong with his head.

"I umm..." said Anders, then nodded his head. "We should go."

For the first time that day, Ivan was in perfect agreement.

Together, they hauled the unconscious Amelie up the steep stone steps. It took far longer to get up than down. Ivan discovered he was exhausted. The struggle in the cave had lasted barely a minute, but he felt like he'd run a marathon.

When they surfaced, the storm hadn't just gone. It was as if it had never been.

The air was eerily quiet. Ivan listened and couldn't even hear the distant rumble of the storm moving on.

The skies were clear, and the moon was up. The ocean had stilled to a gentle roll of wavelets, and even these were dying down.

It was impossible.

Ivan drew a slow breath in, then out.

"Let's get to the boat and get the fuck away from here. In case Magnus and his guys show up again."

Ivan felt like he was floating in a vacuum, only barely in control. Any moment he might do...something stupid. Stupider. *What should I be feeling right now? How do people in the mafia act? Shoot someone, then go get cannoli?* He glanced at Anders, who was watching him cautiously.

"Do you think they survived?"

"You mean all of them except the one I shot?"

Anders winced. "I heard a shot. That was you?"

"Michals tried to grab my pistol. It went off, killed him."

"Not your fault then," said Anders.

Ivan ran his fingers through his hair, trying to stop his mind from flashing back to that moment. He shook his head. There was nothing he could say right now that would make things any better or different.

"Most of them were on the other side of the cave from us," Anders said slowly. "But that rock fall was proper big. I dunno. Maybe they made it. Some of them anyway. With the sea like this, they'll be able to get their boat out of the cave."

They didn't say anything more for the next five minutes. It seemed very important to get to their boat as quickly as possible.

Amelie grew heavier and heavier on the scramble down the moonlit path. Ivan didn't want her to wake up, but he was starting to resent how peaceful she looked, drugged and oblivious. Her heavy punk eyeliner was smudged, so she looked as beat up as Ivan felt.

"Hey," said Anders as Amelie's arm banged against a rock. "Take it easy, ok?"

"I know, I know," said Ivan. "Just, let's keep going."

They both breathed a sigh of relief to see their boat high on the beach with no sinister robed figures waiting around it.

Ivan and Anders swiftly stowed their sleeping passenger in the boat. A sharp burst of adrenaline gave Ivan the strength to push the boat down the rocky beach and into the sea in one rush.

Only after they were out of the shadow of the island, with Anders pulling strongly on the oars, did Ivan start to breathe normally.

"It's going to be a long row back if the wind doesn't pick up," said Ivan.

Amelie was propped in the bow on a folded sail, still asleep. *I hope she stays that way.*

"Anders," he said. His friend looked back at him. "I killed a man. I'm a murderer."

"No, you're not," said Anders. "They were going to kill me. And Amelie. And you. It was self-defence."

"What if some of them survive? And what if they do have someone in the police?"

Anders thought for a couple of oar pulls. "They can't accuse us of anything. Everything's buried under the rock."

"But what if they do?"

Anders had an unidentifiable expression in his eyes. Ivan, who'd known him all his life, couldn't recognise it, which bothered him.

Then Anders said: "I wouldn't care if you had shot Michals on purpose. They were going to kill Amelie, then us. You saw the candles. They've been there loads of times. They've probably killed other people there. They deserved everything they got. I hope they are all buried down there under rock." Anders drew a breath. "It was like a judgement from heaven, the way the roof fell in. It saved us."

Ivan stared down at his hands. He slowly pulled his pistol out of his waistband. "I suppose I should ditch this."

"Yeah, you should. Dunno how you have one, but I'm well glad you brought it."

Ivan tossed the gun into the waters. It sank with hardly a splash, and he didn't feel any different.

"So, um," he said. "What do we do now?"

Usually, it was Ivan who came up with plans and Anders who took charge and made them happen. Right now, though, he felt hollowed out. *I just want to sleep for about a year.* His head ached with big throbs of pain, and his body hurt where he'd been kicked. Even his wrist hurt where the pistol kicked back as it fired.

Anders pulled a few more strokes on the oars, thinking.

"No one knows we were on the island. So we say nothing."

"And Amelie?" Ivan looked at the sleeping girl.

"She probably won't remember a thing."

"Apart from being kidnapped," said Ivan.

"She's working here for the summer to save up for uni, so her family's not around. Her friends here probably think she spent the day hungover. So we put her back in her room before she wakes up and keep a lid on what really happened."

Unspoken between them was the thought *and no one has to know you shot Michals.*

Anders pulled a few more times on the oars, thinking. When Anders was thinking, it usually took him an age to get the words out.

"Hey, I-man," said Anders. Ivan snorted at the childhood nickname.

"Yeah?"

"Thanks for believing me. For coming out here, in this boat, through that storm. For not backing down when we were surrounded and outnumbered. And...for bringing a gun to a knife fight. You savage bastard."

Ivan shrugged. "It's ok. You're a dick, and your rescue plan was total shite, but there was nothing good on TV."

Anders grinned, his teeth shining white under the moon, and carried on rowing.

Ivan watched the dark waters. It was uncannily still. Usually, it took days of no wind for the sea to get this calm. The moonlight shimmered on the water, and he heard the chop and ripple of the oars with perfect clarity.

"You know," Anders said. "The way it happened. Michals dying. Magnus yelling out those words. And then the lightning struck...it was almost like they were connected. As if one caused the other."

Ivan started. It was uncomfortably close to what he'd been thinking.

But that makes no sense.

Anders didn't know about the weird out-of-body experience he'd had. Or had something similar happened to Anders when the lightning struck? Ivan couldn't bring himself to ask.

Instead, he said, "The whole thing was weird as shit. So let's make sure no one knows we were on the island. Especially the little snitch who sent us here."

"We'll need to think of a story for Karl then. But what if other cult members are living around here?"

"You think too much when you row. Let's swap."

Ivan took the oars and bent his back into the slow, steady rhythm. Pull, lift, return. Pull, lift return.

This didn't stop his mind from going back to the moment when he'd stood atop the island, the lightning arcing towards him in slow inches. He'd never seen anything as terrifying or as beautiful. *I'd never been so sure I was about to die. And I didn't give a damn.*

The island was now a distant smudge behind them, and the twinkling lights of their village were drawing closer.

"We'll go ashore at East Bay," said Anders, taking up the oars again. "We can carry Amelie back from there. If she wakes, we'll say we found her out in the forest."

Ivan relaxed back against the boat mast.

"Hey bro, the other day it was you that said nothing happens round here. That living here is like watching paint dry."

Ivan didn't reply.

"Ivan?"

Ivan looked up. He had been tracing a glimmer of moonlight in the water below him. It was leading somewhere hidden, dark, and for a moment, it had been all he saw.

"Yeah, I remember. Turns out I was dead wrong. Clarecross is a cultist paradise. One of the things not mentioned in the guide books. Satisfied?"

Anders smiled his old, easy smile, just a little worn around the edges. "Deffo."

East Bay was a tiny cove surrounded by steep wooded hills. The small port town of Clarecross was just around the next bay. They pulled the boat high up and tied her to an old mooring post.

Ivan shone his torch over the sailboat's hull.

"There," he played the light over some splintered timbers. "That must have been when we ran up the beach."

"We'll sort it," said Anders. He patted the bow. "She'll be good as new. Let's go."

Anders picked Amelie up by the shoulders, and as Ivan went to lift Amelie's feet, her eyelids fluttered. He froze. Amelie opened her eyes for one long moment, looking at Ivan with total incomprehension. Then her eyes closed again. Ivan stayed still for the count of ten.

"Ok?" said Anders.

"Yeah," said Ivan. *I hope.*

For the next ten minutes, they lugged Amelie up the steep switchback track.

"Your girl gets heavier and heavier," said Ivan, wiping sweat off the back of his neck. "Is she ever going to wake up? I'm sure Sleeping Beauty didn't weigh twelve stone."

Anders didn't reply.

"Are you upset because she slept through your daring rescue? Pretty thoughtless of her really."

Anders shifted his grip and grinned. "I finally get to go full hero and...yeah, no one sees it."

"Except the bad guys. And me. You'll always be my hero, Anders."

Anders snorted, and they were silent until they got to the top of the hill. The lights of their little village shone up at them, promising comfort and safety.

"Did you recognise any of them? Apart from Magnus and Michals?" asked Anders.

"Maybe." Ivan had been turning every detail over in his mind. "One of them may have been Jacobsen from the pub. But we'll know more over the next few days, depending on who does and who doesn't come back."

Anders was silent. It was a silence Ivan knew well. Anders was deciding what to say next by trying different things in his head and discarding them.

"Spit it out," said Ivan. "You're thinking so hard I can smell something burning."

Anders shifted uncomfortably and cleared his throat. "It's just....too crazy really. The whole thing. Feels like a dream, and we're going to wake up any moment."

Ivan felt exactly the opposite. Right now was dreamlike. The calm, warm night, the stillness. The cave and the storm, those moments of crystal clarity when he had *understood,* that had been real, the most awake he'd ever been, and now he was drifting away again.

"What do we do if the others come back?" said Anders softly.

"Magnus and Co? Don't know. Can't think right now. I'm tapped out. Let's make a plan in the morning."

"And what if there are more of them? Like this is just one branch of it?"

"Our local franchised death cult, you mean?" Ivan yawned. "It's just what this town's been missing, that and a Starbucks. Right now, I'm just glad we're still alive." *Does that make me a bad person?*

"She's waking up," said Anders, and they hurriedly laid Amelie down on the path.

The two youths faded away back into the forest to watch. The moonlight on the path meant it was quite easy to see Amelie groan, sit up, then turn sideways and throw up.

"Charming," whispered Ivan to Anders.

Anders flinched as Amelie gave another gasping moan and curled into a ball. Ivan put his hand on his friend's shoulder to stop him from rushing back to her. *Bloody hero.*

Amelie stayed curled up for a few minutes. Finally, she got unsteadily to her feet and started walking back to the village. She staggered a bit, moving like a drunk in the last stages before collapse. But she kept moving.

Ivan and Anders followed her silently, staying out of sight. Not that she looked around. Amelie was fixed on the village lights and not much else.

They left her as she came onto the small main street, lit by street lamps.

"She'll be fine," said Ivan. "Just sick, like last night's hangover all over again." He felt a twinge of sympathy.

"What are we going to tell her tomorrow?"

"We went out looking for her, and we didn't find her. That's it. We searched the forest, then when the storm calmed down, we went around the bays. We saw nothing unusual."

Anders nodded. "That sounds fair. So now what?"

"We go home. I may get drunk. Very drunk. What about you?"

A smile ghosted Anders's lips.

"Greg's forty year old whiskey?"

"He's not here to miss it."

Anders let out a gusty sigh. "Right now, I reckon we've proper earned it."

6

A few hours later, Ivan was in a daze. The whisky had helped to numb both body and mind. *But not soul.*

Now, prone in bed, the ceiling swayed gently above him. The light was off, and the last rays of moonlight shone into the room.

Ivan wasn't hungover drunk, just pleasantly insulated from the world. Which is why he felt no more than a distant interest when the shadow shapes started appearing on the ceiling.

He watched them for several minutes before his brain registered that these weren't random patterns of black and grey. There was a mountain, there was a valley. Something that looked like a horse...a horse with wings.

Ivan blinked as the horse took off from one patch of shadow and flew across his ceiling to disappear into the next patch.

He reached slowly over to his nightstand, not taking his eyes off the ceiling, and flicked the bedside lamp switch. It stayed dark, and Ivan remembered he'd unplugged it earlier to charge his phone. Another shape grew out of the large shadow. It was unformed as it inched its way clear, like a dark oil droplet sliding across the ceiling.

This shadow shape was far larger than any of the other ones. It stretched out further and further, taking up a full quarter of the ceiling. Finally, it shook itself free, padding towards the centre of the ceiling.

It's a dog, Ivan thought. Then, *no, it's a wolf.* The shadow's wolfishness was clear in the slope of its shoulders, ragged muzzle, bushed tail and set of its head.

Up until now, Ivan had only ever seen wolves on nature programs. He never expected the silhouette of one to parade across his bedroom ceiling.

He didn't feel afraid, though. Maybe it was the expensive whiskey sloshing around in his veins, but it was like watching a lava lamp. *Should I be worried?*

The wolf turned its head, and Ivan knew it was looking straight down at him. Ice-cold fear spread across his chest, and he rolled over and off the bed as the shadow shape dropped down off the ceiling onto his bed in a black mass. He smelt the complicated scent of fur, fog, and...ceiling paint?

Gasping, Ivan hit the bedroom carpet with a thump and heard his bed springs creak under a weight that wasn't his. He fought clear of the blankets and stumbled back towards the door.

There was a black shape in the middle of his bed, taking up most of it. It was wolf shaped, with a smoke-like vagueness around its edges.

Its ears twitched as it raised its head, and then with a lithe movement, it sprang at him. Ivan sat down hard on the floor, and the shadow wolf sailed over him. But it didn't stop at the door. It went right through his closed bedroom door and disappeared.

Ivan sat on the floor for a moment, thinking.

It shouldn't be possible to feel drunk and sober at the same time. The proof of drunkenness was that he had to muffle sudden laughter at the impossible thing he'd just witnessed.

Very cautiously, he opened his bedroom door and peered down the stairs. They were dark and empty.

Ivan reached behind the door for his long-handled Viking axe. *It just jumped through a door. What's an axe going to do?* He ignored this objection, hefted the axe, and tiptoed down the stairs.

The living room was flooded with moonlight, the french doors making complicated shadows over the carpet, sofas, and a sleeping Anders.

A faint growl came from the kitchen.

Ivan crept forwards, axe raised defensively. There was a rustle in the pantry.

Heart pounding, he peered around the kitchen bench. There was definitely something there. A line from a childhood song kept repeating in his mind. *Who's afraid of the big bad wolf...*

Ivan couldn't make out a distinct shape, as the pantry was deep in shadow. A rattle as cat food spilt out onto the floor. There was a faint crunching sound and then another deep growl.

It touched certain primal parts of Ivan's brain, that growl. It spoke to him of times gone by when man crouched in a cave at night, clutching a crude weapon and hoping nothing large, toothed and clawed would visit and eat him and his family.

He backed slowly away from the pantry and out of the kitchen. Clumsily, he reached out and flicked on the light. In an instant, the kitchen was flooded with the warm golden glow of an incandescent light bulb. The shadows vanished.

Ivan heard a sleepy protest from Anders on the living room couch. He ignored it and edged back into the kitchen to peer inside the pantry.

Ripped up cat biscuit boxes spilt their food onto the floor. *I'm not imagining things, then. So maybe I'm not going crazy? But this isn't normal. Is it? Maybe I am crazy?*

Ivan scraped the biscuits back into their boxes. He looked around the kitchen one last time, switched the light off and hurried back upstairs.

Before he went back to sleep, for the first time since he was seven, Ivan pulled his night light out from a dusty corner of a forgotten drawer and lay down to sleep in its warm, golden glow.

7

The next morning, Ivan opened his eyes and listened to the birdsong outside. For a few precious moments, everything was fresh, and new, and full of promise.

Then he remembered who he was, where he was, and what had happened last night. For a full minute, Ivan stared up at the ceiling. *How do I go on from here?*

Nothing surfaced, and a need to use the bathroom pushed him out of bed. The next surprise was equally unpleasant.

Ivan suppressed a groan as he sat up and swung his legs down to the floor. Everything hurt. Fresh bruises had ripened in the night, muscles had stiffened up, and they were presenting their complaints to him all at once.

Bathroom first, then coffee.

Ivan saw clear evidence of last night's escapade in the bathroom mirror. A nice shiny bruise on his cheekbone and another on his jaw. His pale skin didn't do much to hide the marks. *You definitely look like you lost a fight.*

The eyes that gazed back at him were grey-blue, with an odd darker line around the edge of his corneas that made the blue stand out.

Ivan frowned at his reflection. Lately, he had spent embarrassingly long periods in the bathroom, staring at himself like he was a puzzle to solve. All that had come out of this practice was a feeling that, in some unfathomable way, he didn't measure up.

He prodded his cheekbone, winced, and tried to clean the scrapes on his knuckles. *I guess I'm lucky to be alive at all.*

Downstairs, the living room and kitchen were bathed in golden sunlight. It was full morning, with no trace of mysterious shadow wolves.

Ivan checked the pantry when he went to get the coffee beans, and yes, there were some hastily scraped up cat biscuits and two torn boxes. He resolutely put *that* mystery aside and focused on making coffee.

A faint snore from the couch told him Anders hadn't been devoured in the night by shadow creatures. Ivan ground the coffee, the familiar sound of the grinder and the smell of fresh beans soothing him.

Mug in hand, Ivan sat in the old overstuffed armchair gazing out at the sunlit garden. He sipped his coffee. Under its influence, the world gradually became a better place. But there was something...

He studied the carpet in front of him. There, in the middle of it, where the moonlight would have shone last night, was an impression. The slanting morning sun made it stand out clearly. It was a flattened circle as if something large had curled up there for some time.

Ivan drank a gulp of strong coffee and just avoided burning his mouth. The steam rose from his cup, swirling, the tiny droplets lit gold by the light.

For the moment, he felt blank, empty of thought. *I'm like a railway carriage abandoned in the station. There's a metaphor for life in this village.*

Anders woke as Ivan was downing his second cup of coffee. Ivan watched unsympathetically as his friend rolled over, groaned, sat up, and groaned again.

"I'll make more coffee."

Anders rocked back and forth on the couch, his head in his hands.

"I think I drank more whiskey than you."

"No, you just can't handle it. Also, you may have gotten kicked around a bit more than me."

"A *little*," Anders winced. "I think one of my ribs is broken."

Experimentally, he pulled up his jumper and examined his side. It was an interesting blue and purple colour, and the imprint of half a boot was obvious against his ribs.

Anders grimaced, then nodded thanks as Ivan handed him a hot cup of coffee.

"I reckon," he said thoughtfully, "That we're lucky to be alive."

"The odds were against us," said Ivan.

"Hmmm."

"Massively against us."

There was silence for a good five minutes while Anders drank his coffee and Ivan sprawled on the armchair, gazing into space.

"So," said Ivan. "The plan?"

"Plan?"

"The plan for how we're going to deal."

"Oh." Anders stared gloomily at the sun-bathed living room carpet, not noticing the flattened circle in the middle of it. "That plan."

"What we have," said Ivan, "is a potentially serious situation."

Anders grunted and leaned his head back against the sofa to gaze up at the ceiling.

"The way I see it," Ivan continued, "There are three possibilities. One - everyone died in the rock fall, no one connects us to the missing men, game over, life goes back to normal."

Anders sighed. "That would be grand. I don't think we're that lucky, though."

"Scenario two: Magnus and his evil henchmen come back, and, ashamed of what they've done, decide to mend their ways and spend their evenings doing cross stitch and helping old ladies cross the street."

Anders stared morosely up at the ceiling. "Sounds peachy."

"Three: Magnus comes back with his pals, eager for round two - the knockout phase."

"Mmmm." Anders sounded half asleep.

Ivan stared at the sunlight streaming through the window. He was still detached like things were moving around him, but he was floating above it all. The black shadow of the french door fell across his foot, and he felt it like an almost physical weight.

"Anders," he said. Then louder. "Anders! Not the time to drift off."

"I'm awake." Anders sounded anything but.

"If Magnus and Co return all ready to silence us and ensure their secret cult stays secret, we need to either beat a hasty retreat, defend ourselves, or call in the cavalry."

"Cavalry?"

"Police."

Anders grunted. "If Karl's telling the truth about a cult member in the force, that will get messy."

"Very messy. Starting with me getting arrested for murder. So let's hope for option one."

"That's not much of a plan, is it."

"No," Ivan agreed.

"Maybe," said Anders, "We could...you know...preemptively clear ourselves."

"Like how?"

"Like, remember when we stole the fire truck?"

Ivan smiled. It was one of their most famous childhood escapades. Ivan and his two closest friends: Anders and Owen, had snuck into the station and lifted the spare fire engine key from where it lived in the chief's coat pocket.

Then they'd taken the fire truck out for a joyride. Owen steered, Ivan worked the foot pedals, and Anders had his head out the side window, whooping and hollering for all he was worth.

The joyride had come to an end when Owen lost control and driven off the road into a ditch. Ivan had slammed on the brakes before being flung headfirst into the dashboard. He still had a scar above his left eyebrow as a memento.

"Remember how Owen played that one?"

Ivan's smile slipped.

Owen was Magnus's oldest son, self-assured and able to lie with blue-eyed innocence. He had invented a fourth person, an older kid, who'd apparently driven the truck. At the crash scene, Ivan's head wound bled so much that he'd been sure he was going to die. Anders was freaking out, Ivan was woozy and sick, and Owen had smoothly talked their way out of a tsunami of trouble.

That pretty much sums up my childhood friendships.

"So what, you're saying we should invent some other person that caused all the trouble on the island?" said Ivan.

"Well, if it comes to that, it might help to muddy the waters a little."

"Neither of us is that good a liar," said Ivan.

"Well, if we end up talking to the police, we'll need to come up with something," said Anders.

"Yeah," said Ivan, staring into space. "Something." *Something wicked this way comes.* An image formed in his mind. The island, wreathed in shadow. He shivered.

Anders checked his phone.

"Your girlfriend awake yet?"

"Her name is Amelie," said Anders.

"I know," said Ivan. "I'm still pissed at you, you know."

Anders looked unimpressed. "If being a Viking is what you want to do, why care what anyone else thinks? Fuck 'em."

"Easy for you to say."

Anders grinned, his curls making a blonde halo around his head. "Yup."

Ivan rolled his eyes. "Git. And I still say you called me for help because Hamish was KO'd, and I'm the only one with a boat."

"Not true." Anders was suddenly serious. "I came to you, Ivan, because you're my best friend. And when shit gets real, you're the guy who'll go all the way."

Ivan was still, startled by this sudden admission. "Thanks," he said at last. "And if by 'all the way' you mean killing someone, then yeah, I guess you got that right."

"Shit, I forgot again." Anders looked so mortified that Ivan started to laugh. Anders looked shocked, and then he started to laugh too.

Ivan hiccuped a few times and got the slightly hysterical laughter under control. A tension he hadn't been aware of released, and with it came the first clear thought he'd had all morning.

"We have to go back." He knew it was true as soon as he said it.

"Go back?"

"To the island."

The itch of not knowing if Magnus and his gang had survived was burrowing into Ivan's mind like a splinter.

"If they've survived and are coming back, we need to know."

Anders shook his head slowly. "I don't know. What if we find...bodies? Or worse, survivors?"

"We could take Karl," said Ivan.

Now Anders looked confused.

"That little toerag? Why?"

"Because he's the perfect alibi for why we'd go there: we're helping him look for his dad."

"Can't we go secretly?"

"You can't do anything secret in this town. The only reason no one saw us the first time is because of the storm. And I'm not taking my boat in that kind of weather again."

"What are we going to do about Amelie?" said Anders, tugging at a curl of his blonde hair.

"It really bothers you to lie to her, right?"

Anders nodded.

Ivan growled in frustration. "I know she's your girlfriend and all, but I hardly know her. I'm not putting my fate in her hands. What happened on the island was mental. I wouldn't believe it."

"It's not her fault you hardly know her," said Anders.

Ivan raised an eyebrow at him. "Feel free to invite me along on your next date then."

"Fine, I will."

"Do you know the best way to keep a secret? Don't tell anyone. The more people who know I killed Michals, the more likely it is I'll end up on trial for murder. If Amelie thinks we're lying, she could hang me out to dry."

"No one could prove anything," said Anders.

"Except the kidnappers."

"So...we go to the island with Karl? I still don't understand why you'd want that snitch along."

Ivan shrugged. "His father might still be alive."

"His kidnapping, murdering father."

"I just need to know if they've escaped. We may even be able to find evidence in the cave. That way, if any of them have survived, we can get them arrested."

Anders huffed out a breath. "Fine. But this better not have something to do with...what happened before. With you and Owen."

Ivan didn't answer, so Anders went on.

"And we need to do some repairs on your boat."

"Because you made me take it out in a hurricane."

"No, because you ran it up a rocky beach at top speed."

"Instead of capsizing it."

Ivan's shoulders loosened a fraction. It felt good to joke with his friend again like everything was normal. *Especially when it isn't.*

Anders glanced at his watch.

"I'm due at the store in an hour. I need time to freshen up, look presentable. I'll see you at the boatyard this afternoon."

"Laters."

After Anders left, Ivan stared at the carpet some more. Then he went upstairs to tidy up.

Glowering at the mirror, Ivan tried to brush his hair into a semblance of neatness, but it stubbornly refused to stay put. It was thick but not long enough to brush across in an emo style and hide the fresh bruises on his face.

Back in his bedroom, a small pile of papers confronted him. Ivan groaned. It was his last, long-shot university application. *Soon to be overdue.*

He knew Anders had already been accepted into a university in London, close by where Amelie's family lived.

I guess I know where he's going at the end of summer.

Ivan ran his hand through his hair and tried to muster the motivation to sit down and fill in the damn forms. His mum had been very specific in their last phone conversation. 'You had better get *all* your university applications in, or you'll be getting a job packing groceries at the supermarket when we get home.'

Sitting cross-legged on the living room carpet downstairs, Ivan spread the pamphlets and printed forms in a half-circle around him.

"Regents University London," he read and shrugged.

It already felt like he wasn't going anywhere after summer. Each university rejection letter pulled him further into gloom. *Somewhere there's a supermarket uniform with my name on it.*

Ivan knew he wasn't stupid. It was more...a lack. Of focus and direction. *Maybe Magnus was right about me being an empty vessel.*

Half an hour later, he'd filled out a pack of lies about his ambitions, hopes and dreams. The application was barely passable, but Ivan was done. *It's enough to keep mum off my back, at least.*

Searching for something to eat in the kitchen, Ivan's eye caught again on the ripped-open cat biscuit boxes. Thoughtfully, he took one out and scattered a few biscuits on the pantry floor. Their cat, with typical feline loyalty, had taken to eating at the neighbour's while his mother was away. So if the biscuits disappeared, it might prove...something. *That you've just encouraged the local rat population to move indoors.*

Another inspiration struck him, and he opened a jar of flour from the pantry.

Humming the tune of "Who's afraid of the big bad wolf," Ivan sprinkled the flour on the pantry floor. If the night creature came again, he might get a clue as to what kind of animal it was.

I may have officially lost it, but at least I'm taking the initiative here.

Ivan spared a minute to jot 'keen to take initiative' inside a likely box on his application form. That done, he headed into the garage where his boxing bags and Viking weaponry hung. It would do him good to hit something that didn't hit back.

8

Ivan's phone beeped. He pulled his boxing gloves off and checked his phone.

It was a message from Anders.

> You coming?

Ivan wiped the sweat off his face and texted back.

> Where?

> To fix your boat. Going there now.

There seemed no easy way to duck out of this, so Ivan took a one-minute shower, locked up and walked over the ridge to East Bay.

His boat was still drawn up on the beach where they'd left her after the storm. They slowly rowed her around to the town boat ramp, hauled her up onto a wheeled base, and trolleyed her into his family's boat shed.

Although he complained about his boat, the truth was Ivan had spent some of the happiest hours of his life in this shed, working on it with his grandfather.

Inside was cool and voluminous. Light filtered through dusty skylights high above. Swallows nested in the old timber rafters, and many of the windows were cracked but not broken. When Ivan rolled the big barn doors open, they had a view of the sea. All in all, it was a perfect place to spend a summer afternoon.

Ivan could hear the ocean lapping against the wharf thirty paces away, and the interior was peaceful in a way that made him feel like he'd travelled back in time a hundred years. All his grandfather's old tools were there, neatly labelled and hung in place on the wall, and in one corner was the small portable kiln the old man had used to cast metal hardware for the boat.

Unlike the newer fibreglass and steel boats, Ivan's boat was the traditional kind: wooden, clinker-built, and very, very, heavy.

Ivan thought his yacht was far better looking than the modern boats the villagers used. There was a cleanness to the lines that came from the curve of timbers. *The design is not that different from a thousand years ago when Viking longboats raided this coast.*

For the next two hours, they sanded, scraped, and sawed away, fixing the timbers that had splintered when they landed on the island. The air filled with two of Ivan's favourite scents: the smell of old engine oil and fresh wood shavings.

"It looks good," said Anders at last, running his fingers over the timbers.

"Should hope so," said Ivan, wiping sweat out of his eyes. He'd been lying right under the boat, preparing the surface for sealing.

"The varnish is up there by the soldering iron," said Ivan.

Soon the strong smell of marine varnish covered the sawdust scent. Painting it on made the wood glow golden.

Stretching his tired back, Ivan crawled out from under the boat and rose to his feet. He ran his hand along the bow, thinking of Viking invaders sailing East across the ocean from Denmark and Norway.

Sails for the journey, oars for battle.

The humming sounds of the day brightened while the inky shadows around the boatshed became softer and darker. There was a buzzing in his ears, and even with one hand braced against the side of his boat, Ivan drifted off balance.

Ivan took his hand off the boat, and shadow dripped from it like paint. The buzzing became louder, and Ivan shut his eyes so that he wouldn't feel so off balance. *I'll just walk out into the sunlight,* he thought. *That'll fix it.*

He gave a start when someone grabbed his shoulder.

Anders was behind him with one hand on his shoulder, and in front of Ivan was a three-meter sheer drop straight down into the concrete drydock.

Ivan blinked.

"Uh..." was all he got out before Anders pulled him roughly back from the edge.

"What the hell, Ivan!" His friend was angry. *Frightened angry.*

"I, uh, dunno. I wanted to go out in the sun?"

"You mental or something? You scared the bejeezus out of me!" Anders swiped sweat off his forehead. "One moment, you were by the boat. Then you, you must have gone round somehow because you weren't in the shed, and I had to run outside to find you, and you were just walking towards the dock edge like you weren't even going to stop."

Ivan rubbed his face. His skin was hot, almost fevered. *Maybe sunlight isn't what I need.*

"Thanks, mate. My bad. I think it must have been the varnish. Too many fumes. I feel a bit high right now."

Anders relaxed a little. "Junkie."

But he kept a close eye on Ivan as they went back into the boathouse. They tidied up for the next quarter-hour, neither saying much. As the shadows stretched towards evening, they stood back and surveyed their work.

Ivan patted the boat. "It'll be good for tomorrow. She's not so bad when she's not wallowing in a storm swell."

As he rested against the boat hull, Ivan realised the murmurings he'd heard in his head all day were finally still.

Everything's going to be alright. I'll sort things out.

A mood of pleasant optimism rose in him as he stretched, cracking his neck from one side to the other, while Anders studied him carefully. *Probably looking for more signs of me losing the plot.*

"Time for lunch?" he said.

"Dinner more like," said Anders, checking his watch.

Sun still shone outside, but it was high summer and the days were long.

"I think…" Ivan trailed off. "Fish and chips. At Henrik's. My shout if you do the dishes."

"That was a dad joke, five points to you," said Anders absently. "Let's go."

9

The little village of Clarecross, where Ivan lived, had two pubs. One was posh and catered to tourists, and the other was Henrik's.

Ivan and Anders pushed Henrik's heavy front doors open to warm air, the sounds of many people talking, and the smell of spilt beer.

Ivan still felt slightly off-kilter from the strange experience at the boatyard. He hunched his shoulders, buried his hands in his pockets, and headed for their favourite table in the back corner of the room.

Half an hour later, several people had stopped by their table to chat. The town was full of rumours of how three of their own, strong men, good sailors, had left yesterday, just before a huge storm had blown up out of nowhere. None of the men had been found.

"Lost at sea" was the repeated phrase. Each time he heard it, Ivan's mood went further down. He half expected the five missing men to turn up, covered with rock dust and mauled by the sea, to accuse him of...what? *Foiling an attempted murder and trying to kill them all using supernatural powers... Nope, not that likely, Ivan.*

The ale was not helping, even a little. He could feel the gaze of Magnus's youngest son, Karl, from across the room. The kid was not supposed to be in here, he was just fourteen after all. But no one would refuse him anything this evening. Not with his father missing.

He suspects something. But he can't prove anything. Ivan shook himself. *Why am I thinking like I've committed a crime? I stopped some murderers from killing Anders's girlfriend.*

It didn't help.

Ivan got up to get a beer, and when he looked back, Amelie had joined Anders at their table. She was tucked in close to him. Her face was pale, but her mouth was set in a hard line.

"She remembers being attacked by men in masks," Anders had told Ivan earlier. "They came at her when she was walking to work. Someone jabbed her with a syringe, and she blanked. The next thing she remembers was waking up on the path outside the village."

"That's really all?" Ivan had asked.

"She says that's all. She went to the police, who were useless, and the doctor, who didn't find anything wrong with her."

If I were Amelie, I would keep my cards close to my chest too. He edged through the standing drinkers to the bar and put his tankard down.

He slid some coins across and raised his eyebrows at Henrik, manning the beer taps behind the bar. Henrik was a man of few words, and right now, so was Ivan.

Back at the table, Ivan set the full tankard down and threw himself into the seat facing them.

"So..." said Ivan.

Amelie's hands were clenched on the tabletop. Anders, on the other hand, was trying hard to appear relaxed, leaning back with one arm casually around his girlfriend's shoulders.

Ivan realised he was taut as a wire. *I'm spoiling for a fight. Why?* He was about to say something inflammatory when his classmate Sophie pushed her way out of the crowd and came towards them. Reluctantly Ivan shifted along to make room for her.

"So, you two made up. That's nice." Sophie sat down, her overdone eye makeup and eyelash extensions looking as out of place as they always did at Henriks. "It's all gone a bit crazy now hasn't it?"

"You could say that," said Ivan.

Sophie reached across and squeezed Amelie's hands. "I heard about what happened to you."

"Oh?" Amelie sounded like she didn't want to talk about it, but Sophie had never been one to pick up subtle social cues.

"Oh yes," she said. "Sian at the police station, you know, she does the tea and typing, she said they was all talking about an abduction. And then when she heard it was you, well!" Sophie leaned back in her seat, trying her best to look sympathetic but clearly eager for more information.

Amelie smiled tightly and made a non-committal noise.

"You know what they thought?" said Sophie.

"I'm sure you'll tell us," said Amelie.

"That it could be uni students on a stupid dare. Or," she drew a deep breath, "the Russian mob."

"I think it was probably members of a secret death cult," said Ivan, and Anders choked on the beer he'd been about to swallow.

"You never," smiled Sophie and patted his arm. "You with your imagination. No wonder you're into that weird history stuff."

"If only it was all there was to it," muttered Ivan.

"Now," Sophie went on, "Sian from the police station said they didn't know what to do with it, so they called the headquarters, you know, up the line, and then things really got interesting."

"Like how?" said Ivan, curious despite himself.

She waved a hand. "Lots of typing, memos, conference calls, and all that. Sian had been hoping for a slow day so she could nip out and get her nails done, but no, they had her run off her feet all day, doing this and that."

"How inconvenient for her," said Amelie. Anders tightened his arm around her shoulders, but Sophie went on, impervious to undertones.

"Yes, she said it got especially busy when the new police lady arrived."

Ivan's neck prickled. He'd read somewhere that this was a response from long ago when humans had more body hair. The author thought ancient man had been able to raise his hackles, like a dog or wolf. That's how Ivan felt now. Like a dog that scented danger but didn't know whether to fight, or flee, or even where the danger was coming from.

"A police lady who specialises in uni student pranks?" said Ivan, raising his eyebrows.

"Sian said she had lovely shoes," said Sophie, "and a tailored suit. Not a hair out of place. Made our local boys look well sloppy, I bet."

"Did she say why she was here?" asked Ivan.

"Oh," said Sophie airily, "You know."

Ivan exchanged a glance with Anders, but it was Amelie who spoke next.

"She believed me."

"Who?" Ivan sat back in his chair. "About what?"

"The police detective." Amelie enunciated the word detective very clearly. "She believes that I was kidnapped and taken somewhere." She looked straight at Ivan, jaw set.

It was that moment when we lifted her out of the boat, and she opened her eyes and saw me. No good deed goes unpunished.

Ivan felt his vestigial hackles standing up straight again. He tried to look calm, only as interested as any normal person. *Nothing about any of this is normal!* He firmly told the frantic voice in his head to shut the hell up.

He shrugged. "All I know is that we spent the afternoon looking for you in a stormy forest, getting soaked through. Then the storm cleared, and your boyfriend insists we go out and check all the bays in my boat in case you decided to go for a night swim." *You're talking too much, Ivan. It's a sign of guilt.*

"Ooooh!" said Sophie. "Maybe it was those, you know, the NSA. Like in that series *Cyberdrome*. You know, they take you away if you know too much."

"So not helping," said Anders under his breath.

Amelie jerked her chin angrily, then tucked her pixie-cut hair behind her ears. That movement always annoyed Ivan. He knew he should be sympathetic, but instead, he felt prickly. *Because she suspects me. She's probably grassed on me to this special policewoman.*

"Did they look like the NSA?" he asked Amelie. "The people who attacked you."

"How would I know?" she said witheringly.

Ivan tried to balance a spoon on its edge. The silver bowl of it reflected the pub lights into his eyes. "Do you think they'll come back?" he said.

"All I know is that I'm now packing some pepper spray, a tracking device, and a taser," she said.

"Woah," said Ivan. "Respect."

Anders looked smug while Sophie stared.

"Where did you say you were from?"

"London," said Amelie, and Sophie nodded like it all made sense.

"That's what you get in the big cities," she said.

Ivan saw Amelie try to understand this statement, then give up.

Unlike most people in this town, Amelie was a newcomer. He supposed that was why Anders had latched onto her so fast. She was someone who hadn't known him all his life, someone he could be a different person with.

Maybe that's why I'm jealous. Because it's exactly what I want. A chance to be someone else. Maybe that's why the Viking re-enactments. Huh. Look at me, psychoanalysing myself like a proper grown-up.

"Do you think she'll make any arrests?" said Sophie.

"Who?"

"The new police lady, of course."

"This being such a small town, we probably even know whoever it is," said Ivan.

"Unless they came from out of town," said Anders.

Sophie shook her head. "That's only if it's mobsters or the NSA."

"If it's a cult, they could all be here among us," said Ivan.

"It could be a Wicca thing," said Sophie thoughtfully.

"Vampires," said Ivan. "Not real ones," he said hurriedly, in case Amelie tasered him from sheer annoyance. "But people pretending."

"You're such a pillock, Ivan," said Amelie under her breath. Anders looked like he agreed.

"Hey!" he protested. "I'm trying to be helpful here. Have you been back to the scene of the crime? There might be clues."

"Like the laundry tag off a robe?" said Amelie sarcastically. "Or a piece of paper they just happened to drop with their name and number?"

"I'm not trying to be Sherlock Holmes here, but there might be something," said Ivan.

"Benioff already checked it out," said Amelie.

"Who?"

"Benioff. The detective. And if you make one Sherlock reference, I will kill you."

"Elementa–" Ivan started to say, then stopped himself. "Good to know you've got a proper consulting detective on the job."

Sophie had lost interest in the conversation and was scrolling through the newsfeed on her phone.

"Ooh," she said. "Look at this!"

She held up the bright screen and expanded the picture.

It was a photo of the coast guard searching for the missing men, with a footnote saying there had also been an abduction reported. "Crime expert speculates: could these two incidents be related?" read the article.

"It's like we're on that show," said Sophie. "What's it called? The one on the seaside with the guy from Doctor Who."

Ivan peered over at Sophie's screen. The article was uncomfortably close to the truth. *Did anyone spot us going out in the storm last night?*

All at once, the air in the pub felt too crammed, the noises too loud. Ivan stood up. "Hey Anders," he said to Anders. "Come outside with me a moment?"

He walked towards the door. A whispered argument was going on between Anders and Amelie. Her angry, demanding he stay, him placating, but slowly sliding out of his seat.

Ivan stepped outside, the cool air blowing away the hot fug of the bar. Anders joined him and followed him down the alleyway around the side of the building.

Once they were out of earshot of the people in the bar, Ivan rounded on Anders.

"What the hell do you think you're doing?" his voice was tight, furious. A pressure was building inside his head, and it both frightened and fueled him.

"Nothing," Anders's voice was deliberately slow and calm. He didn't rattle easily. "Just what we agreed."

Ivan shook his head. "You're encouraging Amelie in this kidnapping story. You saw the way she looks at me. She's putting something together in her head—I know it."

"Well, acting so weird makes you look proper dodgy."

For a moment, Ivan considered hitting his friend in the jaw. A nice, clean, right cross. He really wanted to. Then he deliberately took hold of his anger and put it somewhere safe. *In the ocean, where it can't burn you.*

He leaned back against the wall, the pressure slowly draining out of him. "You're right. It's just...well...hard to keep things in perspective."

Anders leaned against the wall with him, his arms crossed. Ivan saw his feelings mirrored there. Tense, worried, and unsure. *Why did Anders have to drag me into this? Then again, if I hadn't been there, him and Amelie would probably both be dead right now.*

"She says she thinks she remembered seeing you."

"Yeah, well," said Ivan. "She did see me."

"I told her you were with me all night, and maybe she heard us in the forest, looking for her. She hasn't come right out and said anything. But I know what you mean. She's angry. And scared. I don't know what she's really thinking."

Ivan was abruptly exhausted. "How long is she going to be here?"

"The summer," Anders sounded defensive again.

"Just...don't tell her anything. Stick to the story." *And maybe all of this will go away.*

"I think you're wrong on that count. But," Anders held his hands up, "I get why you're worried. I got your back, mate. We'll sort it."

Ivan smiled wanly. "Do you have any idea what she's told this policewoman?"

"Just that she got attacked and drugged unconscious, then woke up in the forest dressed in a weird old-fashioned dress. At least, that's what she told me she said."

"Anything about me?"

"I don't think so." Anders didn't sound sure at all.

Ivan straightened, drew in a deep breath, and then blew it out. "I'm going home. Tell Amelie we were talking about something else." He stretched his neck to one side, then the other, hearing a satisfying 'crack' each time.

"Like what?" said Anders.

Ivan shrugged. "Tell her I'm in love with her. Or you."

Anders snorted.

"And, if you can, find out what she told the detective."

"Yeah. See you tomorrow." Anders went back inside the bar, leaving Ivan outside, breathing in the cool night air.

10

A wave of tiredness swept through Ivan as he watched Anders go. He walked down the road to the small village port, where the wharves were silent and dark, abandoned for the night.

Along the largest wharf, the fishing vessels lay quietly in the water. Right at the end of the pier, he sat down. The water was pitch black and silky, with barely a ripple. There were creaks and groans now and then from timber rubbing on fenders and other unidentified movements in the gear and tackle surrounding the wharf.

Ivan fell still, staring into the water. A greenish glow began to spread through the black ripples. It was hypnotic, not quite a light, more of a double image. He had the sense he was seeing it not with his eyes but with his mind, and if he blinked, it would disappear.

So he didn't blink. He just stared, his head gently nodding down towards the water.

All things are alive. The thought surfaced like the gleam in the waters. For a few moments, Ivan had the sense of another world, sharing the same space as the world he knew, full of depth and meaning. A world where the trees, rocks, and water all talked to one another in secret languages he could almost understand. Just a shadow's thickness away.

Footsteps echoed along the pier. He blinked, and the other world was gone.

Ivan stood up to meet the intruder. It was Magnus's youngest son, Karl. The youth stopped for a few seconds, his face shadowed. His body language spoke of uncertainty. Finally, he half leaned, half sat on a stack of crates opposite Ivan.

Ivan, curious but wary, did the same. They sat in silence for a long moment.

"What did you do last night? Did you go to the island?"

Ivan considered Karl. He didn't feel like lying to a boy who may have lost his father for good. Even if said father was a murdering bastard.

"Anders told me you spun some cock and bull story about the island. If you think your father's on the island, why haven't you told the search and rescue crew to look there? Why haven't you gone there yourself?"

Karl said nothing, his face shuttered.

"I can go now and tell the coast guard that's where they should look." Ivan made to get up.

"No," said Karl, rushed.

"Why?" said Ivan.

"I've already been there. There's nothing." Karl looked so miserable that Ivan momentarily felt sorry for him until he remembered what the robed men had been about to do to Amelie. *Amelie and how many others?*

"You know something," he said to Karl. "About the island. Why do you think the missing men went there? Tell me the truth."

Karl sneered. "Why would I do that?"

"Because then I might take you to the island."

Karl's face twisted. "I already told you I went there," he said, voice low and furious.

"You did say that."

"So?"

"So I think you're lying."

Karl stared at him, his jaw clenched. There was a brief scrabble as he rushed at Ivan, fists swinging. It ended as Ivan rolled back on the crates and flipped Karl into the water behind him. There was a splash and then a desperate, thrashing sound.

Ivan rolled back onto his feet and shoved the crates aside. Karl was in the water, but unlike every other villager, he wasn't swimming smoothly to shore. He was flailing and sinking, his face a mask of terror.

Ivan watched him for a couple of seconds, then lay down on the pier and grabbed an outflung arm. Karl seized him with such wild strength Ivan would have ended up in the water if he hadn't already been lying down, braced and ready.

He lifted the terrified boy, pulling him onto the pier. Karl lay there gasping, water streaming off him and pooling on the concrete, his frantic breaths loud in the still night.

Gradually his breathing slowed, and he regained his composure.

"I hate you," was the first thing he found breath to say. Ivan merely waited at a safe distance.

"Fine. I didn't go to the island. I can't sail out there by myself. Even with a life jacket. I just...can't." It was an admission wrenched from him, and Ivan thought Karl would probably hate him more later when he thought back on this conversation. *That's too bad. I need to find out more.*

"What do you think we'll find on the island if we go there?" he asked.

Karl shrugged.

"You planning on rescuing your dad?"

Karl stared at him and then, horribly, began to laugh. It was a thin sound, more like an old man's laugh than a teenager's.

"Rescue...." wheezed Karl. His gaze was burningly intense. "I want to make sure the bastard's really dead."

Ivan stared at him. He couldn't think of anything to say.

"You have no idea what he's like when he's not busy being a pillar of the community," Karl said.

I think I have a pretty good idea.

"My mum actually smiled at breakfast today."

Oh.

"It wasn't always that bad. Not when I was a kid. But some years ago..." he trailed off. "There's this group." Karl's voice had dropped low. Like he was talking more to himself than Ivan. "Dad's one of them. He's gotten to be high up in it, I think. They do things. Old stuff, rituals, rites. Weird shit. But they're not just crackpots. They're powerful. They've been around a long time, and there's groups in different parts of the country. And..."

There was such a long silence Ivan thought Karl had decided not to say anything more. But he kept quiet because he could feel the struggle inside the boy. If Karl did speak, it would be something he'd never admitted before, even to himself.

"When he wanted me to come into the group, I told Da it was stupid, old people's stuff, and I didn't care. Not like Owen." Karl shot him a glance, and a chill crept into Ivan's chest. "The truth is...the truth is I was scared. Sometimes the way they are after a ritual. The way they look. I don't want to know what they do. I think it must be bad."

There was another long silence.

Karl hunched low, not meeting Ivan's eyes, and Ivan recognised the dynamic of a confessional. *Maybe it'll even help him feel better.*

"There's a thing they do each year. On the island. It's very secret, and other men come from other places for it. This year, Da was excited. I heard him saying they'd found something powerful. A way to do a thing they'd been trying to do for ages. And then they went off to the island, and the storm hit out of nowhere, and now they've disappeared. And....and I don't feel bad about it. I know I should, but I don't. I'm glad." Karl's voice thickened like he was trying not to cry.

"I'm not judging you for not wanting Magnus back. I'd rather he didn't come back either." There was a heavy silence. "You must think I'm a total bastard," said Ivan.

Karl was still for a heartbeat, then snorted faintly. "Yeah, you are."

"My boat is old and not that fast. It doesn't weather storms all that well. But in weather like this, I could take you to the island if you like. And we could have a look around."

Karl was staring like he'd never seen Ivan before. "You would do that? Why?"

Ivan shrugged. "I'm curious. I want to know what happened too." He didn't say, 'I also want to make sure Magnus is dead.' The creeping horror of whether living men were stuck in a cave weighed on him. He was still figuring out what to do if they found all five murderous men there, alive. *I just need to know what happened.*

"When?" asked Karl.

"Tomorrow morning."

Karl's face veiled again. For a kid his age, he was eerily good at hiding his feelings. Ivan wondered briefly if he was walking into another trap.

"I suppose I could do that," Karl said at last.

"Come by the boatyard. Early. And then we'll see."

Karl nodded and just like that, got up and left. His shoes squelched faintly on the concrete pier, leaving wet footprints.

Ivan leaned back against the crates again. *Is this a good idea? Or is this my guilty conscience? Do I have a death wish?* Ivan rubbed the back of his neck. *It's just that I hate waiting around for something bad to happen. More than anything. I hate not knowing.*

Ivan leaned back to look up at the stars. As always, he found their vastness both dwarfing and calming. An old poem from English class came into his head:

'To hold infinity in the palm of your hand

And eternity in an hour.'

Ivan sighed, his breath frosting slightly as he breathed out. The tiny whirls of steam glowed orange in halogen street lights. *When it comes down to it, all our problems are really very small.*

Ivan smiled faintly. *I may have just set a bad plan in motion.* He pulled out his phone and texted Anders.

> Going to the island early tomorrow with Karl. You in?

> Mate. You got a deathwish?

> Yeah. And?

> K. cu there

Ivan's thoughts drifted as he walked home, the dark patches between each streetlight becoming longer as he headed out of town.

Curiously, as he entered the shadows between streetlights, he didn't feel less safe. It may have been in his imagination, but as he walked into deeper shadows, he felt the brush of something close against his side. Something large and barely there, but comforting.

When Ivan got home, he didn't bother to turn on any lights. He simply went upstairs, dropped onto his bed, and fell into a dreamless sleep.

11

Ivan woke early to find his room was wreathed in shadows, and he was not in his bed.

He stared at the light fitting a foot away from his face and tried to work out where he was. He had dreamed he'd been floating in an ocean.

Realisation dawned. He was suspended in space a foot away from his bedroom ceiling. In an instant, all the shadows vanished. A moment of free fall and he hit the bed with a tremendous 'whoomph!'

Ivan lay for a moment, still staring at the ceiling, utterly perplexed. Then, in the manner of eighteen-year-olds, he turned over, went back to sleep, and woke half an hour later when his alarm buzzed, remembering only that he'd had a strange dream.

Rolling out of bed, Ivan stretched and yawned. He felt surprisingly good. The ominous events of the past two days seemed a world away, and his room was full of bright early morning light.

All evidence to the contrary, a mood of cautious optimism prevailed.

Today, they would go to the island and find evidence of Magnus's crimes. They would present the evidence to the police. If Magnus was still alive, he would be arrested, and Ivan would go back to having a normal summer. He'd get his last college application in and work out his next move.

Ivan tried not to think of the possibility they might find bodies there, crushed under the fallen rock.

I don't have to clean up this mess with Magnus and his cult, he thought, staring at himself in the mirror. *It's not my job. It's not even my mess.*

The words echoed hollowly round and round in his head, spoiling the bright promise of the day.

Ivan pulled on ripped black jeans, a faded T-shirt and an old football jumper. One black coffee and a text to Anders later, and he was on his way to the boat shed.

His phone beeped as he walked the last stretch of road to the port. It was his mum checking in on him.

> Hi darling, how are you going? Did you get the applications in? How was the end of school? What have you been up to?

I had a brawl with my best friend, foiled a kidnapping, killed someone by accident, am a suspect in a missing person case, and right now, I'm returning to a crime scene where everyone might be dead.

Ivan gave a deep sigh and sent a response.

> Fine mum. Just the usual. Weather's nice here. How's Florence? Hope you're having a great time there with Greg

Anders met him outside the shed, hands tucked into the pocket of a dark blue hoodie.

Ivan unlocked the thick brass padlock and swung the doors wide with a creak of rusty metal.

"Where's the rat?" said Anders.

"Who?" said Ivan.

"Karl."

"I'm right here," said Karl, stepping out from the shadow of some stacked crates. Ivan had to admit it was a cool move and slightly creepy.

Anders snorted. "How long did you spend hiding behind the fish trays, waiting to make your grand entrance?"

Karl ignored him and stalked into the shed. He looked at Ivan's sailboat, his head cocked to one side.

"This thing? That's how we're getting to the island?"

Ivan eyed him. "Plan on backing out?"

Karl glowered. He had on a hoodie, but unlike Anders, the hood was up, shading his face. His thin shoulders were hunched, and his too-short jeans gave him a street urchin look. Ivan supposed he was going for the hipster vibe, but with his pale face and hollow cheeks, Karl looked more like an underage vagrant. *Or an emo teenage vampire caught out in daylight.*

Anders cleared his throat. Ivan knew that sound. His friend made it whenever he was about to say something Ivan was not going to like.

"Yes?" said Ivan.

"Um, we have one more person coming."

Ivan stopped in the middle of putting the padlock back in place. Without turning around, he said: "And who would that be?"

"Ah, you see..." said Anders.

"I'm coming too," said a clear voice, and Ivan whirled around.

Amelie walked forward to stand next to Anders, her dark eyeliner and bleached blonde hair looking out of place in the early morning light.

Anders had his standard avoiding-a-fight hunched posture, trying to pretend everything was fine.

"Anders told me everything," she said, tilting her chin defiantly.

That lying, cheating bastard. Ivan could feel a vein throbbing in his forehead as he glared at them both.

There was a tense silence.

"Anders, come over here for a moment," said Ivan, shooting a glance at Karl. *I don't want him to hear this.* Anders and Ivan walked to the dock edge, out of earshot. Ivan could feel Amelie's glare between his shoulder blades. He didn't care. He was furious.

As soon as they'd reached the dock, Ivan turned to face Anders. His friend was looking defensive but determined. Ivan wanted to hit him. "So," his voice came out hoarse, barely above a whisper. "You thought, Anders, that hauling me into a pit of murderous maniacs wasn't enough. Without asking me, you decided to share our little adventure with the one person who's been telling the police all about me."

Anders hunched his shoulders further. Ivan felt bad, like someone who'd just kicked a puppy, but he couldn't stop himself. *Why am I so angry?*

"She deserves to know the truth," said Anders. "So I told her. The same way I told you all those years ago. Would you rather be kept in the dark?"

That brought Ivan up short. The rage drained out of him like water, leaving a cold empty feeling. He cleared his throat and scrubbed his hand through his hair.

"Yeah, ok. You got a point. But what the hell, Anders? A little warning next time?"

Anders shifted his feet. "She was about to go to the police and accuse you, Ivan. Also, I didn't tell her about Michals. Just…the other stuff."

Ivan shot a look back over his shoulder. Amelie was watching them, arms crossed. She didn't look the least bit apologetic.

"Grand," he said at last. "Ok. Let's just go. We'll sort it out later." He seized hold of the empty feeling, stuffing it deep inside him. They walked back to the others, and Ivan knew his face would be unreadable. *This is why most people don't get close to you.*

Karl had been watching all this with great interest. *Trouble in paradise. Must be nice to see other people's lives aren't perfect.*

Ivan gave Amelie a curt nod.

"We're good. Let's go."

Together, they wheeled the boat out and down the ramp to the water. Ivan pushed her off the trailer and admired the way she floated, shapely and golden with her newly mended hull.

It was one of those clear, cool mornings with very little in the way of wind. Anders climbed on board, turning back to help Amelie.

As Ivan climbed in, he caught sight of Karl's face. The youth's jaw was set in grim determination, and for an eerie moment, Ivan saw Karl's older brother Owen. Anders's warning echoed in Ivan's mind. *Do you really think he can be trusted? Coming from that family?*

Ivan got Amelie to sit in the bow and Karl in the stern. He and Anders each took an oar and started rowing slowly out of the port.

"You're kidding," said Karl. "We're going to row all the way to the island?"

Anders let his oar release a small sharp spray of water to land in Karl's lap. Amelie snickered.

"Watch and learn, grasshopper," said Ivan.

They progressed slowly out to the edge of the headland. The water was liquid glass beneath them, and the only sound was the 'chop sloosh' of the oars. Karl's knuckles turned white as he gripped the stern seat edge. Ivan felt a momentary pang of sympathy as the boy nervously checked over his shoulder how far they were from shore.

Clearing the headland, they caught the zephyr of wind Ivan had seen ruffling the water offshore. He and Anders shipped their oars and raised the sail. The wind was hardly enough to stir his hair, but it glided the boat along at a steady pace. Ivan evicted Karl from the stern seat, took the tiller, and pointed them at the island.

For a time, there was nothing but the fresh morning breeze, the flawless dome of the sky, and the deep ocean blue with the faint track of their wake behind them. Ivan breathed out, his shoulders loosening. *Peace at last.* The breeze freshened, and Karl gave a squawk and hunkered down as the boat heeled over, picking up speed.

Anders grinned. "You been taking swimming lessons lately? If you fall out, we're not turning around to pick you up."

Karl scowled and ducked down further. Gripping the rail edge, his whole body flinched from the water flowing past him, just inches away.

Ivan relented and let him switch over to sit on the high side of the boat. Watching him clamber awkwardly over, clinging to every available handhold, he wondered what it had been like for Karl growing up.

He would have been overshadowed constantly by his older brother Owen, the golden boy, effortlessly good at everything. *And he'd have had no encouragement or sympathy from Magnus. Magnus believed in being strong and taking what you wanted.*

Ivan tried to remember Magnus's wife, Astrid. When he'd all but lived at their house as a kid, she'd always been in the background, a vague figure who never asserted herself. He shivered suddenly. *How much of my childhood happiness was based on a lie?*

The island gradually dominated the view in front of them.

"Where's the sea cave?" Anders asked.

Amelie's jaw tightened as they neared the island. *Does she really not remember anything of what went down?*

Karl broke the silence in a voice so quiet Ivan had to strain to hear it: "Owen said it was just before the next bay. To the left of the landing beach."

"Owen said," Anders said, his voice abruptly loud. He shot a look at Ivan.

A pulse thumped in Ivan's neck. So Owen had been to the cave. Which meant he *had* to have known about his father's crimes. *Or did his father hide that from him too?*

Anders frowned at the island. His friend had made no secret of his dislike of Owen. Even before they'd fallen out, Anders hadn't been part of Owen's gang.

It was strange because, on the surface, Owen and Anders were two of a kind. Both blond, handsome, confident, and good at making friends. But Owen had chosen Ivan, and Anders had always been on the outside, included in their games only when it suited Owen. Looking back, Ivan knew why. *Owen didn't want a friend. He wanted a follower, a flunky. Anders saw through him, but you fit right into that role.* Years later, it still stung.

Ivan focused on the rocky shoreline. The cave had to be well hidden, or it would be more widely known in the village. *Unless you've been living in a town full of cult followers this whole time.* Ivan found the thought weirdly satisfying. If they were going to peel the lid off a conspiracy, it might as well be a big one. *Seems a little far-fetched though.*

"Did he say what to look for?" he asked Karl.

"Just...a part of the landscape that seems dark, repellent. Go towards that part, and there'll be the entrance."

"Repellent," Anders smirked. "Owen said that? What a tosser." Karl ignored him.

As they drew closer to the shoreline, they lost the wind. Lowering the sails and setting up the oars took a minute, and by the time they were ready to move on, they'd drifted close to the rocks. The sun hadn't risen high, and they were in the inky blue shadow of the island, the bright sunlit sea replaced by darker waters.

For Ivan, the island shadows lay on him like a physical presence. *Is this part of what's happening to me?* It was the first time he'd consciously framed it as something happening to him. All the weird sensations, things out of the corner of his eye. *Is there something happening...to me?*

He pushed the thought out of his mind as Amelie spoke for the first time. "There," she pointed. "That rock."

Amelie was right. The rock she singled out was dark and foreboding in a way the rocks around it weren't. Rowing nearer to it was accompanied by a sense of discomfort that escalated to disquiet, then dread, then a near panic.

Ivan gritted his teeth and dragged his oar through the water, propelling them forward. His heart thudded in his chest, and he felt like he was about to throw up. Across from him, Anders looked similarly haggard, and Amelie was a terrified statue, frozen in place.

Only Karl seemed the same, though that could have been because he was already so tense from being out on the ocean.

The prow of their boat drifted slowly forward. As it came to the point where Ivan was sure it was going to strike the rock, it somehow didn't and simply glided deeper into shadow. They slid into the rock like a reflection joining a mirror. For an instant, Ivan saw the boat's prow bend into a vanishing point on the far side of nowhere, and then the boat's momentum carried them through into darkness.

As soon as they were on the other side of the rock, the feeling of dread vanished. They were in a cave lit by the cool blue light of glow worms. The water was perfectly still, mirror black. A droplet fell somewhere to Ivan's left with a loud 'plink.'

Ivan heard Anders slowly breathe out, followed by a low rasp as their boat ran aground. He felt a great reluctance to step off it into the water, but he knew just from looking at her that there was no way Amelie was going to hop off the bow and pull the boat to shore.

Freezing water soaked his shoes as Ivan hauled the boat onto the sandy bank of the cave shore. Phosphorescence bloomed and lit the water green.

"Let's check it out then," he said. They had torches, but Ivan was unwilling to turn on an electric light or speak louder than a whisper.

This place weighed on him. The silence felt like it was waiting.

"I don't like this," muttered Karl. *Join the club.*

Amelie seemed to have recovered her nerve. She surveyed the cave with a scowl. "If there's anyone still here, I won't hesitate to..." She trailed off, oppressed by the heavy atmosphere.

Anders deliberately took out his torch, put the elastic band around his head, and switched it on. The bright white beam banished the ghostly glow-worm light, but Ivan still felt edgy. His hand crept to the hilt of his belt knife. *Better not. This place has seen enough blood.*

Very cautiously, they walked down a short passage and into the cavern where all their lives had taken a detour just two nights ago.

Half of the cavern was still there, but the rest had been obliterated by a huge rockfall. Ivan switched his torch on and turned to face Anders. His friend's face was grim.

Slowly, Ivan scanned around the cavern where there should have been candles, bones, and robed bodies.

There was nothing there. The cave was scoured clean.

Ivan's shoulders slumped. *Well, this plan went nowhere.* He resisted the urge to kick something as he peered at the rocks where the candles had been. They were weirdly shiny with the kind of residue you get from a snail trail. A powerfully strong smell of the sea filled the cave, and everywhere was covered in the same sparkly dried substance.

The rock floor was also scraped clean, but there was one point of interest. On one rock was a perfect circle as wide as Ivan's chest.

"So...not what I was expecting," said Anders. "All the creepy ritual stuff is gone. And now it smells rank."

"What do you think that is?" said Ivan, pointing at the circular imprint. Anders shone his torch on it.

"If I didn't know better," said Anders slowly, "Well, it looks like a..."

"Like a what?" said Amelie.

"Well, like a sucker print from an octopus. Only..."

"What?" Amelie snapped.

"For the print to be that big, the octopus would have to be huge. Like, it would pretty much fill this room."

Ivan tried to imagine a giant octopus (*more like a Kraken*) slithering bonelessly through here. *If that's the case, did it eat Magnus? Do giant octopuses eat people? Or is the correct word giant octopi?*

Ivan sighed.

"Well, this puts us in a worse position," he said.

"What did you expect?" said Karl. "A neatly labelled evidence locker?"

Anders glared at him.

"I'm not sure what happened here," said Ivan.

"What about that rock? At the entry," said Anders. "That was proper weird. Does this cult have...magic powers or something?"

Amelie opened her mouth to say something and then shut it.

"That may have nothing to do with Magnus," said Ivan. "This place looks ancient, far older than whatever Magnus has been doing here. And the...group he's part of is big. Right, Karl?"

Karl nodded. "There are people in other parts of the country. They organise meetings on the Dark Web."

Ivan leaned against the cool, freshly scrubbed rock. He felt flat and foolish, like someone who had put all his money on red, only to have the ball roll one more space and land on black.

"There's not much we can do then," he said. "All the evidence is gone."

Anders huffed a bit and wandered over to where the rocks had crashed down. He kicked at the ground with the toe of his shoe.

Amelie crossed her arms and squared her shoulders.

"We need a plan B."

"Let's bugger off out of here first," said Anders.

"Copy that," said Ivan. Something about this place was still upsetting him. It wasn't necessarily sinister, he realised. Certainly, bad stuff had happened here. *But this place is far older than that. It's a place of power. That's why they chose to hold their sacrifices here. It's not necessarily evil. It's just....old. And powerful. And...*

Ivan realised the cave wall had begun to tilt. Not in reality but in his mind.

Wha—?

The cave wall wasn't tilting.

He was starting to float free of his body. A second later, Ivan was looking down on himself from an uncanny angle.

Shit.

It had happened so easily. One moment listening to this place, and he'd left his body. He felt oddly calm, an observer of his translocation.

If I let go and drift away, what will happen? Will I ever get back?

Like a swimmer fighting against a strong current, Ivan fought his way back into his head.

The place relaxed around him with a feeling almost like a sigh. He opened his eyes again, looking out from his own body.

This place...wants something from me. But what?

"Let's go," he said, sounding raspy.

"What went down?" asked Amelie suddenly.

"Huh?"

"Between you and Magnus. You two definitely have history."

Ivan glanced at Anders, who shrugged, then at Karl, who had his usual inscrutable look on.

May as well. "It wasn't just me and Magnus. It was me and Magnus and Owen. Owen is Magnus's son. Karl's older brother. At the time, what happened didn't make much sense to me. Now it does."

Making sense of the past. Almost therapeutic really...

"What does that mean?" said Amelie.

Ivan glanced at Karl, then back at Amelie. "I'll tell you later." *Maybe.*

Ivan's shoulders relaxed as their boat exited the cave. The sun was higher, and they were quickly out of the shadow of the island. With the sea breeze filling the sails and the warm sun on his skin, Ivan set the tiller. He sat back and found Karl watching him intently. As soon as their eyes met, the boy looked away.

"You know something more, don't you?" said Ivan. "About what Magnus was up to."

They all faced Karl, who'd fixed his gaze on the horizon.

"Karl?"

The boy pushed his hoodie back off his face. In the sunlight, his eyes were a vivid green, mirroring the sea.

"There's his study," the boy said slowly. "If you want to find evidence."

"Evidence like what?" said Anders, arms folded across his chest.

"I think there may be a hidden room behind it," said Karl. "That part of the house is built into the hillside. I once went in the study when he wasn't there, but he'd been in there five minutes ago and hadn't gone out of the study door."

Ivan checked on Anders. His friend's mouth was set in a line, and Ivan could just about hear what he was thinking: *seems like a great way to set a trap for us.*

Ivan gave him a look that said *let's play for more information. We need some leverage, and right now, we don't have much to go on.*

"Okay," he said. "We'll check it out. In fact, we'll go there today. Right after we get back." *Before you have time to tell anyone we're coming.*

12

They tied the boat up to the family mooring and Ivan hopped onto the pier, exchanging the gentle rocking motion of the sea for the solidity of land. They were just turning onto the main street when Anders pushed them all back into a doorway. Ivan made a 'whoomph' noise as Karl's bony elbow shoved into his stomach.

"Wait," Anders sounded strained. And then: "Don't try and look! You'll just attract attention."

Ivan waited, pushed up against the door. *Is it Magnus? Or Benioff, the mystery policewoman...*

The doorway was in shadow, and he tried to imagine it getting more shadowed, hiding them. A few tense seconds later, a group of men walked down the street, heading for the docks.

Magnus wasn't among them. It was a group of his closest friends and some other men he didn't recognise.

"Out of towners," muttered Anders.

Ivan waited a minute longer, then relaxed out of the doorway. *I feel like a kid playing hide and seek. But with higher stakes.*

Casually, without a word, they all strolled down the road to the last corner before the dock and waited. A minute later, a boat engine coughed, and Magnus's boat headed out to sea. Magnus's friend Pedersen was at the wheel, with the other men positioned around him.

Ivan looked at Anders in wild surmise.

"Seems awfully convenient," muttered his friend.

Ivan looked at Amelie. She gave a curt nod.

"Karl, what's your mum doing this morning?"

"She'll be around," he said. "She doesn't go out much."

"Can you show us the study without her seeing us?"

He nodded.

"Then," Ivan drew a deep breath. "Let's do it."

They waited on the corner outside the house as Karl went in.

"I don't like it," said Anders. He'd been saying things like this for the last ten minutes, and Ivan was tired of it.

"I don't like it either," said Amelie. "But it's the best chance we have."

"One of us has to keep lookout," said Ivan. "So we know if they come back."

"When," muttered Anders.

"Grand," said Ivan, not caring if he sounded snarky. "You're it then."

Anders lapsed into grim silence, and Amelie smiled faintly.

Karl returned and jerked his head for them to follow.

"I'll be here then," said Anders. He leaned against the concrete retaining wall that bounded the garden hedge. "Waiting for you all to get caught."

"My phone's on," said Amelie. "Call us if…" Anders nodded.

The strange thing, Ivan thought, was that Magnus's house was a perfect picture of English country tranquillity: neat hedges, a flower-laden garden, a meticulously clipped lawn and spreading fruit trees. The only unusual feature was the large rock mound the house backed onto. That must be where the secret room lay. *You never know what lies beneath the surface of country charm.*

Karl led them up the path to the front door.

"Mum's out in the laundry doing the ironing," he said.

"Is she ironing black robes?" said Amelie sweetly, and Karl scowled.

"She doesn't know about any of that," he said.

I find that hard to believe. More likely, she doesn't want to know.

They heard the chug of the washing machine as they entered the house. It was an old house, several hundred years at least, with the same layered feeling as Ivan's family home.

Generations of feet had worn down the oak stair treads, and the small glass window panes made the garden outside look wavy and strange.

Magnus's study was ordered, with a large mahogany desk at one end. The other wall held a fireplace and a floor-to-ceiling shelf of books.

"Which wall goes back into the hillside?" asked Ivan, and Karl pointed at the one where the bookshelf and fireplace sat.

Ivan grinned at Amelie. "Revolving fireplace? Or a bookshelf that opens when you pull the right book?"

Her lips twitched upwards, and she started prodding the various ornamental pieces of the hearth.

It turned out to be neither. Ivan was prodding different books on the shelf when he stepped backwards and nearly tripped over the fire poker. It clattered on the tiles, and leaning down to pick it up, Ivan saw one mosaic tile shinier than the ones around it. Carefully, he put his finger on it and pushed.

There was a soft *'sprong,'* and a wood panel next to the hearth popped gently open. Ivan grinned, excitement mounting.

"Check it out."

"Wait," said Amelie. "What about booby traps?"

They both turned to Karl, who shrugged.

"How should I know? I've never seen this secret door before."

Cautiously, Ivan swung the panel open. As he did, lights came on in the room beyond. Amelie gasped.

The room beyond was carved into the rock and reminded Ivan eerily of the cave they'd been in that morning. What was helping that memory were the robes on display, hung in carved niches.

There were plain robes like the ones the men had worn the night of the ceremony, but there were also elaborate robes embroidered with gold and silver thread. It looked like real gold and silver, probably sewn a hundred years ago by some cultist.

There were shelves of aged leather-bound books and artefacts displayed on raised plinths. In one corner was a large oak chest. It was, Ivan decided, like a museum, except nothing was behind glass, and it looked rather creepier than the placid and gloomy museums he'd been to.

Feeling like an animal about to walk into a trap, Ivan stepped into the room. He saw Amelie hanging back, *smart girl*, and Karl looking carefully bland.

At one end of the room was a stone altar. As Ivan walked closer, he saw an ancient knife and cup laid together on the stone. He shivered convulsively. The objects *wanted*. They felt almost physically thirsty, and Ivan's treacherous imagination supplied what they thirsted for. With an effort, he shifted his attention to the postern next to the altar.

On it, a large book lay open. It looked ancient, with pages of leather rather than paper. Ivan jumped as Karl put a hand around his shoulder to straighten the page.

"Jeez! Make some noise when you walk, can't you!"

Karl's face was impassive. On his other side, Amelie stared down at the page.

It showed a scene of human sacrifice.

Robed figures circled an altar where a bound man stared up at the sky. A robed figure at the centre had a knife raised high, and it was pretty clear what the next frame was going to be.

"Been there, bought the T-shirt," muttered Ivan, and Amelie shot him a look.

"What? You never asked," he said defensively.

Karl turned the page, and Ivan stared. It wasn't, as he had expected, a gory scene complete with entrails and buckets of blood.

Instead, it showed two worlds, one light, one dark. Where the two worlds met was a human figure, half in shadow, half in light. And through the figure, the dark flowed into the light world, and the light was flowing into the shadow world.

Ivan's skin prickled. From the top of the page, a fork of lighting arced down to strike the figure in the chest.

He became aware of Karl's gaze on him, considering.

"Mean anything to you?" he asked.

"Nope," lied Ivan.

Karl flipped to the next page.

On this page, a man had climbed to the edge of the light world, where the dome of heaven met the bowl of earth. He was lifting the edge of the sky, and a great crowd of creatures poured in from the night outside.

There were earthly creatures, fantastical creatures, beautiful and horrible shapes all mixed together. In the corner of the page, furthest from the light, a nightmare shape of coiling tentacles and hungry teeth unfurled its many limbs. Ivan remembered the giant sucker mark in the cave and shivered.

Beyond the sky's dome, the sun and moon hung together, the one casting light and the other shadow.

"Medieval astrology," said Amelie. "Look, this is interesting but hardly incriminating."

"What about that," said Ivan, pointing at the bottom of the page. There was writing along the bottom, black and cryptic.

"Nordic runes," said Karl. "I've seen Da write like that before."

Next to the printed book runes was a hastily scrawled note in the same script, obviously recent. The author used a blue ballpoint pen.

"Take a photo," said Ivan. "It may be important, and we can get it translated." Amelie snapped a photo.

"Look at this," said Karl. His pale finger pointed to the picture of the day and night. "That's the summer solstice - longest day, shortest night. If my Da's group is planning something occult," his mouth twisted down as he said it, "that could be their chosen day."

"I thought summer solstice would be, well, good energy. Longest day and all that," said Ivan.

Amelie shook her head. "It's a time of change, where things are in balance. The point when the world starts to tip towards darkness. Karl's right—it's a likely time to do a ritual."

Ivan shot a glance at Karl, but the boy didn't react. *Either he knows far more than he's told us or a lot less.* Neither thought was comforting.

"When's summer solstice?" asked Ivan.

"June 21st," said Karl. "That's –"

"Friday," said Amelie and Ivan together.

"Well, damn," said Ivan.

"Ok," said Amelie. "That puts us on a bit of a timeline. But if we're going to bring something to Detective Benioff, it needs to be a bit more concrete than 'there's a secret room with some weird stuff in it.'"

They all stared at the oak chest.

The wood was black with age. Ivan knew from experience that oak this old would be hard as iron. Experimentally, he tried opening the lid. It was locked.

The keyhole was an odd diamond shape, different from any he'd seen before.

"Da always wears a key around his neck," said Karl. He'd been studying the keyhole. "It's that shape."

"Good to know," said Ivan. He was aware of something on the edge of his awareness. Something trying to get his attention.

"Amelie," he said slowly. "Do you think your phone would get reception in this cave?"

"No," she said, going slightly pale.

They retreated outside the room, and her phone immediately gave a faint 'bing.'

Amelie stared up at Ivan, her knuckles white.

"It's Anders," her voice came out in a harsh whisper. "Magnus's men are coming back."

"Quick!" Ivan closed the wood panel door and put the fire poker back in place. Downstairs, a door opened and then closed.

"Shit!" Ivan stared wildly around, heart pounding.

They heard footsteps coming towards the study.

"The window," whispered Karl. Amelie was already there, unfastening the latch, and they all tumbled out, landing five feet down in the soft topsoil of a flower bed. As Ivan pushed the window closed, the door handle was already turning.

Karl crawled deeper into the bushes, and Ivan and Amelie hurried to follow him. They crouched breathlessly in a clump of young spruce.

Silence.

Ivan tried to get his breathing under control. *The worst thing is the fear. I'd rather fight than all this crouching, hiding and waiting.*

Amelie tapped his shoulder and jerked her head to where Karl had continued his crawl around the base of the hill.

Two minutes later, they pushed through a hedge and stepped back on the road. Amelie waved to Anders, who was just about dancing with indecision.

He gave an exaggerated, *oh thank god,* gesture with his arms and came towards them at a half run.

"What the hell happened? I saw the men returning way down the road when I texted you. I was expecting you to come out the front before they entered. I was getting ready to go in after you!"

"We got delayed," said Ivan.

"We're sorry," said Amelie.

Karl said nothing.

"It's like you have a death wish," Anders said, then caught himself. "Sorry, darling. I didn't mean that. Ivan's the one with the death wish. I was just low-key losing my shit here. Did you find anything?"

Ivan's mind flashed back to the picture they'd seen. *A world of light, a world of shadow. And a human, forming the bridge in between.*

"We found the secret room," said Amelie.

"Wow," said Anders. "That's great."

"And we found some writing we need to translate," said Ivan. "Ancient Nordic runes."

"Ok," said Anders. He looked between them, weighing his words. "That's something, I guess. Anything else?"

"There's a chest in the secret room that may be important," said Amelie.

"Did you see inside it?" asked Anders.

"There's a catch."

"Of course there is."

"We need a key to get into it."

"How do you know it's important?" asked Anders.

"It must be important," said Amelie. "Because the key to the chest is always around Magnus's neck."

Anders let out an explosive huff. "This just gets better and better. You nearly get caught breaking and entering—"

"We didn't break and enter."

"*Trespassing* on Magnus's property, and for your encore act, you want to get a key from around his neck? Do I need remind you that if he comes back, he'll be out for blood?"

"We also have a likely deadline," said Amelie. "If the cult is going to do another ritual, we think it'll be this Friday night."

"It's like nobody listens to the words coming out my mouth," said Anders. He slowly shook his head. "Ivan - you can get the runes translated?"

"How does he do that?" asked Karl.

"Ivan is secretly a geek," Anders stage whispered.

"I know some people," said Ivan, trying to sound dignified.

"Very geeky people," said Anders. "Dungeons and Dragons level geekery."

Despite himself, Karl looked interested.

"Well, it's been fun, but I've got things to do," said Amelie. "Keep me posted."

"Hey," said Anders, "what about Magnus's friends? What if they try something?"

Amelie arched one dark eyebrow at him. "Now that I'm on my guard, I rather hope they do." She delivered Anders a swift kiss on the cheek and departed.

The tension dropped as she left. *Am I jealous? Is that what's going on?* Ivan tried to sort out his feelings, but all he came up with was a murky feeling of uncertainty and angst. *How do I know if I can trust Amelie? Or anyone?*

Anders cleared his throat. "I um..."

"Stow it," said Ivan. "Let's go get some food."

He stalked off with Anders and Karl trailing him.

"What's going on over there?" said Anders. They had reached the main street, and instead of the usual relaxed evening shopping crowd, people were hurrying down to the port in a steady stream.

13

There was a change in the air, a stirring sense of excitement as people hustled past them.

Ivan grabbed hold of Jerry, the mechanic's son.

"What's going on?"

"One of the missing men has returned!" the boy said, grinning. "He's alive!"

Something lurched in the pit of Ivan's stomach. They hurried down to the docks, hidden in the crowd.

As Ivan rounded the corner, the sun dipped behind the mountains, casting the docklands into shadow.

Anders whistled through his teeth. "Knock, knock, look who's back," he said.

Oh hell.

There, at the centre of a ring of excited well-wishers, was Magnus. He was standing, legs shoulder-width apart, with his trademark casual arrogance, as strong and confident as when Ivan had seen him two days ago.

Ivan half expected him to be wearing a robe, but he was dressed in dark jeans, seaboots, and a work shirt. Magnus's face was grim, his clothes were salt-encrusted, and there was a big tear in one trouser leg as if it had been caught in something. But whatever it was hadn't hurt the leg beneath.

His boat, tied up at the dock, was gently sinking, and some village men were preparing to haul it up onto the dock.

A woman came out of the crowd, her mouth working in the way one does when trying not to cry. She asked after one of the two other missing men. Magnus, his face grave, said something Ivan couldn't hear. The lady's face crumpled. Magnus put his arms around her, his own eyes squeezing shut against tears.

It was like watching a scene in a stage play. None of it seemed real, not really. *One of them was shot by my gun. Where are the other four men? Were they all in the rock fall?*

Ivan swallowed, imagining what it would be like to be caught under tonnes of rock. At that moment, his arms around the grieving widow, Magnus looked up and saw him.

Ivan felt a jolt in his chest like he'd stuck his fingers in an electric socket. The force of Magnus's gaze hit him like a blow. There was true hatred in the man's eyes, burning white-hot. It was as clear as if Magnus had spoken aloud: he meant to do Ivan harm.

Soon, a voice inside his thoughts whispered, *He will try to take back what you stole.*

Ivan shivered involuntarily. *I didn't take anything,* he thought, but the inner voice was silent.

Maybe I am going slightly mad. Unresolved issues from shooting a would-be murderer. What really happened on the island? Has Magnus killed the other men?

Now Magnus's wife arrived, and Karl was hustled out of the crowd by Magnus's friend Pedersen. They arranged themselves as if for a photo.

Jacob from the tourist shop was heading back from the front of the crowd.

"What happened?" asked Ivan. "Where are the other missing men?"

"So sad," sighed Jacob. "That storm, you know? They were out in it, and lightning struck them. Most unusual. One died instantly, and the other was washed overboard. Magnus nearly died too. There was a freak wave, you know, and the boat capsized. He was only able to right it when it drifted onto the island."

"I see," said Ivan. He put together a different timeline in his head. Magnus probably arrived back this morning while they were on the island. They had just missed being caught by his friends while they were in the cave. He felt cold at the thought of being cornered underground, this time with no chance of escape.

There was a small rustle, and Karl reappeared next to him.

"Your father's back," said Ivan carefully.

"I still want to help you," said Karl.

"Sure you do," said Anders. He started to turn away.

"Listen," said Karl fiercely. "I know you hate Owen and my da. But you should know I'm not my brother. Or my father. I'm...I'm going to get my mum free of him. She deserves to be happy. You have no idea what it's like, living with—" he stopped suddenly, his throat working.

Ivan knew that look. It was the look of someone fighting back tears, who's stopped talking because their throat has clenched up. *Fourteen is such a wretched age. No longer a boy, but not yet a man.*

He made a small shushing gesture at Anders with the hand Karl couldn't see.

"Karl," he said gently. "What you're doing is the right thing to do. And I appreciate it. We all do. I know it can't be easy for you."

"Right," said Karl gruffly. "Damn right."

"We're going to come up with a plan to get the evidence we need to..."

"To get him locked up," said Karl. "I know. That's what I want too."

"The best thing you can do right now," said Ivan, "is to act normal. Keep an eye on what's going on. And if you have information we can use, let me know. You have my number, right?"

Karl nodded.

"Ok," said Ivan. He wasn't sure if he was supposed to put his hand on Karl's shoulder or do something else encouraging. Anders was good at that sort of thing, and he wasn't. But Karl simply vanished into the crowd.

Ivan pushed his thick black hair out of his eyes. Anders was watching him carefully.

"I don't get why you're trusting him. He could set us up so easily."

Ivan shrugged. "I don't think so."

"You had better be right," said Anders. "If this is some sort of transferred guilt thing…"

"It's not," said Ivan. But he wasn't at all sure.

14

"This changes everything," said Anders. "We need to go tell Amelie. She should leave for London tonight. She's not safe here."

Ivan nodded, only half-listening. His thoughts were chasing each other around in indistinct circles. Magnus hadn't come out and accused him of anything, and that made sense, as he was hardly in a righteous position either. But there was something else going on. That look Magnus gave him, how much Magnus *hated* him. It didn't add up. It was as if Magnus blamed him for more than just blundering into his secret cabal.

The other issue, he decided, was the feeling of something on the edge of his awareness. It was maddening how close it felt, yet he couldn't grasp it. Ivan wished whatever it was would stop or come properly into focus.

Anders had said something Ivan hadn't heard and was waiting for an answer.

"What's that?" said Ivan.

"I said, let's go talk to Amelie now." Ander looked more closely at Ivan. 'What's up with you? It's like you're somewhere else."

Ivan half-smiled. Typical Anders - about as observant as a drunken bear. *I must be acting extra weird.*

"I'm fine. And never mind Amelie -– we need to look after us. We're in more danger from Magnus. We're far better witnesses to what they did in the cave."

"Maybe we should tell the police."

"They'll want to know why we've waited so long. It looks bad. Then they'll pin something on me for sure. What we should do is make a real plan to take Magnus down. Otherwise, it's his word against ours, and you can bet he'll have lined up a plan B, C and D to use against us."

Anders frowned. "Yeah, right. He is a crafty geezer."

"Let's go into town to see your girlfriend then."

"Ah," said Anders.

"What?"

"She won't be in town," said Anders. He sounded evasive, which meant he didn't want to go into something, which meant of course, that Ivan did just that.

"Why isn't she in town?"

"She'll...she'll be at the old mill."

"The old mill?"

The old mill was owned by Anders's family. A hundred years ago, this was where the village's grain was milled. In the 80s it was turned into a fancy bed and breakfast. Then the owners split up, following a scandal Ivan had heard several versions of, each more salacious than the last. The mill house lost its luxury status soon after and had gently headed downhill with no one taking care of it.

The dwelling was now Spartan in appearance, the ex-wife having stripped away the crumbling finery. Ivan preferred that way, pared back to its original state. It was a fine, if basic place to stay in summer and unlivable in the winter.

Anders's ears were going slightly pink. "I kind of set it up. As a place to stay. When we got together."

"You sly fox! A secret love nest!"

"Hardly." Anders sounded embarrassed but also slightly pleased.

"We'll go there then. Lead on Casanova."

The path to Amelie's place looped up into the woods and angled around the valley, which was in full shadow now, the gloaming thick around them.

Ivan stuck his hand in his pockets. There was an indistinct whispering in the back of his mind. The most annoying thing was how he could almost understand it, almost catch words and meaning. He shook his head to clear it and inhaled the smell of birch leaves, pine needles and rich forest loam.

Anders, as usual, was focused on his girl. It had always been like this. Anders seemed to attract the opposite sex like a good-natured, blond magnet. Ivan supposed his friend would be quite restful to be with. Much more so than he was.

"She's not going to want to leave," he said. "She'll want to tough it out with Magnus and his gang. She's stubborn like that."

"Well, *you'll* have to convince her otherwise. You're the one who brought her in on this. It's your show."

"Ivan," said Anders. "I had to tell her. I mean, look at what's happening now. We'd have to tell her anyway, right?"

"Whatever," said Ivan. He was not being charitable, he knew. *I just want...* He didn't even know what he wanted. To rewind time? Go back to when he didn't have problems like this? *I just want to have someone fully on my side. My side, and no one else's.*

Ivan heard a raven caw high above. It sounded so much like a warning that his head jerked up to scan for the danger. *If I carry on like this, I'll end up in a straight jacket. Like a juvenile One Flew Over the Cuckoo's Nest.*

He ignored the raven's cry and focused on not tripping over the tree roots that ran over the forest path. Ahead was the fork in the road that would take them up to the old millhouse. The warning cry sounded again.

Ivan stopped in the path. Maybe, just for once, he should listen to his weird premonitions. "We should drop by your place and take your truck."

"Okay," was all Anders said. He was still mulling over what to say to Amelie. They took the other path down to town, picked up Anders's beat-up old Bedford truck (aka 'The Beast') and drove the rest of the way.

As they wound up the hill to where Amelie was staying, Ivan saw why his friend was worried. The old mill house was away from the rest of the village. Staying here, Amelie was isolated, and Magnus loved to prey on the people's weaknesses. *We are all vulnerable when we're alone.*

They knocked on the door.

"Hello?" called Anders softly. There was no answer. Anders tried the door handle. It was locked.

Ivan shrugged. "She's not home?"

"I'll go round the back," said Anders and left Ivan standing at the front door.

Ivan leaned against the wall by the door. The afterglow of the evening gave him just enough light to see the door timbers with their paint nearly all worn off.

Ivan tried rapping experimentally on the door once more, then gave up. He looked up at the dark shapes of the mountains behind him and shivered.

He lapsed into a daydream, thinking over the day's events. Absently, he tried once more to knock on the door, but this time, his hand didn't strike the timber. Thinking the door must have swung open, Ivan walked forward, hands outstretched. His fingers still didn't touch anything, and now Ivan was in the hallway, the thick whitewashed walls ghostly around him.

He walked cautiously forward, feeling worn cobblestones underfoot.

Ivan stepped down into the living room. Thinking there must be someone home if the door was open, he said softly, "Hello?"

There was an indrawn hiss of breath, and a darker shadow moved in the corner of the room.

"Don't move, or I'll shoot."

Ivan thought it sounded like Amelie, though the voice was so hoarse he couldn't tell for sure.

"Hey, it's me," he said, raising his hands above his head like in a cop movie.

Perhaps the sudden movement hadn't been a good idea. The next moment Ivan's ears rang from the noise of a pistol shot.

At the same instant, he was impacted from the side. There was a blow to his shoulder, and the sensation of heavy paws, like something as large as a Great Dane had jumped up on him and was pushing him down.

Ivan's knees hit the floor as the lights came on.

Amelie crouched in the corner, both arms braced as she levelled a pistol at Ivan.

Ivan couldn't think of anything to say. He just stayed frozen, crouched awkwardly on the ground. He didn't seem able to look anywhere but the barrel of the gun.

The perfect black circle of it filled his vision. Time dilated, and his heart hammered once, twice.

Distant shouting as Anders banged on the back door. Ivan hardly registered it.

He and Amelie stayed frozen in a tableau as Ivan stared into that small circle of infinity. *Hold infinity in the barrel of a gun. Did Michals get a chance to stare at his incoming fate?*

Then Amelie blinked, and Ivan found he was able to look at her rather than the gun. Anders was still hammering away at the back door, yelling something indistinct.

Without taking her gaze from Ivan, Amelie called out, "What is it?" Then she jerked the gun at Ivan. "Stay there."

She backed away down the corridor and unlatched the back door. Anders burst in, saw Amelie, saw the gun, saw Ivan, and said, "Shit, Amelie, you didn't..."

"I'm okay,' said Ivan, though he wasn't sure he was. He didn't seem to be able to get up off the floor.

His limbs were heavy, and the walls were wavering around him. On the floor, his shadow rippled like water in a pond.

"I..." he said.

Amelie finally lowered her gun, her expression part horror, part curiosity.

Ivan put his hand on his right upper arm, where he felt a sense of brightness, like that part of him was somehow more open than the rest.

It came away dripping with shadow. He turned his head. Behind him, where the couch should have cast a shadow, was a much larger shadow. It had the sloping shoulders of a great timber wolf.

"I think I might just lie down for a bit," said Ivan and gently collapsed onto the cobblestones. They were cool and soothing on his cheek. *I might stay here for a while,* he thought, and then the lights went out.

When Ivan came to, he was lying on the couch. He wasn't exactly conscious. He was in that state where you hover above sleep but are not yet awake. Everything was clear but distant as if it were happening to someone else.

Amelie and Anders were arguing.

"I can't believe you—"

"*You* can't believe? I can't believe he just came in here. What did you think I'd do? An intruder comes into my house. When the door was locked! And —"

Ivan's awareness shifted. He still couldn't move or open his eyes, but he felt something nose at him. It was the strangest feeling because, in one sense, he knew there was nothing there, but he could still feel the cold, wet nose and musky scent of a wolf as it nuzzled at the hollow of his neck.

It was comforting, and the corners of Ivan's mouth lifted up in a smile.

Anders and Amelie continued to argue in hushed and furious whispers, though every so often, Amelie's voice would peak as outrage overcame her.

Finally, Ivan was able to open his eyes. To his complete lack of surprise, there was no wolf by his couch. Just the brightly lit living room, with the rough brick barrel vault ceiling above, and an old glass light in the centre with a myriad of moths and other bugs whirring around it.

Very slowly, he sat up.

Amelie and Anders both stopped to watch him.

"Um," said Ivan. He flexed his right hand and was surprised to find it worked fine. "I'm okay," he said. It sounded like a question.

They still weren't saying anything.

Ivan tried for something simple.

"What happened?"

"Amelie thinks her bullet nicked you," said Anders while Amelie made an exasperated noise. "And you passed out. But you seem to be alright. But your shadow went all weird. Oh, and we think you walked through a locked door."

Ivan scrubbed his hand through his hair. "Can I have a cup of tea?"

Very slowly, Amelie walked forward. She stopped three paces away from the couch and looked down at him. Her jawline was firm, but her face was otherwise unreadable.

'Yes, Ivan, you may have a cup of tea," she said. Then she went into the kitchen.

Ivan looked at Anders. "Well, that went well," he said. He started to grin, then laugh silently. Anders stared at him in wide-eyed silence for a moment, and then his mouth twitched. He rolled his eyes at Ivan, a slightly wild grin spreading across his face.

Why is getting shot so damn funny? Am I going crazy? Ivan could hardly breathe from laughing, but he couldn't stop. Outside in the night, he heard the hoarse caw of a raven. He couldn't decide if it was an ordinary raven's caw or something more like a cackle.

By the time Amelie returned to put a cup of tea into his hands, Ivan had calmed down. The first sip of hot liquid grounded him. Cradling the cup, he watched Anders and Amelie sit on the sofa opposite him.

"We need to talk," said Ivan. *Four words that never inspire confidence.* His words fell flat in the sudden silence as a drying machine working in the laundry stopped.

"Anders told me Magnus is back. And he told me...the rest of what happened on the island," she said.

"He told you Karl's theory that there's a cult member in the local police? And he told you how Michals?" he said.

She made a small gesture with her hand that somehow dismissed all his nascent guilt.

"So you know why we can't go to the police. And why you should probably head back to London. I mean, this is serious now."

"It was always serious, Ivan. Oh, and I meant to say this before, but I didn't want to in front of Karl. Thank you."

"For what?" said Ivan.

"For trying to save me."

Trying? Ivan had never heard a thank you that sounded less like a thank you and more like an accusation. Sitting next to Amelie, Anders shrugged wordlessly and looked up at the ceiling.

"We do need to talk," said Amelie. "About how we're going to get Magnus and his gang sent to jail."

"Ah," said Ivan. Not his most intelligent reply, but the conversation had shifted to a spot somewhere ahead of him, and he was trying to catch up.

"Actually," said Anders, "I still think you should leave town for a while. It's too dangerous with Magnus out to get you."

"Oh?" said Amelie, raising an eyebrow. "I thought you were here to protect me. Also, Anders, sometimes I feel like you don't see me at all. If you think, for even one minute, I will be turning tail and running away after what they tried to do, well..." she was abruptly silent. "Anyway, you two are in far more danger. You're witnesses."

Ivan glanced across at Anders with an *I told you so* look.

"Well, our evidence-finding mission to the island didn't work out. We got nothing," said Anders.

"Yet," said Amelie.

"Also," said Ivan, "The police inspector lady thinks I'm a suspect."

"That was your fault for acting all suspicious and not telling me anything."

Anders caught Ivan's eye and shot back the *I told you so* look with interest. Ivan gritted his teeth.

"What you're missing," he said, "Is that I *am* a suspect. Because I did it. My pistol went off, while it was in my hands and killed Michals. My illegal handgun."

The words sounded loud in the room.

Amelie shook her head. "That's where you're wrong, Ivan. It was a clear case of self-defence, and you were trying to prevent a murder. My murder. The problem is the lack of evidence."

"As I said," muttered Anders.

Ivan's mind flashed back to the cavern, with his attacker's hands closing over his hands on the gun, the sharp 'pop' of the bullet, and how Michals slumped down, the life vanished from him in one sharp moment.

For a moment, the shadows darkened in every corner of the room. *Not now,* he thought desperately and focused on the bright glow cast by the electric light.

"I think the real problem is that it all sounds completely bonkers," said Anders. "Imagine trying to tell a police officer, 'there's a cult in our village, and they sacrifice people on altars in a cave on the island.' It wouldn't fly. Also, how come you have a handgun, Amelie? For that matter," he turned to Ivan, "where did you get one?"

"That's beside the point," said Amelie, "What we need is to come up with a decent plan. One that works."

Wow, it's like she's giving a military briefing.

Anders cleared his throat. "Involving the chest?"

"Yes," said Amelie.

"We don't even know what's in it!"

"So find out. Get that Nordic text translated."

"Hey, it's been about half an hour since Magnus got back. Cut Ivan some slack!"

Ivan closed his eyes. Opened them again.

"You know, I was...hoping all this would just go away."

"Hope is not a plan," said Amelie.

"You're sounding awfully...organised," said Ivan finally.

"Comes from being a military brat, growing up in a half a dozen army bases up and down the country," she said. "You learn things."

"I'm starting to work on getting organised," said Ivan.

Amelie shot him a look that was half scornful, half sympathetic. "It's far too late for wishful thinking, Ivan. Grow up."

"I've recruited a spy in the enemy camp," said Ivan. "Karl's going to keep us informed."

They both stared at him.

"He's going to help us," insisted Ivan.

"He's a lying rat. That whole family..." Anders trailed off. "You're too trusting."

"No, I'm not," said Ivan. *I probably am.* "He's going to help us, and if—"

"When," said Anders in an undertone.

"He double-crosses us—I have a plan for that too."

Anders gave a faint snort at that, but Ivan ignored him.

"Fine," said Amelie. "Ivan, you get that text translated, we find out what's in the chest, and then we get enough evidence for Detective Benioff to lock Magnus away for good."

"You make it sound so simple," said Ivan.

"Well, it had better be. Because," said Amelie, "I have a lot of other work to do." She sat back, her blonde hair casting a spiky shadow against the whitewashed walls.

"Other work?" asked Anders.

"You know," she said. "The historical remake. The Viking raid. All those Scandinavian history nuts descending on Clarecross this weekend. They'll start arriving tomorrow. Everywhere will be packed, so they called me in to work overtime at the hostel."

Anders smirked. "I think Ivan knows all about this Viking weekend." Then he groaned. "That means I'm going to get roped into work too." His parents ran the general store, and a major event like this meant he'd have to spend hours restocking shelves.

"So you're into war games for geeks?" said Amelie.

"Yeah," said Ivan. It was surprisingly easy to admit it. *Maybe Anders and his big mouth did me a favour after all.*

Anders unconsciously squared his shoulders, making his voice deeper. "Amelie, are you," he hesitated, "ok to stay here tonight?"

Amelie gave him a look. "I have my pepper spray on the bedside table, my sidearm, a knife, and a taser at the ready."

Ivan grinned. "Thorough."

She gave Ivan the first smile he'd had from her since the island. It was a tired smile, but real.

"You know how it is. Get kidnapped by psychos once, and you don't take safety for granted anymore." She paused. "I'm glad I didn't shoot you, Ivan. Just...don't go walking through locked doors again. Or whatever it was you did."

"How did you get in?" said Anders in an undertone.

"Yeah," said Ivan. "About that..." He pushed down the churn in the pit of his stomach. "Ummm..."

"Spit it out, Ivan,' said Anders.

"Ah, nothing really." Ivan studied the ceiling, the moths flying in crazy circles around the light and their blurred shadows.

Amelie fixed him with another one of her trademark looks. "You know Ivan, sometimes you have to trust people. Even when you don't know how it's going to turn out. Especially when you don't know how it's going to turn out."

"I'll take that under advisement," said Ivan.

Amelie and Anders exchanged glances, and Ivan felt a vague sense of unease. What else had they discussed about him?

He cleared his throat. "Then we're decided on what we're going to do next, and Amelie, you're not going to go running off to do...whatever it is you were planning to do. Involving the police."

A ghost of a smile touched Amelie's lips. "You have no idea what I'd planned to do."

Which was not exactly comforting, but Ivan found it oddly reassuring. *Anders has finally fallen for someone with backbone.*

He waited outside while Anders and Amelie said their good-byes. A little of the heaviness that had weighed on him since Magnus's return had lifted. *Making plans is good. Getting allies is good.* And then, more quietly in the back of his mind. *The more allies you have, the more people you'll need to protect. From Magnus.*

15

The next morning, Ivan visited the small town library. He'd gone there with the idea of researching secret societies and sacrificial rites. There was a chance they'd shed some light on what he'd read in Magnus's secret room.

There wasn't much to find. He supposed that was the point: a society wouldn't be very secret if you could read up about it in a small seaside town library.

But there were a lot of books on ancient myths and legends. Ivan found himself reading them for enjoyment, rediscovering stories from his childhood.

His favourites were the Norse legends: Odin, the Allfather, Loki, Freya, Thor, Baldur, one-handed Tyr, the Fenrir Wolf, and the Frost Giants. Gods locked in a struggle with the giants, always tricking and fighting and stealing from each other, waiting for the time when it would all be decided in the final battle, Ragnarok.

The stories were strange and violent, and the gods weren't exactly *good*. You knew they were on the side of humans, but in some stories, Ivan thought the Frost Giants had the moral high ground. Sometimes, the old Norse gods could be real bastards, and other times they were good, noble, and wise.

Ivan remembered a talk at his local high school from a visiting history professor. While the boys behind him were making dumb jokes, Ivan listened.

The professor told them how over a thousand years ago, their town of Clarecross had been raided by the Vikings.

That was the reason for the old town's fortified walls and the paths up to the caves in the mountains. They were where the townsfolk would hide when the Vikings came. Then, for some time in the late 800's, Clarecross had been a Viking town. The Vikings had conquered it and decided to stay. That's why there were so many people with old Norse surnames around.

Ivan tried to imagine how it would feel to watch a fleet of Viking longboats approach. He found he could do this quite well - it was the same fear he had felt creeping through the cave on the island.

He stretched, cracked his neck, and picked up the next book from the pile in front of him. It was a book of local newspaper clippings dating back to the 1930s. Ivan wasn't sure what he was looking for, but he found it in a small article from eight years ago.

'Police baffled by case of missing tourist.' Ivan remembered the event vaguely, but the article filled in the details. A twenty-something year-old tourist from Devon had vanished while on a hike in the hills above Clarecross. Her body had never been found. After a while, with no leads and no clues, her case had simply faded into the background and been forgotten.

Ivan thought of the burned-down candles in the cave on the island and shivered. He checked the date on the article. Jan 10th. *Similar time of year. Could this lady have been like Amelie, but with no one in time to help her?* Ivan wondered how many missing people would emerge if he searched further back in time.

The morning was getting on, and there was the one book he'd saved till last because it looked so promising. It was an old book, covered in dust, and it had been hidden behind some other books in a dim corner of the library. Ivan had only seen it because a cobweb glinted some sun over it, catching his eye.

It was called 'An Anthropologist's View on Nordic Customs,' and it was written almost a hundred years ago.

Ivan blew dust off the cover and let it fall open. The pages cracked open on an etching of figures around a bonfire. There was a hooded figure in the centre, antlers coming from his head. A knife glinted in the horned leader's hands, and a goat lay tied up on a stone altar at his feet.

Ivan rubbed at the back of his neck while the smell of old paper wafted around him.

This illustration certainly looked the part. The caption read: "The Náströnd Cult claims to descend directly from Hel, goddess of death. At the equinoxes and solstices, they practice blót rites: animal and human sacrifice to please the Gods and draw power to themselves. They believed the correct rituals opened a portal to another world."

"Náströnd means the Corpse Shore," Ivan read aloud. *Well, that sounds cheerful.*

A sentence captured his attention. "The Náströnd cult believed in a network of hidden ways that connected all places. One with the correct power could travel unseen on these paths." *Like a supernatural subway. Cool.*

The next few pages veered into an academic discussion of Nordic languages, and Ivan flipped through them with increasing speed.

He stopped when he came to a full-page illustration labelled: 'Iku-Tursas ("The Eternal Tursas") is a malevolent sea monster from Nordic mythology.' The picture showed a ship in a storm, a monstrous Kraken's tentacles embracing it like a lover as helpless sailors clung to the rigging and fell into the sea.

Ivan sat back in his chair and sipped his coffee. The library had a small cafe just next door, and if you were in Mrs Nilsen the librarian's good books, you were allowed to bring your coffee in and drink it while you read.

Ivan wondered if he'd miss the library if he left town. Most people his age did leave, and not many came back. *Still wondering how you'll manage out in the big wide world?*

The sunlight filtered through the library windows, catching dust motes and illuminating them golden. Someone was browsing the shelves to the side of him, but Ivan didn't register who they were.

He was lost in a present daydream. For a second, the motes of dust shone brighter, suspended in space. He could feel that *something* again, that feeling of connectedness, and subtle pressure, like something pushing in on him. The glowing dust motes were cast into darkness as someone stepped in front of the window.

It was the visiting police detective.

She was wearing an elegant suit, her shoulder-length ash-blonde hair flawless. She had a coffee in one hand. Ivan felt slightly affronted that Mrs Nilsen the librarian had warmed to her so quickly. *Maybe she has a special coffee-inside-library badge in her wallet.*

While he stared at her, she said, "Mind if I sit down?"

Ivan looked around. The other small tables were empty. He opened his mouth to say something (he wasn't sure what,) but she was already lowering herself into the chair opposite him. He hastily shut the Nordic book and slid 'Arthurian Legends' on top.

"Doing a bit of research?" The lady sat back in the chair, hands cupped around her coffee, her elegant features matching her suit. She smiled in a friendly way, but her light grey eyes remained keen, undermining her casual posture.

"You have the advantage of me," said Ivan. *It must be from reading old books all morning. I'm talking like someone in a Regency novel.*

The detective was nonplussed for a moment, and then she gave a surprisingly husky laugh. Despite himself, Ivan liked the sound of it.

"I see. My name is Natalia Benioff."

"Agent Natalia Benioff? Detective Natalia Benioff?"

Her smile vanished. "I've been here long enough for word to get around. Not surprising in a small place like this." She had a precise way of talking, as if she had the whole shape of each sentence already mapped out before she began.

Natalia Benioff put her coffee down on the table, and small changes in her posture added up to make her seem much more businesslike. "You are Ivan Luca, and I have some questions for you."

Ivan studied her. She was younger than he'd originally thought - the well-cut suit and hair made her look older and more professional. *She's in her twenties,* he thought. *Mid-twenties probably. So, not that experienced.*

"I'll tell you what," he said. "How about a trade? You answer three of my questions, and I'll answer three of yours. Only true words spoken."

She glanced down at the books he'd been reading. "Very appropriately mythological. It doesn't work that way, though. The information flows from you to me. Not the other way round."

Ivan shrugged. "I'm not obligated to answer any of your questions."

Her eyes narrowed. Ivan had the feeling he was being reassessed. Most people around here tended to discount him. With his dark hair and slim build, he fit naturally into the shadows. People especially overlooked him when he was with Anders, who was well-built, handsome, and liked talking.

Right now, though, he was being studied very closely. He found it both gratifying and alarming.

"Very well," she said. "You start."

"No," said Ivan, unsmiling. "I go second."

"You may not answer my questions if you go second," she said, frowning.

"Pinky promise?" Ivan raised an eyebrow at her, extending his little finger. "Also, you're the one wanting to ask questions, not me. You may not answer mine if I go first."

She waited a long moment, then nodded. She didn't extend a hand to complete the pinky promise, and he lowered his hand onto the table.

"Very well. Proceed." She picked up her coffee cup and took a sip, keeping her eyes on him the whole time.

Ivan leaned back in his chair and half-closed his eyes. Around him, the glowing dust motes were back. He watched them hang in space, creating a suspended web. He could feel the distances between them, sense how they drifted together and apart. *Everything is alive.*

There was a faint humming in the air, and the noise of it buzzed right through Ivan's head. A dreamlike feeling settled on him like a cloak.

"You didn't come here because of the three missing men," he said. A small voice in the back of his mind was frantically telling him to shut up, but it was far away, and he paid it no attention.

"You came here to look into a wider pattern of disappearances. Something that's been going on for years."

Detective Benioff had gone still and was regarding him closely, her grey eyes unblinking. The dust motes hung around her in a golden corona. Ivan regarded them, and her, with equal benevolence.

"First question. How am I involved?"

"Surely you'd be the best person to answer that," she said tightly.

Ivan raised his eyebrows at her. "You get three answers in return."

She sat back, spreading her hands on the table. "People agree that you and your friend Anders were out on the night the men disappeared. You say you were searching for Amelie. But she doesn't remember seeing you."

That statement jangled in Ivan's mind. It was, at best, a half-truth made to obscure something else.

"You'll get back the same quality answers as you give."

Her expression didn't change, but there was a minute tension, then controlled relaxation in her shoulders. *She has a firearm in an underarm holster.* Her jacket was cleverly cut to conceal it, but Ivan saw it in his mind's eye as clearly as if she'd taken it out to show him.

"Your second question," was all she said.

"Why are you here?" he asked.

She huffed out a surprised breath. "In a philosophical sense?" her mouth twisted. "Why are any of us here?" She leaned back in her chair, regarding him clinically. "As you said, I am looking into a wider pattern. People disappearing, never seen again. If you know anything about it, your silence may cost lives. Not coming forward makes you an accessory." Her gaze was hard.

The dust particles shimmered above her, flickering in a beam of sunshine. Behind her, Ivan saw a little girl in a red raincoat. She was about eight years old, with a pretty face and straight blonde hair. Her eyes were blue and curious.

Why is the kid wearing a raincoat? It hasn't rained for days. There was something strange about the girl that Ivan couldn't quite place. *I think she's connected to the detective. But how?*

"Who is she?" he asked.

"Who?" Benioff sounded puzzled.

"The girl," said Ivan. He looked over Benioff's shoulder again. The girl was gone, perhaps ducked behind some shelves. "The girl in the red coat."

"What?"

"The girl in the red raincoat," said Ivan.

Benioff looked at him in bewilderment, dawning realisation, then sudden intensity. All traces of politeness vanished from her face. Ivan could see she was scared and at the same time very angry.

"You're playing a dangerous game, Ivan. I don't know where you got your information, but I would advise you not to cross me. The consequences will be more than you can handle. If you were involved in any way in…" she paused for a moment, then her face returned to its usual smooth facade.

Benioff pushed her chair back and stood. "If you are in any way involved in these disappearances, or if you obstruct my investigation, I will see to it personally that you are put away for a very long time."

She shot one more hard glance at Ivan, then left. The scent of her—freshly laundered linen and a curious aroma of nutmeg and cinnamon, hung in the air after she was gone.

Ivan sat peacefully in the library for a moment, watching the dust motes dance. Then, abruptly, he fell out of whatever dreamlike state he'd been in.

His heart pounded like he'd run a mile in the snow. A bolt of electricity shot through his head, and he curled down over the table, narrowly missing hitting his coffee cup with his face. He groaned as the shock faded, then groaned again as his mind ran through the conversation he'd just had.

"Shit!" Seemed to sum up his feelings quite well. "What the f—!" *And who was that girl?* He got up and quickly walked around the bookshelves where he'd seen her. There was no one there. *Am I officially losing it? For reals?*

The answering silence was not comforting.

Ivan swigged the last of his coffee, which had gone cold, and threw it in the recycling bin as he left the library. Outside, he ran his fingers through his hair, tugging at the roots in a vain attempt to clear his head.

I just seriously pissed off a police detective. Great way to keep a low profile, Ivan.

He looked around, but Detective Benioff was nowhere in sight. Ivan grimaced, took a side alley and headed for home.

Unease wormed down his spine. *A man who probably wants me dead is back in town. Should I even be spending time alone at home?*

Part of him tried to say he was overreacting, while the other part remembered the look Magnus had given him.

"*When someone shows you who they are, believe them.*" It was one of his mother's favourite quotes, and right then, Ivan missed his mum and Greg more than he'd ever thought he would. *But I'm glad they're not here right now. I'm glad they're far away and safe.*

16

Ivan opened the oak front door of his family home and waited for the familiar comfort of home to sink in. The last few days had been too huge and strange. He felt like a boat that had lost its moorings, drifting dangerously close to an unknown cavern.

He took the stairs two at a time to the second storey, then more slowly, he climbed the steep ladder-like stairs to the attic. This had been his bedroom ever since he was six. The high, sloping wooden ceiling dropped down almost to the floor, and it smelt of cedar, and home, and safety.

A wave of tiredness engulfed him, and Ivan flopped down on his bed in a patch of sun and fell asleep.

In Ivan's dream, he was walking through a battlefield. The dead lay everywhere. There was smoke billowing through the air, and the smell of blood and mud, and death.

In his dream, this didn't bother him. He simply walked a path through the bodies as if he had done this a hundred times before. He was searching for something. Something he had lost a long time ago and now needed urgently.

Harsh cawing sounded overhead. Flocks of black birds were circling above him. *Crows or ravens,* he thought.

One swooped and flew directly at his face, wings flapping, sharp claws outstretched.

Right on impact, Ivan threw up his arms to shield his face and woke up, heart thudding in his chest.

He yelped to hear the harsh cawing again and looked around wildly to find where it was coming from.

There was a sharp tapping at the little attic dormer window.

Cautiously, Ivan crept over. An enormous black bird perched on the sill. It was fiddling with the window catch with its beak, trying to get it open. *Too big to be a crow,* he thought. *Must be...a raven?*

The raven stared straight at him with the brightest, most knowing eye Ivan had ever seen on bird or beast. He took a step forward to open the window, then immediately took a step back.

What was he thinking?

Ivan crossed his arms.

The raven ducked its head at him expectantly.

"I'm not letting you in," Ivan said.

The raven put its head on one side and looked at him first through one eye, then the other. It rapped sharply on the window with its beak.

Ivan was startled into laughter. The bird had all the brisk certainty of an official investigator dressed in black.

That thought sobered Ivan. *There's that fancy police inspector in town. What if she connects me to Michals's death?*

He jumped as the raven gave another sharp caw. It clacked its beak at the fastening as if to say, "Well, go on!"

Fascinated, Ivan reached slowly for the window catch before he stopped himself.

"You'll just flap around and make a mess," he said. He didn't entirely believe this. The bird was too focused and aware. "Besides, you're awfully big."

This was closer to the truth.

The raven fluffed its feathers impatiently.

Ivan said, "I'm sorry," and went downstairs.

Part of him wanted to go back to sleep, but he knew he couldn't with a raven glaring in the window like an indignant relative, demanding to be let in. Instead, Ivan made himself another coffee.

The kitchen relaxed him, all golden wood and solid stone, timeworn and homely. Ivan's home had been a farmhouse for four centuries. All its farmlands were now sold off, but the house still had a generous spread of garden around it.

Ivan spent the next half hour cleaning the kitchen. While they were gone, his duties were simple: looking after the house and garden. Pick up some paid work here and there and stay out of trouble. Enjoy the last of home before he left for university. At least, that had been the plan. *I didn't factor in murderous cults. And the possibility I might not get into any universities.*

With the chores done, there was nothing to distract him from the worries that had chased around in the back of his mind all day.

I need to try and make sense of the last few days. Ivan took a pen and paper and went outside to sit in the afternoon sun. He was faintly disappointed the raven had gone. Leaning over the solid outdoor table, he listed everything he knew about what had happened.

He tested each statement as he wrote it down, weighing up its completeness and truth.

1. *Magnus and his friends are part of a secret society*
2. *They probably kidnap and sacrifice people.*

Ivan crossed out 'sacrifice' and wrote 'murder.'

1. *This society probably has something to do with the old Norse religion from when Vikings lived here.*
2. *Something very strange happened in the cave when the lightning struck.*

Ivan crossed that out and wrote instead.

4. *Something very strange happened when Michals died. Then lightning struck because I told it to...*

He hesitated at that last statement, shook his head and plunged on.

1. *I got woken up by a bossy raven*
2. *I'm seeing things from other people's pasts and shadows that seem real. I think...*

Ivan chewed on the end of his pen. The sunlight was warm on his back, and the coffee was good and strong.

He turned over the page and wrote:

What to do:

1. *Go very far away? (London or overseas)*
2. *Tell Benioff what happened in the cave?*
3. *Talk to Karl - see if we can find out more about what Magnus is doing now*
4. *Find out what's in Magnus's chest*

All these ideas had serious problems. He crossed out talking to Benioff. *She's sure I'm a suspect now. Whatever I said really pissed her off.*

He crossed out 'going far away' as well. That would be a sure sign of guilt, and who knows what kind of case Magnus and his cult could cook up against them while he and Anders and Amelie were away. He lightly underlined 'Find out what's in Magnus's chest.'

Ivan relaxed back on the garden bench, wondering how the hell they were going to find out what was in the chest if Magnus had the key around his neck all the time.

He half-closed his eyes, feeling the summer air stir his hair. His fingertips prickled. The humming of the insects got much louder, and he had the feeling of the world holding its breath like something was about to happen.

The moment was shattered by a knocking at his front door. Ivan got up and padded through the house to answer it.

As he flicked the latch up, he had a sudden vision of half a dozen hooded and robed men waiting to grab him. But it was too late, he was already opening the door, and it was only Anders.

Anders's face was strained. Ivan realised he'd looked that way since their trip to the island. His friend was not made to keep secrets, and it was taking its toll. *Maybe he should have thought about that before charging off to be a hero. We should have talked to the police at the very beginning.*

"Heya."

Anders followed him through to the kitchen, helped himself to a can of soda, and then they went into the back garden. Ivan sat back at the table and relaxed in the sun, but Anders couldn't settle. He kept pacing the brick patio, brow furrowed.

"What's wrong?" said Ivan.

Finally, Anders gave a big sigh and sat down opposite Ivan.

"We're properly in the shit, Ivan."

Ivan raised an eyebrow.

"That woman, you know. The detective. She's just been grilling me."

Ivan shrugged. "She talked to me too."

Anders shook his head. "You know what she wanted to know? All about you."

"Where was I the night the men disappeared?"

Anders huffed out a breath. "All about you. Where you lived in the past, what you do, who your parents are, your school, your hobbies. Like she was building a file on you."

"Did you ask her why?"

"She said you were a person of interest in an ongoing investigation. And threatened me with obstructing police enquiries if I didn't answer her."

Ivan slowly released a breath.

"I have to agree. We are well in the shit. Or more accurately, I am."

Anders raised his can in a half salute.

Ivan slumped forward, leaning his elbows on the table. Then he tilted back his can, and let the last of the cool soda slide down his throat.

The situation was like a wave, he decided. A big wave. And they were on a boat. Try to run away, and you get flipped. Turn to either side, and you get flipped. The only way through was forward. Ride the wave, with just a fingernail grip of control. *Like the freak wave that pushed us up the beach at the island.*

"What do we do about the police lady?" asked Anders.

"Natalia Benioff?"

"On a first name basis already?"

"I'm a person of interest."

"Well?"

Ivan rubbed his jaw. "It's true what they say — no good deed goes unpunished."

Anders started to say, "For fuck's sake—," then his eyes widened. "Ivan," he said in a hushed monotone. "Why do you have a giant raven in your garden?"

Ivan wanted to turn to where Anders was staring, but a chattering sound and rush of wings made him flinch, and then freeze. He heard Anders gasp and the scrape of his chair as he pushed it backwards, away from Ivan.

But much more immediate was a clawed grip on his shoulder. Ivan had the feeling the owner of the grip could make it a lot harder and sharper if they wanted to, but for now, it was gentle.

Very slowly, Ivan looked to his left. Sure enough, the raven was perched there on his shoulder. He'd never seen one this close before, and it was *big*. And, he swallowed, its beak was very strong and black and sharp. The raven ruffled its glossy black feathers and gave a soft caw. It sounded satisfied.

"Maybe it's escaped from a zoo," said Anders. "Or a circus. A wild raven would never do that."

"Not helping," muttered Ivan. He thought of how sharp its beak and claws were and how soft his face and eyes were. He kept still and tried to figure out what to do next.

"Stay put." Anders backed away slowly and then ran into the house. Ivan went statue-still as the raven nibbled very gently on his ear for a few seconds, then stropped its beak on his hair.

"Nice bird," said Ivan faintly. "Good raven."

It looked directly into his eyes, ducking its head. It made an enquiring noise deep in its throat.

"I'm sorry," said Ivan. "I don't speak raven." He was feeling less frightened, and more curious. Something in the raven's eyes was so intelligent. *Like it could speak to me if it wanted to.*

The raven made another noise. It felt like a conversation Ivan was only hearing one side of. The conversation finished just as Anders re-emerged with an absurdly fragile butterfly net.

A final beak rattle, a push on his shoulder, and the raven took flight. It gave a reproachful caw as it soared upwards and into the wooded hills behind the house.

Ivan let out a shaky breath. "Well," was all he could think to say.

Anders, his eyes wide, picked up a long black feather from the ground by Ivan's feet and handed it to Ivan.

"Wow," said Anders. "That just happened."

Ivan took the feather and ran his finger along it, admiring the perfect design. Each pinion latched into the next one, so they moved as one, light and strong.

"I think," he said at last. "Things have started to get weird."

17

"Have you got a translation yet?" Anders's voice on the other end of the phone sounded eager.

Ivan took another sip of his coffee, leaning on the kitchen bench. It was Thursday morning, and he was still surfacing from a troubled sleep full of unsettling dreams. *Magnus is back, and he hates me. If he's after me, I need to do a better job of watching my back.*

"Yeah," asked Ivan. "Do you want to hear it?"

There was a pause. "I'll swing by your gaff and pick you up," said Anders. "Ok? We all need to see this. Also, Amelie's given me a list of stuff to get before the weekend."

Ivan rubbed his eyes. "Fine," he said. "See you soon."

A few minutes later, Ivan heard a rattling roar as Anders's truck, 'the Beast', swung into his drive. He opened the house door for Anders, who pushed past him.

"Need the loo, be right back."

Ivan leaned against the threshold and waited for his friend, trying to ignore the persistent feeling of time running out.

Anders reappeared and grinned at Ivan. "Let's go see some Nordic runes."

At Anders's truck, Ivan went to jump into the passenger side, then recoiled backwards in shock.

"Did you leave a window open?" he asked.

"What is it?" said Anders.

Cautiously, Ivan looked into the front seat. There, crouched like a small black thundercloud in the old truck's interior, was a shape remarkably like a raven.

"It's the raven," said Ivan, and Anders groaned.

The raven moved then, and Ivan saw the sharp outline of its beak and the glint of light reflecting off its black eye.

"Good raven," he said soothingly and opened the door. "Shoo?"

Anders opened the door on his side and waved his arms like an usher.

The raven made an enquiring noise, and Ivan had a sudden pang of sympathy for the bird. Wherever it had come from, it was all alone now.

"I think it's –" was as far as he got because, with a crisp flap of its wings, the raven took flight. Ivan flinched backwards, but it was too late. The raven had settled on his shoulder. This time, the firm grip on his shoulder didn't fill him with fear. It felt familiar and right.

Anders laughed uncertainly. "That bird's got the hots for you, all right."

"Shows it has good taste."

Carefully, he slid onto the bench seat of the truck. The raven ducked low on his shoulder and then hopped down onto his lap. Very cautiously, Ivan stroked the coal-black feathers on its back.

"Make sure you keep the window open on your side, too," said Anders. "I'm not driving with a deranged bird flapping around in here."

The raven clacked its beak at him sharply.

"Manners, Anders," said Ivan.

They drove into town with Anders's truck rattling down the bumpy cobbled road.

"You know, it's not every ride you can see the road through the floor," said Ivan.

Anders changed gears with a grind. "The Beast is going to keep going for the next sixty years."

The raven sat on Ivan's thigh, claws tightening painfully whenever the truck lurched on a pothole.

Anders hauled on the Beast's steering wheel as he swung them into a car park.

"This going to take long?" said Ivan.

"Patience, laddie. Got to pick up some things from the shop. Be right back!" He swung out onto the road, leaving Ivan with a raven on his lap.

As Ivan got out of the truck, the raven hopped up onto his shoulder and perched, swaying. Ivan thought a raven on his shoulder would attract attention, but he needn't have worried.

The Vikings had started to arrive in town. The streets were filled with loud and cheerful folk dressed in costumes. Most of them were dressed as Vikings, but there were some startling variations. Ivan saw people with Celtic woad, some shaman types, and even the odd highlander. There was chain mail, leather vests, clanging swords, axes, bows, and spears.

Everyone seemed in a good mood and excited to see one another. Despite the tension that had been eating into him all day, Ivan could feel himself getting swept up in the holiday atmosphere.

Ivan had registered and paid the Vikon event fee weeks ago. He remembered the mixture of anticipation and worry over whether his school friends would recognise him in costume. Right now, the fear of being seen in Viking gear felt like something from the distant past, unconnected to any of the recent upheavals in his life. *I guess dealing with a mad death cult takes priority over joining Vikon this year. Buggar*

A girl about Ivan's age in a shield maiden outfit grinned up at him and said, "Great raven! Wish I'd thought of that! Where did you get it? And where's the rest of your costume?"

She had blonde curly hair and fierce black eyebrows, and Ivan didn't know where to begin answering all this. It seemed, though, that he didn't need to because she went on talking.

"You must be throwing in with us in the Raven Clan this year. Have you seen the other side yet?"

Ivan shook his head.

She wrinkled her nose. "Bunch of Náströnd warrior priests. Boring! They didn't put much effort into their costumes. Cheapskates and slackers!"

"How's that?" asked Ivan, a vague prickle of unease worming its way down his spine.

She shrugged. "Go take a look. They're already setting up over at the football club. That's their HQ. They're all in the same dark robes. No imagination. Bit of a downer if you ask me."

"Oh," said Ivan. *Oh shit....*

Her smile bubbled up again. "Still, our lot more than make up for it! Plus, you never know what might be under those robes. Maybe there'll be a big reveal." Her dimple never left her right cheek while she was saying this.

"Hey, um..." Ivan said, pausing. The shieldmaiden had warm brown eyes, and they shone as she waited for him to go on. "Where is the Raven Clan setting up?"

"We're in the town hall."

"You know, there might be some trouble. From the robed guys."

Her eyebrows quirked as she grinned. "I should hope so! That's what we're here for. *You* know."

She reached over and patted his upper arm, and a tingle, almost like an electric shock, ran down his arm. "Don't worry, raven boy. I'll come rescue you if you need it."

For the first time in what seemed like an age, a warm, glad feeling spread across Ivan's chest. He couldn't think of anything to say, and for once, that was just fine.

They both stood there for a moment, smiling like idiots, and then someone yelled something from further in the crowd, and the girl's head whipped around to listen.

"Gotta go!" she said. "See you 'round." She vanished into the helmeted, be-ringed, fur-clad crowd milling around them before Ivan could think of anything more to say.

He looked sideways at the raven. "Our side?" he said.

Its eye sparkled at him as much as the shield maiden's had.

Anders reappeared, pushing his way between two burly men in full Norseman garb.

"Let's go do runes and kick ass," he said.

Ivan rubbed his forehead. *Dozens of guys in black robes. Shit. Are they all Magnus's group?* "We're not in an action game."

"Look around you and tell me that," said Anders.

Ivan's phone made a faint 'bing.' It was a message from Karl. *My father thinks you took something from him. He's really mad about it. Be careful.*

He held the phone up for Anders to scan.

"Do you know what that means?" Anders asked.

Ivan thumbed a quick 'thanks' in reply.

"I have no idea," he said, ignoring the tingle between his shoulder blades. *Like I have a target on my back.*

"I didn't know you were a bird fancier," someone murmured behind him.

Ivan jumped as Detective Benioff appeared at his shoulder. Standing next to her, Ivan realised he was just a little bit taller than her. She'd seemed taller, sitting across from him in the library.

Benioff tilted her head, and an elegant fan of hair came loose to shadow her face. "It's a raven," she said. "Unusual bird to have as a pet."

Like a mirror image, the Raven tilted its head to stare back at her.

"It likes to keep an eye on me," said Ivan, "just like you." He smiled his fakest smile.

Benioff frowned, then moved on up the street. Ivan let out a slow breath.

Beside him, Anders was slowly shaking his head. "I don't know whether you're brave or stupid. I'm going for stupid. We need to keep on the down low."

"She started it."

"C'mon, we're meeting Amelie at the Millhouse," said Anders.

The Beast chugged and spat black smoke as it started up. Anders's teeth flashed white as he grinned at Ivan. "Let's see what you got, bruv."

18

"So I got the translation off some friends on my Vikon chatroom."

"And that means?" said Amelie.

"Ivan has next-level geek friends who know Klingon and Elvish," said Anders.

They gathered in the kitchen of the old millhouse and watched Ivan scroll through a long conversation thread on his phone.

Ivan frowned at the screen. "One of the members here is a professor in Norway. That's who did the translation."

"If you're trying to make your chatroom sound cool, it's not working," said Anders at the same time as Amelie said: "What do the runes say?"

Ivan paused. "Can we fire up your laptop? I think we should see this on a bigger screen."

Amelie flipped open her laptop, and Ivan typed in the various logins. It loaded up slowly, the internet signal patchy up in the hills.

Ivan watched the gothic font of the website's front page appear, feeling both self-conscious and a little bit proud of what he'd managed to find out. The raven on his shoulder leaned forward to peer down at the screen. *Can ravens read Nordic runes? Probably.*

"Ok, so," Ivan scrolled down to where he'd posted the photo they'd taken of Magnus's book.

"Hang on," interrupted Amelie. "Is this a private chat?"

"You have to be a member," said Ivan.

"She's got a point," said Anders. "Nerds who translate ancient Nordic in their spare time may also do a little ritual sacrifice on the side. As a weekend hobby."

"Paranoid much," muttered Ivan. "It's too late now. I can delete the thread after we read it if you want me to."

"Yes," said Anders and Amelie together.

"Fine, stop raining on my parade. Guys, this could be something."

With the cursor, he highlighted one phrase in English. The lettering was tiny, white on a black screen. Anders bent in closer.

"Gamelord372," read Anders. "That's your Nordic professor? Sounds like he's a real party animal."

"Actually," said Ivan, "I think *she's* a professor at the University of Oslo. Just a guess, though."

"Gender stereotypes can be so misleading," murmured Amelie. "What's Ivan's online name?"

"DreadlordConqueror2." Anders smirked. "Fierce."

"I chose it when I was twelve, alright?" said Ivan, his ears reddening a little.

"I don't know which is worse," said Anders. "That it's Ivan's geek name or that there's two of them."

"Look, do you want to hear this or not?"

"Read out the translation, Dreadlord Conqueror," said Amelie. She was trying not to smile.

"Fine. This is a translation of what was printed in the book. I'll read out the margin note after." Ivan cleared his throat. "Here goes:

'When moon rises at summer's peak,

The midnight river will flow between worlds,

The Ox of Death —'"

"Wait, what?" Anders snorted a laugh while Ivan glowered.

"It's a mythological term." Ivan scrolled down. "'The Ox of Death' is one of the names of Eternal Tursas, aka the Father of Diseases. I read about it in the library this morning. It was kind of weird for it to show up again like this."

"Yik," said Amelie. "Nice picture."

One of the chatroom members had posted a picture of a tiny ship sailing serenely on a grey-green ocean, oblivious to the huge tentacled monster reaching up from below.

"That's it," said Ivan. "Great Tursas. Monster of the Depths. Supposedly responsible for the Black Death and every other plague before it. Listen to the rest of the translation:

'The Ox of Death awakes with lightning,

And shadows swallow the earth.'"

"Well, that sounds cheerful," said Amelie. "Summer's peak - that's still Friday, right?"

"Yup," said Ivan. He had a sinking feeling. The 'awakes with lighting' line had stirred up memories like silt, clouding his mind. "So, in plain English, Magnus and his cult are going to do some major league wicked stuff on Friday night. When the moon rises. I guess it's nice to have a timeline. But there's more."

"More what?" said Anders.

"I talked to one of the Vikings in town, and she said their rival clan is arriving, and guess what?"

"What?" said Anders.

"They're all dressed in black robes."

Amelie narrowed her eyes. "That could be a coincidence."

"Or not," said Ivan.

"What did the margin scrawl say?" said Anders. "We're guessing Magnus wrote that?"

"Most likely," said Ivan. He scrolled down some more. "There's some argument about whether it's meant to be 'shadows swallow the earth' or 'shadows cover the earth," he said.

"They both sound bad," said Amelie. "Do we actually believe any of this?"

There was a small silence.

"Anyway," Ivan carried on, "the note that Magnus wrote says: 'The island is the place. And I shall keep safe the key, hidden that which is locked.'"

"That makes no sense," said Anders.

"There's another translation," said Amelie, pointing.

"Yeah, that." Ivan scrolled down. "MrGreyMouser says the better translation is: 'The island is the focus, and locked in the chest I hold the key.'"

Ivan tapped his fingers on the table and then turned to meet Anders's eyes.

His friend was silently asking him a question, one that Ivan didn't want to answer.

Because the answer is yes, we probably do need to get that key and find out what's in the chest. And what I really want is to go home and draw the blinds and sleep till this all blows over.

"I guess we need to open the chest in Magnus's secret room after all," said Ivan. "So we'd better figure out how to get that key."

"The one around Magnus's neck?" asked Amelie.

Ivan heaved a deep sigh. "Yup."

"We shouldn't take the key because then he'll know it's gone and guard his chest twice as carefully," said Amelie. "We need to make a copy of the key."

"Smart," said Anders.

"Ok," said Ivan. "So, how can we make a copy of the key?"

"And get it off his neck in the first place," said Anders. "Without getting killed, that is. Or tipping Magnus off."

"This," said Amelie. "Is where I have an idea."

I just know I'm not going to like this idea, thought Ivan.

She told them her idea.

Ivan didn't like it.

Half an hour later, they'd hashed out the details of Amelie's plan.

Amelie had made them some quite excellent coffee and produced shortbread biscuits. Ivan thought they may have been in apology for her truly terrifying plan. He nibbled at his biscuit while their talk turned to a question he wished they would ignore: did Magnus have magic powers?

Ivan shook his head. "I think he's dangerous, but mostly because he's got guns and knives and a bunch of followers. He's delusional."

Amelie tilted her head to one side as she regarded him. "Are you sure about that?" she asked.

"What do you mean?" asked Anders.

"Where did the raven come from?"

"It just showed up," said Ivan, feeling a little like a traitor to the Raven. But he didn't want to say, 'I had an out-of-body experience where I felt like I was part of the sky, then I kind of got hit by lightning, and saw some shadows come to life, and got knocked over by an invisible wolf, and then this bird arrived, and it all adds up to me losing my mind.' 'Just showed up' seemed safer.

She shook her head. "I'm not buying it, Ivan. Ravens don't just 'show up.' Weird stuff has been going on around you for the last few days. Walking through locked doors. Being adopted by ravens. What else is going on?"

Amelie and Anders both turned to face Ivan. *I bet the raven's looking at me too.*

"Hey," he protested. "It's not like *I* know what's going on. Magnus is doing the weird stuff. You should ask him."

"Karl said Magnus thinks you stole something," said Anders. "That's what you're talking about. Right, Amelie?"

"So," Ivan hesitated. This was the hard part. It was what he'd been avoiding thinking about. "I have an idea about what happened. But it sounds a bit mad."

"All of this is bare mad," said Anders fervently.

"Yes, but this is extra crazy. Remember in the cavern, just before the lightning struck?" Anders nodded. "What did Magnus say?"

"He said: 'The blood sacrifice is complete,'" said Anders slowly.

"And he held his arms up like he was expecting something. And...I felt like I was in two places at once. It was...I felt like I knew everything. Well, lots of things. Did that happen to you?" Ivan heard his voice trail off. Talking about it out loud sounded lame.

Anders shook his head, so Ivan pushed on. "When the lightning struck, it was like it hit me because I was also above the island. And then the cave came down. Now Magnus is back, and he thinks I took something. What does it all add up to?"

"He was doing the ritual on the island to get something. Maybe it was some sort of occult powers. And now he thinks you stole something..." Anders's eyes widened. "Ivan, you must have superpowers!" Anders was grinning broadly, and Ivan was a little relieved to see he didn't take this seriously.

But Amelie nodded slowly, like this made sense. "He wants the weird stuff to happen to him. Which means," and now she fixed Ivan with a look that pinned him to the sofa, "that the weird stuff must be a lot more useful than what you're doing with it."

"Hey," protested Ivan weakly. "Good job blaming the victim here."

"There are no victims, Ivan," she said. "Only people who play the cards they're given and people who fold."

"Apart from being a raven magnet, I haven't been able to do anything unusual. Not on purpose."

"By accident?"

"Hard to say." Ivan thought about the lightning, the girl in the red hood he'd seen in the library, how angry that had made Benioff, and the weird murmurings on the edge of his awareness. A vague memory prodded him about waking up floating on a sea of shadows, but it refused to come clearer.

"You need to start experimenting," said Amelie briskly, as if this was just another item on their to-do list.

"All I know is that when weird stuff starts happening, I start losing my grip."

"On what?"

"Reality." There, he'd said it. "Guys, I think I'm going crazy." It felt surprisingly good to finally say it out loud.

"Ivan, you're such a drama queen," said Anders calmly.

Ivan spluttered with indignation, and Anders carried on.

"You're not crazy because one, you know this stuff is weird. So you have insight. Two, there's a raven." He pointed at the Raven on Ivan's shoulder, who blinked back at him with black eyes. "Three, Magnus and a host of henchmen are after you. And while I'll admit they are a bit mental, they're not imaginary. Therefore, you're not going crazy. You're just..." he paused.

"Just what?"

"Experiencing a reality we can't usually perceive," said Amelie. "Like seeing more of the light spectrum."

"Differently normal. Otherwise known as crazy," said Ivan. "Also, it's not light I see. It's shadows."

"Whatever, bro," said Anders. "The main point is that Magnus thinks you have something valuable, which must mean powerful because he's that kind of nutjob. So you need to get busy learning what it is and how to use it."

"Before we're all dead," said Amelie.

"So, no pressure," finished Anders.

"Thanks, guys, that's touching. When, though?" said Ivan.

"Well, we have about two hours before phase one of Operation Key Snatch," said Anders. He grinned. "No time like the present."

19

Ivan walked out of the millhouse and stood in the centre of the small patio.

"You know how crazy this all sounds. You want me to learn how to use..." Ivan waggled his fingers to indicate an unknown superpower mode.

Anders snorted. "That's so going down as your signature move."

Not quite the support I feel I need right now.

"We don't think you're crazy, Ivan," said Amelie. "It's just a theory we need to test. Like a scientific experiment."

Also *not the support I need right now.*

"So...what do you suggest?" said Ivan.

"Let's approach it logically," said Amelie.

Yeah, cos this is so *logical.*

"What have you done so far that could be..." she waggled her fingers in an imitation of Ivan.

"Superpowers," said Anders, with a broad grin that was half mocking, half wistful.

"Yes, superpowers," said Amelie.

Anders counted off on his fingers. "Well, there was that cave collapse. You said you thought you were in two places at once then."

"I didn't *do* anything," protested Ivan.

"Then there was that weird-as thing at the docks."

Amelie arched an eyebrow at Anders.

"Ivan disappeared from the boat shed and turned up outside it. Then he nearly walked off the pier, " Anders explained.

"That doesn't sound very useful," said Amelie.

"So not my fault," muttered Ivan.

"And the time you walked through Amelie's locked door and got shot at," said Anders. "And then there's the raven that shows up whenever it wants to and eats your biscuits," he added, seeing the raven sneak the last piece of shortbread out of Ivan's hand.

"It's hungry," said Ivan. "There's not enough carrion in this town."

Amelie considered. "When you list it like that, it doesn't seem all that impressive."

"Thanks. Really," said Ivan. "That makes me feel much better about being top of Magnus's hit list."

She shook her head. "We must be missing something big then. Magnus strikes me as a very calculated, power-hungry kind of person. Not one to bet on low odds."

Ivan thought back to the picture they'd found in the secret room. A night world joined to a day world with a human conduit. That seemed big, alright. *Too big to be true. Too big for me.*

"Tomorrow is Friday," said Anders. "It's when the occult shit is meant to hit the fan. So," he pointed at Ivan, "Start working your stuff, boy wonder."

It reminded Ivan of the times he'd been forced to perform in school plays as a kid. Thrust into the limelight, hating it, wanting to run back into the shadows. *The shadows, huh? Seems to be something of a theme now.*

He took a deep breath and let it out. The raven perched on a rock a few feet away, watching the proceedings with interest.

Throw me a bone here, Ivan thought.

As if it had heard his thoughts, it winged over to his shoulder, claws digging in briefly as it steadied itself. Ivan put his hand up and lightly brushed the feathers on its back.

He closed his eyes and fell still, trying to recreate how he'd felt every time something weird had happened.

Ivan deliberately relaxed his shoulders, arms, and hands. He tried to summon that *shift* of vertigo that accompanied a change in his perception.

It didn't happen.

He was too rushed, on the spot, *observed.*

Ivan opened his eyes. Anders and Amelie were watching him, and while they both had matching smirks, they looked tense. *They're afraid. Afraid for you, or afraid of you?*

The raven stropped its beak on his hair, and Ivan tried to calm his paranoia.

"Umm, maybe if you both just go away for a bit, I'll see what I can do. Without you watching me."

"Ivan has performance anxiety," said Amelie, though she did say it with an encouraging smile.

"Attaboy," said Anders, and they both went away into the kitchen, bearing the empty packet of biscuits and coffee cups.

Ivan sat down on the ground and let his head drop down. The raven leaned close to him, its soft feathers brushing his ear.

He stayed like that for a while, counting his breaths, and gradually began to feel that *internal* sensation of being inside his body as well as outside of it. The rushing of his blood in his veins, the beating of his heart. Organic motions that had happened every second of his life but had never paid any attention to until now.

In the most relaxed way possible, Ivan reached out in a direction he knew didn't normally exist, and *pulled*. There was a sensation of great distance, nearly infinite space, and Ivan was floating in the middle of it, calm and detached.

He heard a gasp and opened his eyes.

He was still sitting cross-legged but was now floating three feet above the ground, with a mist of shadows around him. The raven was on his shoulder, but now it was darker than black, dripping shadows with a density to them that shouldn't be possible for a creature in the real world.

The next moment Ivan plummeted down, landing painfully on his tailbone.

He growled a swear word, then said 'sorry' as the raven cawed at him reproachfully. It had taken flight as he crashed down, and it now landed back on his shoulder, feathers fluffed in disapproval.

"Holy shit," said Amelie, half whispering. It had been her gasp that distracted Ivan. She and Anders had come out the kitchen door and were standing on the edge of the patio, staring at him. "I mean, it's one thing to have a theory about something and another entirely to see it..." she trailed off.

"That was sick, bruv," said Anders, grinning. "Do it again."

Ivan got up, shook out his legs, and resisted the urge to rub his tailbone. It was aching fiercely.

"I...guess I can try again. It's not easy, though," he said. "That is, I don't think we can rely on it. On Friday, I mean. I have to be super calm to do anything, and super calm is not what I am anytime Magnus is around." Ivan had to prevent himself from looking around nervously as if saying the name would conjure Magnus up. *I don't think I'm ready for any of this.*

Anders just smiled in his best captain of the football team manner. "You'll get it, wonderboy. We'll leave you to it."

He and Amelie disappeared inside again, but Ivan was fairly sure they were watching him through the kitchen window.

He sat down again, facing away from the house and tried to recapture the feeling of space inside him. It was no good.

His thoughts flitted here and there, and most of all, they kept going back to two images: Anders and Amelie lying helpless on the cave floor and Magnus's face as he flicked his coat back to reveal his knife.

Whenever that image came up, Ivan's heart pounded, and all calmness fled.

About an hour later, Anders came out of the house. He tried not to show it, but Ivan could see his friend was disappointed.

"No worries, I-man. Everything's ready. Time to go into town and get that key. It's showtime," Anders punctuated that last sentence with a filmstar smile, teeth flashing white.

"Yeah, and I hope we get out with all our teeth," said Ivan gloomily. He extended a hand, and Anders pulled him to his feet.

20

"This is the worst plan ever," said Ivan. "I can think of half a dozen things that can go wrong without even trying."

"There are some tricky parts," said Anders.

Now they were getting to the execution of the plan, Ivan felt slightly sick. *It's like the feeling before a wrestling match but multiplied by ten. Maybe eleven.*

"You have a better plan, say it," said Amelie. She was upbeat about the plan, mostly because it didn't involve her potentially losing all her teeth. "I'll be waiting just around the corner."

"Keep the engine running," said Ivan. "We might be followed by an angry mob."

Amelie looked doubtfully at her car.

"It's a rental," said Ivan. "Rentals are great for being chased by angry mobs."

"That's a fact," said Anders. "Rentals can do anything."

They parked up. Ivan tried to get the raven to stay in the car when he got out, but it clacked its beak at him and flew away. *Smart bird. That's what I'd like to do.* Anders stood across the bonnet from him. His friend now looked about as sick as Ivan felt.

"So...I'm low-key freaking out now," said Anders.

Ivan plastered on a cocky grin he didn't feel and rapped on the car bonnet.

"Just back my play. We got this." *Shit. I really hope so.*

"Yeah, just like last time," muttered Anders. "Okay, let's go get smashed."

At midday, *Henrik's* was always crowded. And on Thursdays, it would have the slightly on-edge feeling it always did when Magnus was at his usual place by the bar.

As long as Ivan could remember, Magnus had spent every Thursday afternoon there. It was a power play, pure and simple. Magnus would sit in his chair, a chair no different from all the other chairs except that it somehow belonged to him, and hold court.

People would come to talk with him, trying to look confident or nonchalant. They would leave pleased that he'd talked to them and that everyone else had seen what good terms they were on.

Occasionally, Magnus would say a few quiet words and the person would leave looking pale and shaken.

As kids, Ivan and Owen would sit together in the corner of the pub, allowed in only because they were with Magnus. They'd drink soda and watch the comings and goings. Owen would feel proud because it was his dad at the centre of it all. And Ivan would feel proud because he was allowed inside the bar, Owen was his friend, and nothing could touch him.

Remembering it all, Ivan cringed inwardly. Even when he'd been old enough to come here by himself, he hadn't been inside *Henrik's* on a Thursday since Owen left.

Standing outside the door with Anders, Ivan could feel his heart drumming away in his chest. But he knew from experience that none of this would show on his face. Not to a stranger, anyway.

Ivan squared his shoulders and pushed the swing door open. Warm air, laughter, the smell of spilt beer and loud conversation rose to engulf him. *Steady...now comes the fun part.*

With only the tiniest hesitation, he walked over to the bar and sat in the chair next to Magnus.

"A beer, please," said Ivan, pointedly ignoring Magnus.

The loud noise of talking died as people took note of what was happening.

Henrik slid Ivan's coins off the counter. He looked at Ivan from under his bushy eyebrows, not saying a word. But Ivan heard the message: *watch your step, boy.*

Well, too bad, thought Ivan. *This shady shit has been going on far too long. I wonder how many of you here knew what was happening on the island and did nothing?*

The butterflies in Ivan's stomach took flight, their tiny shadows flickering across the shiny bar top. Ivan was flying too, both richly amused and savagely intent.

"So," he drawled, "I hear you took an extended fishing trip, Magnus. Too bad your friends didn't make it back."

Now the silence rolled out like a mushroom cloud. The drinkers were cupping their hands around their tankards, ready to move back at the first sign of trouble. Henrik gave Ivan a disappointed look and started clearing the nearest glasses off the bar top.

Magnus's eyes were heavy-lidded.

"You would know as much about that as me, Ivan."

"Ah yes," Ivan drew a shape with the beer spilt on the bar counter. He wasn't even thinking about it, but when he shot a glance across at Magnus, the older man was staring at what he'd drawn. Ivan looked down: he'd traced two intersecting circles. *A day world, a shadow world.*

Ivan leaned back in his chair, giving Magnus an insolent smile. "I was thinking you must be feeling a little put out right now."

"Do go on." Magnus's voice was honeyed, and Ivan knew he was at his most dangerous when he was most polite. The back of his neck prickled.

"You do all this work in secret for years. You're ready for the big breakthrough, the final showdown, the big kahuna, and then, shazam!" Ivan snapped his fingers. "A couple of teenagers blunder in and ruin it all."

Ivan didn't know exactly what he was saying. He was plucking words out of the air with the aim of annoying Magnus into violence. But it seemed to be doing the trick. The older man's bear-like shoulders had gone rigid with anger.

"Ivan Luca, I advise you to choose your next words very carefully." Magnus purred. He sounded calm, but there was a harmonic underneath that resonated danger.

Time to poke the bear. To his right, Anders was squaring up, eyeballing one of Magnus's cronies. *This is about to get messy. Well, in for a penny...*

"Y'know," said Ivan, his tone deliberately light. "I was wondering how Owen fits into all this. Were you hoping to get something for him too? Pass it on? Family legacy? Too bad it didn't work out —"

His words were cut short because, in a surge of movement, Magnus's hands were around his throat.

It was the moment everyone in the bar had been waiting for.

There was a roar of anticipation from the drinkers and the scrape of chairs as people stood up to get a better look. Ivan knew they were all looking forward to seeing this young upstart get taken down and taught a lesson. *Well, time to give the folks at home what they're waiting for.*

Ivan and Magnus were both on their feet, straining against each other. Anders braced off the bar and kicked the man lunging forward to grab Ivan from behind. The man staggered back and upset the table behind him to shouts of outrage.

Ivan had no time to spare. The grip on his neck was getting tighter, and spots appeared in his vision. *You have seconds before you pass out. Do something!*

He surged forward and sent a vicious knee into Magnus's groin.

The older man buckled over, wheezing, and now Ivan's hands were around Magnus's neck, searching. *There!* His fingers hooked onto the chain with both hands. Someone hit him in the side, and he careened back into the bar, but his grip held firm. The chain snapped and came away with him, and there in his hands was the key.

A man came at him with a bar stool, and Ivan ducked. The barstool crashed into the bar, smashing glass. *Sorry Henrik!*

Vaguely, Ivan wondered if he'd ever be allowed back in here. Behind him, Anders's shirt was torn, and he had a bloody nose, but he was still on his feet. *Almost time to go.*

Magnus was upright again, looking murderous. Ivan faced him, arms up defensively, the key hidden in his hand.

Ivan blocked the first punch, but the second caught him on the cheek. It hurt like white fire. Then Magnus's hands were choking him again. *Does he only have one move?*

This time, Ivan kept one hand pulling down on the chokehold while the other searched desperately under the bench top.

Got it!

Under the counter, where he'd stuck it when he first sat down, was a small container lined with plasticine. He pressed the key into it, snapped it shut, and then opened it again. The key dropped onto the floor, and Ivan shut the container tight, shoving it in his pocket.

We may not have thought this next bit through properly. Namely, the escape part...

Magnus's grip around his neck was starting to *hurt*.

A sound cut through the noise of the fight and the shouting crowd. It was the sharp crack of a cricket bat being smacked onto a vinyl counter with a certain emphatic but controlled force.

Silence fell.

Henrik stood behind the bar, calmly holding a cricket bat in his right hand and slapping the end of it into his left. In his huge hands, the heavy bat looked like it weighed nothing.

"It's time for you to go, Ivan," he said. "And Magnus, whatever the boy said, I expected more of you."

With a grunt and one final twist, Magnus let go, shoving Ivan back.

Ivan rubbed his windpipe, staring at Magnus. Magnus didn't say anything, but the fire in his eyes told Ivan this wasn't over. Then Magnus's gaze fell on the key lying on the floor, and his hands flew to his neck. He swiftly scooped the key up, pocketing it.

His chest heaving, Ivan took stock. There were two broken chairs, a lopsided table, and lots of broken glass. Ivan nodded to Henrik. *I'm sorry.* Just for a moment, Henrik's eye, the one Magnus couldn't see, flicked down the tiniest wink. Ivan felt a warm glow. *At least not everyone in this town is on Magnus's side.*

Anders shoved a guy's arm off him as he pushed himself back from the bar.

"Let's go."

Ivan felt the eyes on his back as they left the bar, each step crunching on glass.

As the door swung closed, he heard the noise start up again, like a kicked hornet's nest. The door pulled open again, and they both flinched around, expecting more trouble. Ivan relaxed only slightly as Detective Benioff stepped out to join them.

Ivan hadn't remembered her being there. She must have blended with the background, difficult to do in the pub's mostly male crowd.

Her elegant shoes clicking on the pavement, she fell in step with them as they walked towards Amelie's car.

"That was quite a disturbance," she said. Her blonde hair fell across her face, and she flicked it back.

"I think you'll find it was more of a ruckus," said Ivan. Beside him, he saw Anders's eyes go wide, but he couldn't help it. It was like his mouth said these things before consulting his brain.

"I wouldn't have thought this was your style, Ivan," said Benioff.

Ivan thought of the small silver box of plasticine nestled in his pocket and this time managed to keep quiet.

Before they reached the corner, Benioff swung in front of them, blocking their path.

"I don't know what you're up to," she said, "But a word of warning. The man you picked a fight with? He is *not safe*. You should be more careful."

Ivan caught Anders's gaze. Anders was silently asking: *Can we trust her? What does she already know about Magnus? Should we tell her more?*

Ivan kept his face expressionless. *Stick to the plan.*

"Detective Benioff, I appreciate the warning, but we're not up to anything. We just...said the wrong thing, that's all. We'll be more careful in the future."

"If you say so." Benioff arched an eyebrow, clearly sceptical. She raised a pale finger. "One moment." She fished in her pocket and drew out a business card with a number on it. "For when you run out of clever ideas and need rescuing. And Ivan," she pulled the card back slightly as he went to take it, "I meant what I said about trying to keep me in the dark. You don't want to end up on the wrong side of the law. It's not a pleasant experience. You're just one very small step away from ending up in police custody. Several search warrants are being processed as we speak, and one of them might be for your house."

Ivan nodded slowly and took the card. "Good to know, detective."

They walked to the corner, Anders limping slightly, Ivan pulling him to go faster. Ivan felt a flood of relief to see Amelie's car. They jumped in.

"Floor it," said Anders, and she did.

"How did you go?"

Ivan took out the container and opened it. There were two fresh, sharp imprints of the key in the plasticine.

"I did this while being strangled by Magnus," he said.

"Congratulations."

Ivan leaned back, an absurd feeling of pride in his chest. His neck and throat ached abominably, and his cheek throbbed, but they'd made a plan and executed it, and now they had an edge. *Hopefully.*

Benioff worried him. *What does she think she'll find at my house?* He shuddered to think what his mum and Greg would say if they found out he was under police investigation.

"If Henrik hadn't stopped the fight, they would have beaten us to a pulp," said Anders. "I would have gone home with all my teeth in a jar." He sounded less than pleased.

Amelie reached over, turned Anders's face to hers, and then whistled at the damage.

"You boys sure know how to start a fight."

"Ruckus," murmured Anders.

Ivan grinned. "Magnus is usually a much better fighter. He was so mad he couldn't think of anything but trying to strangle me. Because..." he trailed off. *Because I think he really* does *want to kill me.*

"Because he's an A-1 capital asshole and needs to be put away for a long time," said Amelie.

"Hear hear," said Anders.

"So let's go make this key," said Amelie, and the little car she'd hired for the summer revved and shot up the hill to the mill house.

21

Ivan watched as Anders carefully tamped sand into the casting container. Halfway down was a resin model of the key, created from the plasticine mould. A few feet away, Amelie was tending their burner, its butane fire cherry red as it slowly melted a bundle of old keys.

"Done."

Anders carefully cracked the mould, revealing two halves of tightly packed sand. He popped the resin key out and gently shaped two channels out from it - one to pour molten metal down and one to vent superheated air.

Ivan stared curiously at the two negatives, two halves shaping the space where the key had been.

It was tugging at his memory somehow. *Two worlds, one a shadow of the other.*

"And then you pour the molten metal in, and it makes the key." Amelie had come over to stare down at the mould.

"Yup." Anders carefully put the two halves together. Now all Ivan saw were the two holes, one to pour and one to vent. "How's the molten metal going?"

"Almost there," said Amelie.

Ivan felt the heat from the furnace from four paces away. The air rippled and shimmered around it, and the small vessel that had held the keys was now full of a glowing gold liquid.

Anders grabbed the iron tongs, black with carbon, and carefully fitted them around the vessel.

"Remind me how you know all this?" said Amelie.

"Ivan's grandad," said Anders absently. "He used to cast metal cleats and other pieces for his boat when we were kids. This is all his gear." His whole attention was fixed on the small container with its molten payload.

Anders carefully carried the ladle over to the mould and poured the molten metal into the hole. It flowed like fire, disappearing down into the darkness. He kept pouring until the glowing, sparking liquid came back up through the vent hole.

With a sigh, Anders sat back on his heels and put the tongs down.

"That's done. Now we leave it a while to cool, then quench it in water."

"Time for tea then?" asked Amelie.

"A cold bevvy is what I'm after," said Anders. "After you, milady."

Ivan stayed behind as they left, watching a small crust form on the molten metal. He had to resist the urge to reach out and test just how hot it was. *It's very hot. You'll burn.* But deep down, he wondered if perhaps he wouldn't. He felt like a space was opening up inside him, a hidden space, like the key-shaped hollow deep in the sand.

He could almost feel the shape of it: a space of potential that could be filled with something else. *Or through which something could flow.*

Ivan couldn't put a finger on which sense he could feel this space with, but it was there. *As sure as Sunday.* He put his hands in his pockets to stop himself from dipping a finger in the molten metal to test the theory.

Strange you should be making a key when you are a key. The thought came to him as clearly as if someone had spoken behind him. Ivan actually looked around, but Amelie was busy packing away the small furnace, and Anders was off in the kitchen.

I'm trying to concentrate here, he thought back at it. Then, *I really am losing it.*

Ivan shook his head to clear it and went inside to get a drink.

Amelie was leaning against the counter, cup in hand, regarding him coolly.

"Don't think I've forgotten," she said.

"Forgotten what?"

"You were going to tell me the story. Of what went down between you, Magnus, and Karl's older brother. What's his name...Owen?"

Damn. I hoped she had forgotten.

"Well?" she prompted.

"Fine. Okay." Ivan grabbed a glass and filled it with water. He took a sip.

"Stop faffing Ivan," said Anders, "and tell the story."

Ivan scowled. *Easy for you to say.* "Back in the day, Owen and I were best mates."

Anders snorted faintly at this. Ivan ignored him.

"We did everything together, and I thought we'd always be tight. But when Owen got to his eleventh birthday, he started acting strange. Brooding. He almost told me something a few times, then changed his mind. And then..." Ivan cast his mind back. This part of the events was clouded in his memory. *For a lot of reasons.*

"I must have seen something one day when Owen and I were out playing. To this day, I can't remember what it was. My memory's fuzzy around that time because...well, we'll get to that. But I'm guessing it must have been to do with his father's...habits. His cult. Whatever."

Ivan took another sip of water, feeling the coolness slide down his throat. "The next day, Owen shows up at my house, friendly as can be, wants to go play on a swing we built up in the forest. We hadn't gone there in months, but he was strangely insistent. So I went along with it. And then...." Ivan paused. Saying this out loud was like pushing through a barrier.

"Well, I went first on the swing, like he wanted me to." *Because I always did what Owen wanted me to do.* Ivan pushed his hair out of his eyes, sensing the hushed silence of his audience like a physical weight.

"When I was out over the ravine, the rope broke. I didn't die, but...it was close. I got knocked out. Owen must have run home without telling anyone, but Anders came and found me. The next bit I can't remember clearly. I was concussed badly. Anders helped me out of the ravine. But later, after I'd recovered, Anders showed me the rope from the swing. He'd used it as a sort of sling to help carry me home. Part of the rope was frayed. But most of it had been cut."

Amelie made a small sound.

Ivan stared at the glass in his hand. "I don't know who cut the rope. It could have been Owen. It could have been Magnus. But Owen knew enough to make sure I got on the swing first, and I fell for it. Literally."

"You don't get dad joke points for really dark jokes," said Anders.

"Yeah, right," said Ivan. He concentrated on drinking his water and tried to push all the black thoughts and memories back down into the shadows. *How does it feel to be betrayed by your best friend?*

"You must have seen Magnus and his cult doing something criminal," said Amelie.

"Mostly likely. It makes sense with what we know now," said Ivan. "I guess the fact I can't remember what I saw is why Magnus left me alone all these years. Until now."

"What happened to Owen?" asked Amelie.

Ivan shrugged. "I was out of school for six months, and when I came back, Owen had left. Gone to some fancy boarding school." *I haven't seen him since. I don't know what I'd do if I did.*

Anders glanced at his watch. "It's time."

The tension in Ivan's spine increased. *If this doesn't work, we're back to square one. And the clock is* seriously *ticking.*

Anders knelt down and carefully pried open the mould. There was a cracking sound, then shifting sand.

Ivan heard both himself and Amelie let out a breath. The key shone dully amongst the sand, a complicated creation still attached to the metal from the pouring and vent holes. Anders knocked the sand from it and held it up to the light.

"It worked." He didn't sound surprised, just satisfied. "Here." Anders handed the key to Ivan.

It was still warm to touch, like a living thing. The key was an old design, one Ivan had never seen before. The head was a thick triangular shape with symbols cut into the ring at the top.

His fingers dragged along the rough edges, feeling where the fine sand had stippled the surface. He compared the heft of it to how Magnus's key had felt in his hands. This one was slightly lighter, but the shape was identical.

This key is going to get us into a lot of trouble.

Anders selected a file and took the key off Ivan. He sat down on one of the old millstones and started gently cutting away the excess metal, then smoothing the edges and corner of the key.

Amelie came over. "Think it'll work?" she asked.

"Deffo," said Anders. "First time."

"Here." Amelie handed Anders a necklace woven from string, the kind fishermen make to fill time at sea. He threaded it through the keyhole, knotted the ends and handed it back to her.

"You ok to keep it safe for now?"

Slowly, Amelie took the necklace and put it over her head. She dropped the key out of sight under her t-shirt in a strangely ceremonial gesture.

"So, we have a key. And a chest to break into. And an enemy to frame. That's what I call a well productive day." Anders was looking pleased with himself.

"Are you staying for dinner?" asked Amelie.

"Nah, I'll head home," said Ivan. He supposed Anders and Amelie wanted time together, and he could do with some time to himself.

"If you're sure," said Anders carefully.

"Yup," said Ivan. "Well done us. I'll see you tomorrow for the next step in the plan."

He gave them a half wave and headed down the driveway. One curve of the road and the mill was out of sight, hidden behind a tall stand of trees.

22

Ivan walked along the forest path, heading home. The shadows were long now as the sun slowly sank to dusk. Everything was cloaked in a dusty gold as the last evening sun filtered through the trees.

He breathed in the rich air, enjoying the musty tang of pine needles. He was just starting to relax when a stinging blow hit him on the side of his head.

Ears ringing, Ivan stumbled and fell on one knee. Quick footfalls approached through the forest. Several figures were pounding toward him. Ivan heaved himself to his feet, swaying, and the world tilted again as something hit him on the side of the head again. A rock flung with great accuracy. He caught a glimpse of one of Magnus's friends, his sling just loosed, a glitter of triumph in his eyes.

Ivan collapsed in the path, his face in the pine needles. They still smelt good.

Hands hauled him up, and he found himself face to face with Magnus.

The bearded man's face had a smile that twisted unpleasantly at the edges.

"Bind him," he snapped to the others. "We'll do this quickly."

Someone tied ropes tight around Ivan's wrists. He thought to push his wrists apart as they did it, but the rope was so tight all it did was make sure his circulation wasn't completely cut off.

Somewhere in the back of his head, an urgent voice was telling him to do something, now, something strange and specific. But he couldn't make out the exact shape of it over his own hammering heart and the woozy ache in his head.

Two men grabbed his arms and started marching him up a path deeper into the forest, away from the village.

They stopped at a bend in the path. Magnus was ahead of Ivan, his broad back slightly hunched. His hands kept clenching and unclenching. *Why am I noticing small details like this? Is my brain recording my final moments for posterity? That makes no sense...*

Magnus grabbed Ivan by the hair, pulling his head up.

"You're going to give back what you stole, boy."

Ivan said, "I didn't steal anything," and his voice sounded distant to his ears. The blow from Magnus hit him in the mouth, snapping his head sideways. Ivan tasted blood.

Magnus grabbed the top of Ivan's head again, forcing him to look up. "You took what was rightfully mine. Mine and my family's."

Ivan had never seen such fury held in such a tight grip. He tensed, anticipating another blow, but Magnus carried on talking instead.

"All that power, sitting in your worthless body. You have no idea how hard I worked, how much I sacrificed..." His eyes bored into Ivan's, and the thought surfaced that maybe Magnus had gone mad. *Being stuck in that cave might have cracked his mind.*

But perhaps Ivan was mad too because, for a moment, he thought he was somewhere else, was some*thing* else. The ground rushed under his tireless feet, the air was a huge complex ball of smells, and there was a surge of power with each leap of his steel-sprung muscles.

Ivan blinked and spat blood onto the pine needles. *Maybe I'm about to die, and that was a preview of my next reincarnation.* The thought seemed incredibly funny, and he struggled to keep a hysterical laugh inside him.

Magnus had gone quiet, looking at Ivan's blood on the forest floor.

"Blood," he said, "is how you're going to give me back what you stole in the cave." Magnus smiled then, a quick flash of white in his beard. "You have no idea, Ivan, how much power is inside you. And now I have you here, helpless, unable to tap into it. I think I almost prefer it this way. The prey caught in the trap, the hunter victorious."

Ivan tossed his hair back and pitched his voice to carry.

"Do your flunkies know about the cave when your brilliant plans ended with five of them dead? Do they seriously think you'll do anything for them once you've got what you want?"

Magnus's expression went distant, almost serene.

"Ivan, this is why you are not worthy to wield this power. You don't understand the sacrifice it requires. It's not your fault. Most humans live tiny lives that don't amount to anything, and they prefer it that way." Magnus sniffed the air, a predator scenting blood.

"Poor Ivan. Always alone, always on the outside. Your so-called friends can't help you. Their feeble schemes have led you to this defeat. Only the strong are worthy of power because they can see things as they are and act accordingly. I know. I have seen the truth."

"Which is?"

"This world is a thin veneer over an abyss of darkness."

Ivan spat more blood onto the forest floor.

"Meh," he said. "You sound like a bad melodrama."

"Perhaps I'll write it in blood across your butchered corpse." Magnus fell silent, his black eyes hooded. He leaned close, and Ivan shivered as his hot breath whispered in his ear.

"You have no idea what *else* we awoke that night. I was lying trapped under the rockfall. The others would have left me, the cowards. But I found help. Oh yes," Magnus's eyes glowed, dark and vibrant. "Help came for me out of the darkness. Help, and the promise of great power. There are things you don't know about, Ivan. Things you dream of and wake screaming. They're all real, somewhere in the dark."

A mad glint flickered in Magnus's eye as he stepped away from Ivan. He rubbed his knuckles, and then straightened Ivan's coat in an almost friendly way.

"And so now," Magnus said, "you have to die. And one day, when the monsters reach out to take this world, I will be waiting to defend it. Or my son. Or my son's son."

"What if your son only has daughters?" said Ivan. But he was thinking: *is he talking about something real? The giant tentacle marks...the cave scraped clean. What does Magnus know?*

Magnus gestured. "Tie him to that tree. And afterwards, we'll make sure his friends are silenced too."

Two men started to drag Ivan to the tree. He tried resisting but was still weak from the blows to his head.

Out of the corner of his eye, he saw Magnus flip his jacket back from the hunting knife that hung on his belt. The knife that was always extremely sharp.

"Da, what're you doing?" Karl's voice was breathless as he arrived. It sounded like he'd been running hard.

His father kept staring at Ivan. "I didn't tell you we were here, Karl. But maybe it's for the best. You said you were old enough now to do a man's work. Well," he indicated Ivan, "Watch and learn. This is what happens to those who stand in our way."

Ivan closed his eyes, feeling the surge of head sickness merge with adrenaline. And there again was that strange other sense of rushing through the forest at great speed.

I'm about to die. I wonder how much this will hurt.

"It's a funny saying, 'slit your wrist,'" said Magnus. He motioned for two of his followers to hold Ivan's bound hands in place. "It's never been about slitting wrists—that would be foolish. To get the blood inside of you to the outside, you need to slit the forearm."

Ivan struggled then, but the men holding him never loosened their grip. One of them rammed his head back against the tree trunk, and the other held his wrists in an iron grasp. Straining so the tendons stood out from his neck, Ivan looked down. He saw Magnus push his knife deep into Ivan's left wrist, then draw it slowly up his forearm.

He heard Karl cry out and a sharp pain as his own body finally registered the injury.

Magnus stepped back, looking satisfied, and knelt to hold a stone cup under Ivan's arm. Ivan recognised it as the cup from Magnus's secret room.

With a soft pattering sound, it was rapidly filling with blood. It was Ivan's blood, dark red and arterial.

"I've bled out animals many times before," Magnus said softly. "Animals caught in traps, like you. The carotid artery in the neck is faster, but the radial artery is...more effective for my purpose."

Ivan's vision had giant spots of colour in it, like exploding stars. *So that's why they say you see stars when you're hurt...*

He closed his eyes as his fate washed over him. *I'm going to die by my life draining out into a cup.* In the blackness of his mind, a door formed high above him. Ivan felt light, floating. In the dark inside his head, he drifted up level with the door. It began to open, and Ivan spiralled towards it.

With total sureness, Ivan knew all he had to do was let go, and he would be gone. Cut free, he would float through the door, never to return to this world.

It seemed like a fine idea.

He could still feel the sting in his arm and the light-headed blood loss. *I don't have long now.*

And then a presence was with him in the darkness. It was huge and shadowy, yet somehow comforting.

I know you. As his heart pumped his blood out with a steady pulse, he thought: *I'm glad you're here.*

Mentally, Ivan gathered his strength. His *will*. He pushed back through the door in his mind, and it felt like trying to open a door against an ocean of water. *I'm going to face this. It's my life. My final moments. I wouldn't change any of this for all the world.*

The wind was rushing through his hair, and a hundred sensations merged into a whirl of sound and colour. His eyes blew open, and the dark shape was still with him, but now it was here, in his world, crouched just across the clearing.

With a growl of pure menace, the black shape leapt on top of the nearest man, who screamed and fell to the ground.

It was huge and wolf shaped. Ivan had seen wolves on TV, but this wolf was different from the ones he'd seen. They were grey; this one was charcoal black. They were big; this one was huge. And this one cast shadows that were darker than any he'd seen in the real world.

It came back with me. The shadow wolf. Fuck yeah.

The wolf barrelled into the next man, knocking him down and tearing at his arm as he cried out in pain. The two men holding Ivan let go.

The creature growled again, so deep Ivan felt it in the pit of his stomach. A heartbeat later, Magnus screamed. The wolf had sprung on him and had its teeth set in the arm he'd flung up to protect his face.

There was a sickening crunch, and Magnus screamed again. The wolf whirled away from him and positioned itself in front of Ivan, its deep growl reverberating around the clearing.

"Shoot it," Magnus yelled at the others. "Pedersen, use your gun!"

The wolf moved faster than Ivan could believe, and Pedersen cried out as it caught his hand with the gun in its jaws and bit down. There was a crunch, and Pedersen staggered back, clutching his hand to his chest. His eyes wide, he dropped the gun from his shattered fingers and ran, stumbling through bushes.

The men holding Ivan scuttled over to Magnus and hauled him up. Magnus had his knife out, but the hand clutching the hilt was shaking.

Ivan's attackers backed away as the wolf advanced, its growl coming from a deep primordial place where wolves were king and men were food.

Magnus shot Ivan a look of pure hatred, and then all the men ran, crashing through the undergrowth. Ivan saw Karl, his eyes wide, staring at the wolf for a frozen instant, and then he too fled.

Ivan listened to their progress through the forest as he slowly sank to the ground, his back against the tree trunk, head spinning. The expression on Magnus's face as he ran away struck him as the funniest thing he'd seen in a long time.

He started laughing helplessly, gasping for breath as the huge black wolf padded back to him. It cocked its head to one side, regarding him quizzically. *Is this euphoria from blood loss? Am I going into shock? How bad is the damage?*

Ivan sucked in a long breath, slowly coming under control. The forest spun gently in his vision as the Wolf came closer. Its face was level with his, its yellow eyes intent. Ivan should be terrified, but the Wolf was so big and real. *And I feel like I know it from somewhere.*

His eyes drifted shut as the wolf closed the gap between them. A brief snuffle as it sniffed him, a cold, wet nose and the hot wolf breath on his skin. There was a brief tug, pressure, and a snap as it bit through his bindings.

"Thanks," said Ivan. He slowly raised his arm. Blood was still coming out from the wound in spurts. *This is bad.*

Shakily, Ivan pulled off his jacket and wadded it up to press on his arm. *Apply pressure, stop the bleeding.*

He leaned back against the tree trunk, feeling dizzy. The wolf looked at him, then sniffed at his arm. With a jerk of its head, it shoved aside Ivan's jacket and licked his arm. There was a sharp feeling in Ivan's arm, not painful, just cold, like he'd dipped it in icy water. A hissing sound, and the skin around the wound went black, then blue, then gradually faded back to his normal pale skin tone. The bleeding stopped.

Ivan stared. "Thanks," he said, then closed his eyes again and waited for the world to stop spinning.

A warm weight settled by his leg. Ivan opened his eyes. The wolf was sitting with its back to him, ears pricked up, scanning the forest.

Magnus and his gang will be back with guns soon. Better get going.

"Hey," he said, and the wolf turned its head toward him, golden eyes looking at him seriously. Ivan lifted his head and straightened, which was not easy with his vision still wobbly.

The wolf was up in one fluid movement, regarding him steadily.

"Let's go," said Ivan.

Very cautiously, he laid his hand on the wolf's shoulder, then put more weight on it as the world tilted. The creature's shoulder was level with his waist, the biggest dog he'd ever seen. *It's not a dog, you idiot. It's a fucking* wolf. *Holy shit.* Ivan shut his eyes and hoped the feeling of dizziness would pass soon. Then, one step at a time, the Wolf walked home with him.

On the way, Ivan texted Anders and Amelie.

> Magnus is hunting for you both. Don't go anywhere alone.

His phone pinged almost immediately with questions from both of them, but a quick 'I'm ok' message was all Ivan had energy for right now.

When they came to his house, Ivan felt like he'd left it a lifetime ago.

His hands shook as he unlocked the front door. The wolf by his side growled softly and padded inside in front of him, sniffing the air.

Ivan stood in the doorway with his mouth slightly open, staring at the wolf. He hadn't expected *that.* He wondered, slightly dazed, whether the Wolf would like roast beef or chicken like it was an unexpected dinner guest.

He entered, closed the door and locked it. At the snick of the lock, the Wolf looked back at him but didn't seem unduly worried.

Ivan let out a long, slow breath. Nothing in his childhood home looked right, with a wolf in the foreground. It was a real, fully grown timber wolf with a mane of shaggy black fur and intent golden eyes. *And it has extra shadows.*

"My life is getting extremely weird," Ivan said. The Wolf cocked its head at that, and Ivan faced it.

He gave a little bow. "Thank you for saving my life."

The wolf gave a little huff as though mildly amused. It continued sniffing its way through the living room.

It was so tall it could easily rest its chin on the dining room table, and it did so, eyeing the fruit bowl.

It made a circuit of the dining room and kitchen and at last settled on the three-seater couch in the living room, filling it entirely. Ivan had a brief moment of hysterical laughter that never left his mouth, imagining trying to shoo it off the couch. In this house, dogs weren't allowed on the furniture. *But it's not a dog.*

The wolf remained lying on the couch, watching as Ivan made tea and pressed some ice wrapped in a tea towel to the bump on his head. He willed his hands to stop shaking, but they wouldn't.

I'm not used to being a target for murderers. Amelie was handling it better than me.

Tea in hand, he sat on the couch opposite the Wolf, regarding it soberly.

"What on earth are we going to do?" he asked.

The wolf watched him. It seemed so calm, the opposite of how he was feeling. Ivan found its presence steadied him.

He decided to confide in it some more.

"Since going to the island, I shot a man, and I had an out-of-body experience where I may or may not have been hit by lightning. At least four other of Magnus's cronies have mysteriously disappeared, I'm hearing weird voices in my head and knowing things I shouldn't know. A raven adopted me for a while, I've discovered a secret death cult in my village, and I've been rescued from said death cult by you." Ivan let the rest of his breath out. "Oh, and a police detective, who's actually quite attractive, thinks I'm involved in the disappearances and wants to arrest me."

The wolf regarded him silently. It seemed to be listening, but Ivan had no idea what kind of advice it would give him. *If I could speak wolf, that is.* The tune from "Who's afraid of the big bad wolf" popped into his head, and the wolf cocked its head at him, almost as if it could hear it.

A thought struck Ivan. He set his tea down and went over to the bookshelf, pulling out the old, cloth-covered book his dad used to read to him when he was a child.

It was a book of Norse Myths and Legends: bloody, strange, and magical. Years later, when he'd read the book for the first time himself, he realised how many gory bits his dad had edited out of the stories. Ivan flipped about one-third of the way through, and there it was, just as he'd remembered.

He studied the illustration of an old man, hat brim pulled low over his face, one-eyed. On each shoulder was a raven, and a wolf on either side of him. He held a staff, and the illustrator had managed to add a ghostly impression of a spear to it.

Underneath the illustration, in copperplate font, was written: Odin, the Allfather, Lord of the Norse Gods (see Aesir,) King of Asgard, travelling through Midheim, Earth.

"This is mad," said Ivan. "I'm not mad, am I?"

The Wolf's eyes met his. To Ivan, it looked a trifle smug, lying there on the plush couch. He had the sudden urge to touch its fur and reassure himself it was real. But he didn't because a) he was still a little nervous of it, and b) if he was mad, he couldn't trust any of his senses, and c) even from here, he could feel the heat from its body and smell its musky wolf scent.

Anyway, if I am mad, I'm not the only one. Ivan gingerly felt the side of his head where the first rock had struck him. There was a big, tender lump there. *I'm very, very lucky to be alive.*

Ivan picked up his phone and called Anders.

On the other end of the line, Anders sounded slightly breathless.

"You'll never guess what's going down," he said.

Ivan rolled his eyes at the wolf on his couch. "Try me."

"Magnus and his mates claim they've been attacked by a wolf! I thought it was total rot, but then I saw the bites. They seem to think it's near your place, so you should be careful." There was a hesitation on the line. "How come you texted Magnus was looking for us?"

Ivan slumped against the kitchen bench. "How far away are they?"

"They were getting tooled up, is the last I heard. They had to get patched up first, though," Anders sounded pleased. "They've got rifles, compound bows, traps, knives...you know how those boys love their toys. There's more of them too." Anders was starting to sound worried again. "Some out-of-towners showed up. I thought they could be planning one of those 'stray bullet' hunting accidents for you. Or all of us."

Ivan eyed the Wolf again. It looked back, unconcerned. "It's a bit more complicated than that. Hey, can you get here real fast? In your truck?"

"For sure."

"Ok. I have news for you too. But first, we need to go somewhere safe. Do you think Magnus and his crew know about the mill house?"

A brief silence on the other end of the line. Then: "I don't think so. We've always kept on the down low."

"Good. See you soon." Maybe Amelie liked wolves. You never knew with a person.

For the next few minutes, Ivan paced around the living room. His mind supplied him images of Magnus and a horde of hunters arriving at his door, armed with every hi-tech killing implement you could get at a hunting store or more likely, order over the dark web from Russia.

He felt a shockingly strong surge of protectiveness towards the Wolf. It had come from god-knows-where to protect him. But even a wolf that size would have no chance against assault rifles.

"We have to go," he told the Wolf. "Trouble is on its way."

The Wolf's golden eyes were calm. *It's so regal,* Ivan thought. At ease on the sofa, it transformed it into a throne. It didn't appear ready to move.

"Please?" said Ivan. "They have guns, and there are lots of them."

It flicked an ear.

Ivan checked his phone again. He'd had it switched off all afternoon while they'd made the key. There were half a dozen missed calls from Karl on it, starting from early afternoon, then a text saying, "Don't go anywhere alone. My father is hunting for you." Ivan felt a tiny bit better. *I was right to trust Karl.*

Anders would be here in about half a minute. *I have no idea how to get the Wolf to come with me. How do I get it into the truck? I don't even know its name.*

Instead of trying to cajole the Wolf, he headed for the door. The Wolf was off the couch in an instant, padding at his side.

Ivan cautiously cracked the door and listened. The Wolf poked its shaggy snout out the door and listened too. Far more effectively, Ivan was sure.

It was a quiet summer evening, the air rich with the scent of the forest. The Wolf pricked its ears, and a few seconds later, Ivan heard the roar of the Beast.

23

Anders's Bedford pulled into the drive with a skid, and Anders hurried over to Ivan's front door.

"They're saying some crazy things at the pub...Woah!" Anders reeled back as the Wolf poked its head past the door.

"That's...Geez, Ivan. What the hell!"

"It's ok," said Ivan, hoping it was. "Look, we need to leave before they get here."

"Is it safe?" Anders said nervously, peering at the Wolf's huge head.

"I think so," said Ivan. "As long as you don't try to kill me."

Anders silently backed away as Ivan opened the front door, and the wolf stepped out into the summer night.

Ivan found he didn't like being out in the open. He kept wondering if he was going to feel the sudden impact of an assault rifle. *But Magnus said he wants my blood. So no guns. Not like that anyway.* The thought wasn't very comforting.

Ivan opened the truck door and swung up into the front bench seat. The Wolf hesitated a few seconds before flowing up onto the seat next to him. Ivan heard the suspension creak as the wolf settled. Very gingerly, Anders opened the driver's door.

He saw Anders's shoulders tense as he got into the driver's side, as if he expected sharp teeth to sink into him any moment. But the Wolf sat still, just as regally as it had on his sofa.

As Anders closed the door, the front of the truck was abruptly full of Wolf. The feeling Ivan had from it now was a hidden amusement mixed with unease at being in such a confined space.

"It'll be alright," he said.

They took the back road, lights off in the twilight, watching carefully. Wherever the hunting party was, Ivan saw no sign of them as they navigated up to the windmill.

Anders slowed as he drove up the rocky driveway and guided the truck towards the small garage.

Ivan opened the truck door, and the Wolf rose up. Ivan was struck again by how very large it was, and how quiet. It slipped out of the truck and leaned gently against the side of his leg. Quite warmed by this display of affection - or was it possession? he gestured towards Anders.

"This is my friend Anders. He is one of the good guys."

Anders laughed a little shakily. "Bro, I think your Wolf wants to…"

The wolf reared up, and Anders took a startled step backwards. The wolf came down with its paws on his shoulders, and Anders froze. His terrified face slowly transformed as it sniffed him carefully, then gave his face a long, wolfish lick.

As the Wolf strolled back to Ivan, Anders's face was a gleaming picture of joy.

"It's a real timber wolf. And it's on our side. That's bare wicked. Ivan, we can't let Magnus and his gang find it." He studied Ivan in the fading light. "Bro, what happened to you?"

"Let's go inside," said Ivan. He was suddenly very tired. "Then we need to make new plans."

Inside was warm and dark. The lingering glow of sunset was slowly fading into the summer night.

"Amelie's working late," said Anders. "She's preparing for the Viking event. There's loads of them staying at the hostel. She texted to say, '*make yourselves at home.*'"

Somehow, Ivan doubted she'd been thinking of a giant wolf when she said that.

Anders lit the fire - the only means of cooking in this house and set a kettle to boil. While it sputtered and steamed over the fire, Ivan told Anders what had happened in the forest. He paled when Ivan showed him his forearm.

"So the wolf saved you?" said Anders. He prodded at the wound on Ivan's arm, but it already looked like it had been healing for several days.

"Yes, and now Magnus wants it dead. And he certainly wants me dead."

"This is all totally mental. What the hell are we going to do?"

"I don't know," said Ivan. He leaned back into the couch, feeling weary, shaken loose, like a tooth ready to be pulled.

The dancing flames illuminated the Wolf as it gazed lazily into the fire. Very carefully, Ivan reached out and stroked the thick fur around its ears. *I wonder if cavemen felt like this with the first tame wolves, the great ancestors of dogs. Although...I'm not sure this wolf is tame, exactly. I wonder why it came here.*

There was a tapping on the window, and they both jumped. The Wolf's head whipped around to see the intruder, and then it relaxed.

Ivan got up and walked over to the window. A single eye, black as the night outside, peered in at him. Feeling dreamlike, Ivan undid the window catch. The night took shape with two wing-beats as the Raven flew inside. Its talons gripped, then loosened as it settled on his shoulder, claws grasping his shirt in a way that was already familiar.

Anders's mouth shaped a perfect 'O' of surprise. Ivan's mouth lifted in a smile.

The Wolf blinked, or was it a wink? Ivan sat down again, feeling the Raven's feathers brush against his cheek and the fire heat his face as he leaned back and closed his eyes.

"I know who you look like," said Anders. "Wodan. Odin. But younger and way more emo."

"Thanks, mate."

"And Odin only had one eye. I remember," Anders carried on, "from a book I had when I was young. He always had these two ravens with him. Thought and Memory."

Ivan opened his eyes. Before Anders spoke, he'd felt like he was diving into a deep pool, dark and clear.

"That's a peng picture," said Anders, taking his phone out. "One for the ladies." Ivan shook his head, but Anders took the photo anyway.

"Don't upload that," he said.

"Too late," said Anders. "With the hashtag #don't mess with this guy, he's got a Wolf. Just kidding! It's tagged 'Voted most likely to really piss Magnus off.'"

Or die before the summer solstice.

"Very funny," said Ivan.

"I feel bad, bro. I got you into all this," said Anders.

Ivan shook his head. "Don't be like that. What's been going on with this cult...it's wrong. We have to stop it. Somehow. And anyway, I've been in this, sort of, for a while."

"Since Owen."

Ivan nodded.

They heard a car door slamming and then the front door opening.

Amelie gave a squeak at the sight of the Wolf, then froze as it trotted demurely up to her and nosed her palm.

"Is it...what the hell, Ivan?"

"It's a wolf ok?" said Ivan. "A really smart one. See? It likes you."

Amelie slowly relaxed as the Wolf returned to sit next to Ivan by the fire.

"I've never seen a wolf before," she said. A wondering smile spread across her face. "It's amazing. But how do you know it's safe?"

"Ummm. It saved my life, ok? And it seems to like Anders too."

"Hmmm."

She didn't say anything complimentary about the raven, which Ivan felt was unfair.

Anders told her what happened while Ivan kept back, stoking the fire and boiling more water. As the story built to a climax, Ivan watched her hand stray to her side, where he was sure she was carrying a handgun.

At the end of the story, Amelie met his eyes.

"This is..." she started again. "I'm sorry."

"This is not your fault," said Ivan. "It's senior psychopath and his delusional quest for power."

"Still," said Amelie. "This is..." she trailed off. "Bad. Very bad. How are you?"

It was the simplest of questions, yet Ivan felt unable to answer it. *I thought all that stuff from my childhood was over, old history. Dead and buried. And now it seems like it's going to keep coming back until I...what? Die? Defeat Magnus? I'm just so fucking tired right now.*

"I'm tired," he said.

Anders and Amelie exchanged a significant look.

"We need to go to the police," said Amelie. "Benioff will believe me."

"I...no," said Ivan. "We just need to move forward with our plan very carefully."

"Ivan, you're not making sense," said Amelie. "Magnus nearly killed you."

"I just..." Ivan's thoughts circled in confusion. *Why can't we just go to the police?* It did seem like the simplest solution. But every part of him resisted that course of action.

"If we tell the police," he said at last, "either they won't believe us, or they'll bundle us off into some sort of protective custody. And Magnus won't stop. He'll have a dozen witnesses ready to swear he wasn't anywhere near me today. And then he'll come after us again sometime in the future."

"You want to beat Magnus yourself, is that it?" said Amelie.

"No," said Ivan. *Maybe.*

"Are you afraid he'll win?"

"No," said Ivan. *Fuck yes, I am.*

"You're not trying to shield him or something, are you?" said Anders.

"No!" said Ivan. "I just...think we need hard evidence before we go to the police. Or he'll get away. Again."

"Yeah, we've seen that happen before," muttered Anders.

"I have a plan that I think will work," said Amelie. "Though I understand if you're not up to helping with it."

"I'm up to it," said Ivan.

Anders frowned. "Maybe we *should* go to the police now. This whole thing is fucking crazy."

Ivan rubbed his forehead. *What I did back there, the way I knew the wolf was coming. It must mean something.* "I think we can do this," he said. "Find the evidence to take Magnus down, with no way out for him."

"If you're sure..." said Anders. He didn't sound certain.

"I'm sure," said Ivan. He squeezed his eyes shut. When he opened them again, both Anders and Amelie were looking at him with mixed expressions. Doubt, concern, resolve, understanding, trust. Ivan's jaw clenched. *This is my call. I won't let them down.*

"Let's do it," he said.

"Alright, bruv," said Anders. "Hey, we got this."

"We better got this," said Amelie. "Because if something happens to me, my dad will come here and kill everyone responsible. That's no exaggeration. It's a promise."

The tension slowly drained out of the room. Amelie leaned back against Anders, and he smiled.

"What I want to know," said Ivan, "is why you're not getting the first train out of here? No, why aren't we *all* getting the first train out of here?"

"Because trains don't allow wolves on them," said Amelie.

Ivan scowled to show her this wasn't funny. "Don't tell me you're staying for blondie there because I won't believe you."

Amelie smiled and put her arm around Anders. The smile made her suddenly younger and a lot more relaxed.

"Anders is the love of my life, and no, I'm not staying for him. I'm staying because I was raised never to run from a fight.

These bastards tried to kill me, and I intend to pay that back. With interest. Also, this holiday is finally getting interesting."

"Surely you're not just along for the ride," said Ivan.

"Bought my ticket in full," said Amelie. "To see the trainwreck." Though she did smile a little when she said it.

They both looked at Anders, whose ears had gone red.

"Poor darling," said Amelie, ruffling his hair. "You didn't know?"

"About being the love of your life?"

Amelie smiled a little dangerously.

"I guess," said Anders, "I'd better...um...make sure we all get through this alive then."

"I'm relying on the Wolf for that one," said Ivan. He hummed under his breath, *'Who's afraid of the big bad wolf,'* and Anders grinned.

They all turned to look at the Wolf, who gave a deep sigh and lowered its head down to stare at the fire, its ears twitching slightly as the flames flickered and danced.

"So what's your plan?" said Ivan.

"We know that Magnus has a chest that's always locked in his secret room," said Amelie.

"We do,' said Ivan.

"So we break into the room. If the chest contains something to incriminate Magnus, job done. We call in Benioff and get Magnus arrested."

"And if it doesn't?"

"We set a trap to frame Magnus, baited with what he wants most."

"What's that?" said Ivan.

"You," said Amelie.

The silence after this statement was the slightly awkward one of three friends, two of whom had nearly died in the last few days, contemplating baiting a trap with one of them. *I guess I now know who's the most ruthless of the three of us.*

"I don't like it," said Anders. "It's too risky."

"We'll only do it if the first plan fails," said Amelie. "And the first plan will work."

"It had better," said Ivan.

"I'm too old for this shit," said Anders. "No, really," as Amelie put an arm around him and kissed the side of his neck.

After a dinner of tinned baked beans warmed on the fire (the Wolf disdainfully refused its share), the flames burned low. The Raven went to roost on the windowsill, Anders and Amelie disappeared to the room up in the windmill tower, and Ivan took a bedroll out of a cupboard and curled up next to the Wolf. It gave a satisfied growl and leaned back against him. Ivan fell asleep to the sound of the fire crackling and the Wolf's quiet breathing.

24

Ivan half woke much later, in the dead of the night, because the Raven had stalked down from its resting place. It was standing near the Wolf, which had propped its head up to look at it.

Hovering in the dreamlike state between sleep and waking, Ivan was sure some sort of communication was happening between the two creatures, but he couldn't tell what.

A log in the fire crackled, and the Wolf gave a deep bass growl Ivan could feel thrumming through his chest.

The Raven stared into the fire, the flames reflecting off the perfect black orb of its eye. With a whir of wings, it disappeared into the darkness.

The Wolf laid its head down on the rug, and the solid weight of it leaned against Ivan's chest. As he drifted into sleep, he wondered if he would remember in the morning.

On waking, Ivan drank strong black coffee boiled on the revived embers of the fire. The Wolf had gone, Ivan supposed, on some foraging trip. He tried not to worry too much about it encountering Magnus and his band of murderous hunters.

The memory of last night tugged at his mind, a persistent thread he needed to unravel.

There was a feeling inside him, a building pressure in his head. It tugged at him like he would become unmoored if he didn't hold on. *Hold on to what...*

The Raven balanced on Ivan's shoulder as he drank the coffee. He was no longer as nervous of its strong black beak and sharp claws. *I guess I know it's an ally.*

Ivan stretched and winced. His body was stiff and sore from Magnus's attack yesterday.

"Do you like coffee?" he asked the raven. "I can put some in a cup for you."

The raven eyed him with its bright black eye.

"How about toast?" said Ivan. He took another sip of his coffee, the liquid nearly hot enough to burn his tongue. "I think you and the Wolf know a lot more than I do about what's going on."

The raven wiped its beak on his hair. It felt like being patted on the head as if he were a dog or small child who'd learned a new trick.

Ivan buttered his toast and swept the crumbs into the sink. He walked outside into the slightly chill morning air. The sun was up, and the slanting morning light turned the edges of everything gold. It must be very early, as the days were long this time of year.

Ivan sipped his coffee and bit into his toast. It was a traditional loaf covered in seeds, and the butter had melted to drip onto his fingers.

"Firstly," he said conversationally to the raven, "I want to know where the Wolf has gone. I don't want it getting shot by Magnus and his friends."

The Raven fluffed its feathers and clacked its beak.

"Secondly, I need to know more. About what's coming at the solstice. And what you think we can do about it."

He held up the last corner of toast. "Go on." It vanished from his fingers like a magic trick, and he heard the bird crunch it lightly in its beak before swallowing it down.

"Coffee?" Ivan held up his cup of steaming black coffee. A pause, and then the Raven delicately dipped its whole body down and scooped two beak fulls of coffee.

The Raven settled back on Ivan's shoulder and leaned its body against his head. He savoured the moment. The early morning air, the bright sky, the feeling that anything was possible. He closed his eyes against the sun's rays, and it was like closing one door and at the same instant, opening another.

In Ivan's mind, a dark storm cloud blew towards him. Black ribbons of smoke trailed through his fingers as he raised his hands. A searing pain and his fingers lengthened into flight feathers, each pinion as perfect as the feather the raven had dropped in his garden, what seemed like an age ago.

A harsh cry tore from his throat, and now Ivan was flying up the mountain valley at the end of the village, faster than any bird. Up ahead, a rocky mountain face loomed, and he flew straight into the slick black rock. In an eye blink, he was passing through a dark, twisting tunnel that opened out into a central cavern with a black lake.

At the lake's edge, dread surged through him. He was digging in his mental heels, trying not to move over the lake, but he couldn't stop himself. It was like a bad dream, where you're magnetically drawn to the one place you don't want to go.

Ivan drifted over the lake, and, quite helpless, his mind's eye moved to look down. There, darker than midnight, something stirred in the inky depths. Something very old, very powerful. *Something hungry.*

Ivan sensed it becoming aware of him. One vast eye was opening. In another instant, it would see him.

With a wrench, he tore himself free of the vision and opened his eyes, gasping for breath. He was back in the peaceful mill garden, the early morning sun starting to warm him.

The Raven made a curious, chortling noise deep in its throat and looked sideways at him. *Did it see what I saw?*

"Thank you," said Ivan. "I think."

He went back inside for more toast and coffee. His mouth had run quite dry. *Be careful what you ask for.*

The sun grew warmer as it rose, and Ivan rested in it, trying to soak up the feeling of life and light. The Wolf came out of the trees and sat with its back to him, resting against his knee.

Anders and Amelie finally emerged, coffee mugs in hand.

"Morning, bruv," said Anders. "Time to get tooled up for the plan: phase one."

Ivan nodded. He gently stroked the fur between the Wolf's ears.

"Please stay here," he said. "And look after Amelie." It flicked an ear at him but didn't try to follow.

25

Anders pulled into the parking lot in the middle of town.

"It's a shambles in there. All your Vikings mates are in the main shop, knocking over displays with their battle axes and buying phone chargers and whatnot. We better make sure they don't buy up what we need."

Ivan tried to give a carefree grin. It didn't work. He had a sinking feeling about their plan. *But it's the best we've got.*

"Right," he said. "Let's go shopping."

Ivan and Anders walked down the main street. Every minute or so, they had to move out of the way of costumed Vikings. Most of them seemed to have real beards. Some had long hair braided in a Norse style.

"You'd make a good Viking," said Ivan. "You could grow your beard."

Anders grinned. He did look the part, broad-shouldered, blonde and blue-eyed.

Ivan sighed, thinking of the money he'd spent signing up for Vikon. *Galen must be here somewhere. I wonder what he looks like. To think my biggest worry this weekend was that my classmates would recognise me in Viking gear.*

The electronics and outdoor equipment shop was brightly lit, almost surreal in its lack of shadows. The assistant looked like she was going to stop Ivan from coming in with the Raven, but Anders gave her such a sunny smile she decided not to.

Ivan wandered through the aisles while Anders picked out the cameras they needed for their plan. When he looked up, Anders had gotten sidetracked and had a baseball bat in his hands, testing the weight of it. Ivan shook his head and wandered on, browsing the aisles.

"Look at you two, all matchy matchy," said Anders, waving a hand at Ivan and the Raven. "I still can't believe it's adopted you."

Ivan caught a glimpse of himself in a store mirror, and it was true. His black hair blended perfectly into the raven's dark feathers.

"Why do you think it's so keen to hang around?" he asked.

"It can smell death on you," said Anders in a dramatic whisper.

Ivan's shoulders tensed. "Too soon, bro," he said.

Inevitably, they found themselves drawn to the hunting section. Ivan stared at the sleek knives in their sheathes and the precision hunting bows, all anodised steel and carbon fibre for lightness and strength. In the gun cabinet, rifles were neatly laid out, with price tags and brand names. He shivered.

"Let's get out of here."

With Anders's bag of supplies, they stepped out onto the street, dodging a lady clad in what looked like a purple silk tent and a horned Viking helmet.

Ivan kept watch on the main street while Anders sauntered down Blackburn alleyway. There was a rubbish bin near the end, and Anders used it to climb up onto the sloping roofs that pitched down to enclose the alley. He spent the next few minutes setting up cameras and carefully connecting them to his cell phone. Then he jumped down and joined Ivan, leaning casually against the wall as they surveyed his work.

"The cameras will turn on as soon as any of us is near," he told Ivan. "There's a proximity setting, and the cameras will send the video feed straight up to the cloud."

In case none of us makes it out alive, thought Ivan. *Great.*

"Is there an easier way to do this?" he wondered out loud. Anders shrugged.

"Amelie programmed a message to be sent to Benioff tomorrow with links to the video feed. Just in case...you know."

"I feel so cheerful right now," said Ivan. "Let's go get a pint."

Ivan hesitated for a moment outside *Henrik's*, then shouldered through the doors. The pub was empty of Magnus's crew, however, there was a group in Viking gear in one corner.

At the bar, Henrik made no mention of the raven perched on Ivan's shoulder. He wiped down the counter before fixing Ivan with a steady gaze.

"Surprised you'd show your face in here so soon," he said.

"Yeah, well," said Ivan. "Thanks for saving our asses the other day."

Henrik shrugged. "It's my bar. I call the shots."

Ivan grinned. *Was that a pun? From Henrik?*

His smile faded as the weight of what they planned to do this evening settled on him. *There are so many things that could go wrong.*

He shifted his arm on the countertop. Even though the wound had closed over unnaturally fast, it still ached where Magnus had cut it. *Face the facts, Ivan. You're scared.*

"You look like you could use a drink," said Henrik.

"Thanks," said Ivan. His forearm throbbed again, and the back of his head ached in sympathy. "Hey Henrik, do you ever wonder if you're up to a certain task? Like, you're not sure if you've got it in you? Say you have something big to do, and you feel, well, kind of empty." Magnus's words from the cave echoed in his head. *'You're an empty vessel, Ivan.'*

"Hmmm." Henrik studied Ivan for a moment. Then he took down a glass tankard from the shelf. For a big man, Henrik moved deftly in the space behind the bar. He gave the tankard a cursory wipe with a dishcloth and set it on the drainage grill under the beer taps. "You're worried you might come up empty when you're up against a big challenge."

"Yeah." Ivan let out a breath, feeling the tension in his shoulders ease a fraction.

"Y'know," said Henrik, positioning the tankard under a beer tap, "you're assuming being empty is a bad thing. Sometimes an empty vessel is just what you need." He pulled the tap lever, and golden liquid poured down. "How else are you going to get the beer in?"

Despite himself, Ivan smiled. "Cheers, mate."

"On the house," said Henrik, setting the tankard down in front of Ivan. "Now, you want some lunch to help fill that empty place inside?"

Back at their table, Ivan watched Anders. His friend was strained, picking at his food, and pushing it around his plate instead of eating it.

Ivan held a chip up to the raven, feeling the sharp tug as it speared it neatly out of his fingers.

"Are you ready?"

Anders started, then frowned. "Yeah. Maybe. We're well in it now. What if the chest doesn't have anything useful?"

"Then we'll have to go on to plan B. I'm pretty sure Benioff will back us up. Just...we need to be careful what we tell her. She's smart. And suspicious. If we do plan B, we need to tell her just enough to get her on board, but not so much she guesses what we're up to."

Anders gulped and nodded, his hair falling across his face.

"What if...we can't stop them in time from...you know."

"From bleeding me out properly this time?" Ivan regretted saying it when Anders Adam's apple jumped as he swallowed convulsively. "Look, I know this plan has risks. But it's the best one we've come up with so far, and if it works, we'll get Magnus put away for a long time. I can't have him hovering around town like a...a robed nutter with a very sharp knife. He knows where I live." *Where all of us live. And where my family will be when they get home.*

Anders nodded, but the set of his shoulders was far from happy.

The Raven let out a harsh caw, the first noise it had made all morning. Ivan started, but no one at the other tables even looked up. He reached across to finish Anders's chips.

"Hey!" Anders protested.

Ivan shrugged. "You weren't eating them." He became aware they were being watched, and not in a friendly way. He took out his sunglasses and held them up, pretending to clean them. In the reflection was a robed man, hood drawn too far forward to make out a face.

He caught Anders's eye and flicked his gaze sideways.

"Dodgy geezer in the robe? I see him. Time to go?" said Anders.

"Yes. Let's get back to the car, then lay low until evening."

They left the bar as it got even busier, fur-clad barbarians mixing with blue-skinned Scottish woad and Saxon warriors. Ivan tried to head back to where they'd left the car, but every time they turned, knots of robed and hooded men got in their way.

This happened three or four times in a row when the Raven croaked in his ear, and Ivan realised they were being herded uptown in the direction of the football club. *That's where the Valkyrie girl said the robed men had their headquarters.*

Ivan grabbed Anders's elbow. "We have to make a break for it before they hem us in."

Anders nodded, his jaw set. The ratio of robed men to Vikings was growing steadily.

Anders headed purposefully towards a knot of hooded figures, shoulders squared, as if he were about to barge them. They saw him and braced. He took two steps straight at them and then darted sideways.

At the same time, Ivan dashed in the opposite direction. It was exactly how they used to make a break on the football field, and Ivan was briefly satisfied as he and Anders ran behind the startled monks and headed full speed back the way they'd come.

A shout came up behind them, and suddenly there were robed figures everywhere, pouring out from side streets. Ivan dodged one, and sidestepped another, but they kept coming.

Someone grabbed Ivan around the waist from behind. His arms pinned, Ivan kicked desperately at the other robed man running towards him. The man staggered back, winded, and Ivan stomped down hard on the first attacker's foot. The grip around his waist vanished as the man let him go with a hoarse cry.

That only bought him a few seconds' respite as three more robed figures ran purposefully towards him.

"Here!" Anders yelled, and Ivan dove towards the sound of his voice. Back to back, they faced a growing ring of robed figures. They were surrounded.

"Shit," breathed Ivan. Adrenaline washed cold across his chest, and his sides ached from too much running and not enough air.

"Plan?" gasped Anders. "I got nothing."

Ivan tensed as the figures surrounding them gathered for a final rush. They would go down fighting and be dragged away, and then...well things would go downhill from there.

Behind them came a horn blast so loud it shook all the shop windows.

The robed figures whirled around, and Ivan seized Anders's arm. Together, they charged towards the noise, knocking down two robed men caught off guard.

Ivan staggered as a hand caught his ankle and kicked backwards into its owner's face. The grip released, and they were momentarily free, running back down the street.

"Woah!" Ivan stared in amazement.

Coming towards them on the main street, huge and majestic, was a Viking longboat. For a moment, the illusion was complete. Then Ivan saw the ship was mounted on a truck, the keel split to let the driver see out to steer.

There was a cheer from all the people on the boat as Ivan and Anders ran towards them, and someone tossed down a rope ladder for them.

There was a chorus of boos and jeers as the robed men advanced, and then a barrage of water balloons and flour bombs drove them back.

Another horn blast shook the street, and Ivan saw a man on the aft deck with a giant ram's horn connected to an even larger bass amp.

"About turn, Dave!" someone shouted down to the driver, and the boat swung ponderously around and started back down the street.

Ivan gripped the railing as the boat juddered. All along the sides of the boat hung round painted shields, and lined up along the shields were heavily armoured Vikings. Up in the rigging, the Raven perched, scanning around with a satisfied air.

"Told you I'd rescue you," said a familiar voice.

Coming towards him was the shield maiden he'd spoken with earlier, accompanied by a very tall, very broad, very well-built man. He was one of the Vikings who sported a real beard and long plaited hair.

The shieldmaiden grinned up at him, her dark eyebrows arching under her curly blonde hair.

"We thought the robies might try something sneaky. We're not officially begun yet, but we were on the lookout while taking this for a test run," she patted the gunwale of the boat. "Lucky we did," she said. "Your bird caught our attention, and then…"

"We could see what was happening from up here," rumbled the big man. "You two weren't even in proper costume yet. Not at all in the spirit of the thing. We weren't about to let them steal a march on us. Damned cultists."

"Thank you," said Ivan. He was still catching his breath and couldn't begin to think how to explain what had been going on.

"Yeah thanks, mate," said Anders.

The big man stuck out his hand. "I'm Jarl Galen. And this," he nodded towards the Valkyrie, "is Ida. She's my right hand—"

"Woman," finished Ida, smiling and sticking out her hand to Ivan.

"Ivan," said Ivan, shaking her hand and then Galen's. "Hey, you're Galen from the Vikon forum? You didn't say you were a Jarl. That's a war chief," he told Anders. "Like a Viking duke."

Galen shrugged and grinned. "It's both an honour and a penance to lead this misbegotten band of mongrels. So you're Ivan. Well met, brother. And your friend?"

"Anders." Seeing Anders and Galen shaking hands was like a glimpse into the future, where Anders met his larger, more muscled and bearded self.

Ivan watched shop signage pass by at eye height. It was a pleasant way to travel, and he relaxed, feeling safe, at least for now.

"Where are we headed now?" he asked Galen.

"Back to base," he said. "It's time to make plans. We kick off officially in four hours, so there's lots to be done. Although," he frowned, "things aren't usually quite this lawless. We're going to have to be on our toes this meet."

Ivan nodded politely. Again, he was lost for words as to how to explain the difference between normal Viking re-enactment priests and a horde of murderous robed men intent on raising evil power with blood sacrifices. So he kept his mouth shut.

"And you two," said Ida, her dimple showing again, "need to get into costume."

"Umm…" said Ivan and Anders at the same time.

Ida laughed. "Don't worry—we'll sort you out."

Behind her, Galen mouthed silently at them "Be afraid. Be very afraid."

26

The longboat swung into the town hall car park to accompanying cheers from the people gathered there. There were dozens of cars, with people unpacking, getting changed, hauling out cooler bins, sleeping bags, swords and axes.

The big Viking grunted approvingly. "We'll match them in numbers, at least."

Around them, the Vikings were disembarking from the longboat, climbing down the ladder, catching their weapons on things, and hugging people in the car park.

"What did you do to upset the robies so much?" asked Ida.

Ivan rubbed the back of his neck. "It's a local thing," he said. "Magnus, one of their main people, has it in for me for me and my friends. He's one to hang on to a grudge."

Galen frowned. "Personal feuds should not be carried over into Viking events. If anything else happens once we start, I will talk to the marshalls." He swung himself over the side of the ship onto the ladder. His armour was real and clanked as he climbed down.

Ivan thought if Galen had been with them in the street before, they could have broken through the crowd of robed men using him like an assault tank.

"You'd better stick close to us this weekend. These things can get quite...intense," said Ida.

"Right, intense." Ivan smothered a smile, thinking of the madness of the last few days, but Ida caught his expression.

She raised her eyebrows. "Oh, you think because this is re-enactment it doesn't get real?"

"No, no," said Ivan hurriedly. "This is great."

She was slightly mollified. "Is this your first Viking event?"

Ivan and Anders said "yes," and "no," in unison, and Ida's mouth quirked upwards. Ivan found he was smiling along with her.

"Well, come and check it out then," she said as she swung lightly over the gunwale. "There's just time to kit you out before the kick-off."

"We, ah, have some things we need to do," said Anders.

"Just stay till evening," said Ida. "It'll be fun, I promise."

"That'd be grand, thanks," said Ivan. "Anders, we don't have to be anywhere until nightfall."

The Raven flew to Ivan's shoulder as he reached the ground, drawing admiring glances from the people in the car park. Ida looked smug.

Inside the town hall was mayhem. The hubbub of people all talking as loudly as they could engulfed them as they entered the wooden hall. Someone had put wooden shields and spears up over the door and a huge banner that said 'Raven Elag & Vikon.'

What seemed like yards of furred cloth of various types was being cut up for last-minute costume alterations. There was leather everywhere and steel clanging as Vikings compared ceremonial weapons. Someone was brewing an enormous pot of coffee in the kitchen.

Two men and a woman in one corner were arguing over an enormous flow chart. Ivan gathered it was their way of keeping track of the plans for the weekend.

As they walked past, one of them complained, "Those damned cult priests, no sense of the historical story arc at all. There were only meant to be six of them, not a whole bloody tribe!"

"Yes," said the woman. "What about the pitched battle? How's that going to go with them all in robes?"

"I'm sure we can work with it," said the third one soothingly.

In another corner, two serious young men were cataloguing first aid kits. "Jarl Galen, we need more Steri Strips," called one as they wove their way through the assorted gear. "Remember last year when JT lost half an ear?"

Galen grinned and nodded, not breaking stride. Ida took a square of cake as they passed the refreshments table, and a moment later, so did Anders and Ivan. It was a rich chocolate coffee cake, homemade.

"Raveka is our cook and secret weapon," said Ida. "She spends the whole weekend in the kitchen, where her rule is absolute.

She cooks up marvels to strengthen us as we plan and execute victorious conquests, and we could never triumph without her."

Biting into the cake, Ivan had to agree. It was delicious. Through a mouthful of cake, Anders shot Ivan a look that said: *what are we doing?*

"This is as good a place as any to lay low until we're ready," murmured Ivan.

"Seriously?" said Anders.

"You did say you wanted to get tooled up," said Ivan. He was starting to enjoy himself.

"Right." Ida put her hands on her hips. They had arrived at their destination. "Time to get you two sorted."

"Wait, what now?" said Anders.

"Costumes," said Ida. "Don't worry—you can take them off when you go. If you don't have some sort of gear though, you'll ruin the atmosphere."

"Um, I dunno if we—"

"If you two want to stay, you have to look the part."

"Yeah, but we—" Anders seemed to have forgotten that Ida was the one who'd ordered them to stay in the first place.

"It'll be fine, Anders," said Ivan. He tried not to let Anders see how amused he was. *Who knew this was how I'd end up at Vikon after all? With Anders.* "Just go with it."

"Works for me," said Ida. "Efraim," she called to a tall, skinny red-haired man. "I have two greenies to get kitted out before kickoff time."

The red-haired man stalked over. His eyes narrowed slightly as he took in Ivan's Raven and Anders's shoulders. They widened as the Raven cocked its head and stared back at him.

"Oh, excellent," he breathed. "I like. I like very much. You," he pointed at Anders. "A classic Viking, young Danish warrior seeking to make a name for himself in battle."

"DreadlordConqueror2," murmured Anders, and Ivan growled, "Shut up," back at him.

Efraim shouted, "Judy! Fit out our young Adonis here in full warrior kit: jerkin, mail, helm, shield. And..." he hesitated, "either broadsword or a single-headed axe. Whatever fits. And don't forget the makeup!"

"Wait, what now?" Anders's attempt to back away was brought up short by a table stacked high with bits of body armour.

"This way, young man," Judy turned out to be a slightly harried woman clad entirely in flowing blue veils. Anders shot Ivan a worried look as she took his arm.

Ida was laughing silently. She patted Anders on the shoulder and whispered, "Can't wait to see the finished product. With makeup!"

Ivan gave his friend a thumbs-up and a cheery grin as he disappeared into the crowd.

Efraim fixed his attention on Ivan. "Well," he said. His long fingers made to reach out and touch the Raven, but then he changed his mind as he eyed its strong beak.

"What to do with you..." Efraim put his head to one side, chin in hand, measuring Ivan up with his eyes. Ivan felt himself being catalogued, mentally undressed, and dressed again in something quite different.

"I was thinking sorcerer or soothsayer, but we have entirely too many of those already," Efraim's expressive mouth twisted in disapproval. "And I think we can do better. I'm getting a strong vibe of…" he waved a hand. "I sense a mystery about you, a deep mystery, a hidden calling. A great power, an unknown potential. Something dark. Shadowy. From another world. Yes," he said to himself. "I like that."

He gestured at Ivan. "All in black. And I'm going to use some kohl for your eyes. Real men wore battle paint in Viking times. I'm thinking a touch of goth flavour. With all the mystery stuff I mentioned earlier." He flourished one hand. "You'll thank me later." He whirled around and started pulling things out of boxes.

Ida gave Ivan an appraising look, then left to talk to someone dressed in a leather skirt, two leather straps, and not much else.

Ten minutes later, Anders and Ivan met by the cake table. Anders grinned sheepishly. He wore a brown tunic with leather arm guards, a fur waistcoat, and twin swords crossed behind his back. Someone had tied fur shin guards over his jeans with crisscrossed leather thongs.

Ivan wasn't sure how he felt about his transformation. As promised, he was all in black. Worryingly, Efraim had started off fingering some very fluffy black furs, promising they'd 'end up looking gothic.' But in the end, he'd opted for something simpler.

Ivan had on a black tunic belted at the waist with a wide leather belt. Efraim had let him keep his dark jeans but swapped out his sneakers for leather boots that fit him perfectly.

"You can wear this jacket," Efraim had told him, handing him a black padded cotton jacket. "But I'd rather you didn't. And take this," he passed Ivan a black polished wooden staff that tapered down to a narrow end.

He'd dismissed Ivan with a wave and turned to fix the helmet on an armoured man who couldn't move without something clanking.

"What's your outfit about?" asked Anders.

Ivan shrugged. He felt strange, both more like himself and not. *I'm not sure...but it feels right.*

"Efraim said I'm a raven speaker from the far North," he said.

"What's that then?" asked Anders.

"Someone who, in the heat of battle, becomes the mouthpiece of Odin himself, god of war, knowledge, and death."

As Ivan said this, there was a shift in the room, just for a second. The fluorescent lights still hung down, shedding cheerful white light, but they seemed less radiant, and the chatter of the people retreated behind a layer of silence. The air thickened as an oppressive pressure built from outside.

Ivan swallowed, but it looked like Anders hadn't noticed anything, so he pretended he hadn't either. He scooped up a piece of cake and bit into it.

"The sword they lent me is real," said Anders, biting into his slice of cake. "It's not sharp or anything, but it's proper steel. Tell you what—this Viking thing is more savage than I thought."

"Huh," said Ivan. He felt absurdly pleased. "I said you'd make a good Viking."

"Yep. Also, Amelie said she'd meet us just after sunset. In town."

"Who's Amelie?" said Ida, popping up between them.

"My girlfriend," said Anders. He unconsciously squared his shoulders, looking proud.

"Cool, do you think she'd like to join us?"

"Err...I think she's working today."

Ida turned her attention to Ivan.

"Do you have a girlfriend who might want to come?"

"Um...no. No girlfriend."

Ida's eyes sparkled. "Good to know." She glanced over her shoulder. "I'm going to help provision the ship, but I'll see you back here at seven for announcements." She ducked away.

"She likes you," said Anders. He had a knowing smile.

"Huh?" Ivan stared at him.

"Don't give me that shy bollocks. She wanted to know if you had a girlfriend. That means she likes you, Raven Speaker boy."

"Oh," Ivan didn't have any idea what to say to that. His head was full of being hunted by Magnus, crazy visions in the mountains, wolves, ravens, policewomen, and hordes of robed men. He didn't know where to fit in Ida with her dimple and her fierce eyebrows. She didn't seem like the kind of person you fit around other things anyway. She needed her own particular space.

"You should go for it. She's well fit."

"Shut up, Anders."

Ivan was on his third piece of cake when someone began bellowing 'silence!' from the front of the hall. The shout was taken up by everyone, creating a deafening noise that gradually died away.

"Friends, clansmen," shouted the speaker. "Vikings!" Everyone cheered.

It was Galen, now clad in a steel helmet, his axe held ready in one hand.

"Welcome to the Twelfth Annual Viking Summit!" More cheers. "First, Blair here has a few housekeeping items."

A grey-haired man in a leather tunic ran through a series of information chunks ranging from the ordinary to the bizarre.

"Edith is in charge of first aid. Raise your hand, Edith," was followed by, "And I want to remind you normal combat rules apply. No head strikes, strictly shoulders to knee. And..." his gaze swept the room, "No repeat of last year's exploits. Ted and Tim are in charge of pyrotechnics that may," cheers, "or may not" groans, "occur. That goes double for any trebuchets you lot may have decided to smuggle in." Laughter. "Any questions?"

There was a babble of concerned voices.

"Ah, yes. That." Galen stepped forward to answer the questions. "Apparently, there's some mixup with the opposition fit-out. They're simply not following protocol or any of our historical guidelines." A rising hubbub of voices greeted this. Galen raised his voice.

"We shall keep up our side of things regardless. We take the high ground! It's a better place to rain down hell on your enemies," he added to general laughter.

Someone next to the speaker said something in his ear. Galen nodded and carried on.

"We know there's been some local trouble. So I want to make it clear right now, that anyone transgressing our rules, even if provoked, will be immediately expelled from this weekend." He said this over another storm of protests. "Any unofficial raids, skirmishes, or retaliatory strikes will result in immediate expulsion."

Silence greeted this final statement. "That is all I have to say on the subject." With great dignity, he turned to go, then abruptly whirled back around.

"We shall be victorious!" he bellowed. The responding roar of approval half deafened Ivan. "Forward the Raven Clan!"

Vikings all around Ivan roared, stamped and shouted, clashing weapons against their armour and shields. Ivan caught Anders's eye and grinned. His friend had just chest bumped a man who was about as round as he was tall, covered with beads, carved bones, and chain mail. Anders was starting to get into the festive mood.

Ivan jumped when the Raven jabbed him in the ear with its sharp beak.

"What?" he said, puzzled, and it bobbed its head meaningfully towards the door.

Ivan wove his way through the milling crowd and exited the hall. He looked up the road to where the football club lay, with Magnus and all his robed cult followers.

At the top of the town was the bright blue and white roof of the club. His gaze went higher, and Ivan's mouth went dry.

Far away, the mountains marched into a steep valley. High on the upper slopes, a storm was brewing. Or perhaps not just a storm. A darkness. Ivan remembered his dream of the thing in the mountain lake and shivered.

"But what can I do?" he said.

The Raven turned to him. Ivan let his mind fall still, shutting out the noise from inside the town hall. In the quiet of his mind, he heard a voice that was not his own.

It's gathering power but can't break through. Yet.

"How do I stop it?" said Ivan. "It's coming at moonrise, isn't it? Like the runes said."

In the stillness, the answer came quietly.

The fight will not be easy. There will be a price to pay, as always.

Ivan let out a small huff of breath. *More cryptic than a fortune cookie.* But if the Raven heard that, it gave no sign.

Back inside, the preparations were heating up, resembling the start of a rowdy party. Anders and Galen were squaring off, swords against axe, in what looked to be a crash course in Viking combat.

"Are you going to join us for the pitched battle tonight?" asked Ida. She'd done her sudden appearing trick and was standing alongside him.

"Maybe," said Ivan. "We...have to do something in town first."

"Your local trouble?" Ida looked sideways at him.

"Yes, that."

"Well, our scouts are out right now, keeping tabs on what the robies are doing. Once it's full dark, we'll be doing a night raid. It will," she grinned, "be epic. But whatever. You gotta do what you gotta do. That said if you need to sneak back into town without attracting attention, leave at the same time we go for our sortie. The robies will be very distracted. You'll see. Also, what's your character name?"

She had this way of changing course mid-sentence that threw Ivan completely off balance.

"Err...Ivan?"

She rolled her eyes. "Ok, Raven Boy. It's just not very...Norse."

Ivan, slightly stung, said, "It's Rus. Some Viking mercenaries went there, you know."

"'spose so. And you do have a raven, after all. That's some high-level street cred right there."

The fierce call of a ram's horn half deafened him. Someone bellowed, "The Twelfth Raven Clan Viking Fest has begun!" Everyone cheered, and the cheer turned into a chorus of fierce 'hoo's' and stamping that shook the wooden hall.

Ida grinned at him, her eyes sparkling, and Ivan found himself smiling back.

This is going to be a night to remember. He thought about the darkness gathering in the mountains. *I hope we all live to remember it.*

27

Ivan snagged a fourth slice of cake and a coffee. He shared the cake with the Raven as he and Ida sat on the hall entry steps, watching the long summer sunset begin. Streamers of cloud turned slowly pink as the sun flared.

Five Vikings came up the steps, moving in such a furtive way it immediately drew the eye.

"Who are they?" asked Ivan.

"Our scouts," said Ida. "They'll share their reports soon."

Several iron-helmeted Vikings had made a wood pyre in one corner of the car park, and now they lit it, the flames climbing merrily.

"Do they have permission for that?" said Ivan.

"Of course," said Ida airily. "Gerard does all that. He's very big on us being good guests who get invited back. He does a speech every year about it, which, fortunately, we have missed."

Ivan stowed his staff by the longboat mast and spent the next half hour helping Galen connect up LED-powered flaming torches in the rigging while Anders was co-opted into hammering together some sort of siege weapon.

A crowd gathered by the fire where a robed man was reciting the Hávamál epic poem.

Ivan checked his phone. He felt a little guilty hiding it in his costume, though he'd noticed a few other Vikings with phones taped surreptitiously to scabbards or hidden in furry pouches.

Anders climbed up onto the float with Ida.

"We have to go soon," said Ivan.

"The scouts are going to tell us what they saw," said Ida. "Come and listen."

Round the fire, a tableau had formed. The scouts were reporting, with the shortest one as the spokesperson, and the others in a huddle behind him, muttering to themselves. They did not look upbeat. Under a thin layer of bravado, they looked worried. *As if they've seen something unsettling.*

A man dressed in opulent furs was speaking.

"Report, ye scouts, to us, the Raven Elag council, what thou hast witnessed of our enemies," he said, arms held theatrically aloft.

Bad acting must be a requirement here, Ivan thought, then felt rueful. *It's still better than hanging out, drinking beer, and watching rugby.*

The lead scout shifted from foot to foot, glanced back at his fellow scouts, and cleared his throat.

"Umm...well..." he searched for inspiration in his boots and started again. "We five didst travel, with um, great stealth, into, unto the realm of the Shadow Cult."

"Why do these lot sound like they're in a Shakespeare play?" whispered Anders. Ida snickered.

"Wast thou observed in your mission?" demanded the councillor.

More looks were exchanged.

"Ummm. Maybe? Probably not, though."

"They were quite busy," put in another scout defensively.

The councillor huffed in frustration.

"We didst see the most terrible things," said the lead scout.

"It was bloody awful," muttered the other scout, just loud enough to be heard.

"Yeah, that poor goat," muttered another. "I still think we should have called Animal Rescue."

They went quiet when the councillor cleared his throat loudly and banged his staff on the ground.

"Tell us what you hath seen, leaving nothing out. I charge thee," he said, putting the last sentence in as an afterthought.

And so, with rambling interludes, interjections, and slipping in and out of thee's and thou's, the story came out.

The robed monks had set up some kind of pyre on the football field.

"The football club won't be happy about that," muttered Galen.

The monks had a goat tied up in front of the club, and one of the scouts had spotted some suspiciously sharp and shiny-looking knives on a makeshift altar.

Half the audience thought the scouts must be mistaken, and the other half approved, saying it showed real authenticity and made up for the monks' boring costumes.

None one believed the monks were actually planning to sacrifice a goat, no matter how freaked out the scouts were. *But I bet that's exactly what they have planned.*

Near sunset, all the robed men had gathered in a formation and started some sort of swaying, deep-toned chant.

This was where the story became confused. The chant seemed to have affected the scouts. They reported variously feeling 'awful,' 'dizzy,' 'creeped out,' and 'just bloody awful.'

Around the fire, Ivan saw everyone was glad the scouts were finally getting into the spirit of things. Maybe the robed cultists wouldn't be such a dead loss after all.

But Ivan could see the scouts weren't pretending. They were genuinely afraid. And they were both ashamed to admit it and wanting the other Vikings to take them seriously.

Then one of them said, "But what about the bloody great dark cloud gathering above them? What the hell was that?"

The Raven stirred on Ivan's shoulder, and the hairs rose on the back of his neck.

"What did the cloud look like?" he asked and abruptly found himself the centre of attention.

"The Raven Speaker asks," said the councillor, pleased.

Ivan could feel his cheeks redden. Expectant faces ringed the fire. *They almost do want to believe all of this*, he thought disgustedly. Right behind this thought came another one: *well, they should*. And with that came a cold warning.

Unwillingly, he stepped forward, the heat from the fire on his already hot face.

"Behold, the Raven Speaker," said the councillor pompously, bowing and stepping back.

Ivan frowned at him. *I'm not good at this—whatever it is.*

"What did the cloud look like?" he asked the head scout. The councillor smirked at his lack of proper theatrics.

"Ah, it was a bloody big black cloud...o Raven Speaker," said the lead scout after a moment's hesitation.

"Was it only over the footba— over the robed ones' headquarters? Or was it coming from elsewhere?" asked Ivan.

"It went up in a big black column, but the cloud was coming from up in the mountains. Big black stream of it, flowing down. Like special effects, if you know what I mean."

Ivan realised everyone expected him to make some sort of pronouncement. His mind was blank. 'That doesn't sound good,' just wouldn't cut it, he knew. Nonplussed, he turned to the Raven, more to play for time than anything.

The small voice in his head that wasn't his own said acerbically, 'Well, isn't this a pretty mess we're in now.'

Not helping! He thought back at it.

"Er," he said. "Well done, scouts. I have much to think on, and will do something about this, ah, very soon." He did a sort of bow and backed away.

Anders was grinning at his discomfort. "Wise words, O Raven Speaker," he said.

"Stow it, you Conan wannabe," said Ivan. "Also, this is bad. We'd better get on and shut things down before they turn truly pear-shaped."

"Alright then." Anders shouldered his shield and cast a brief look back at the hall. Ivan could tell he was thinking about the chocolate cake.

Ida appeared at Ivan's side and put a small piece of paper into his hand.

"What's this?" he asked.

"My number," she said. "In case you need rescuing again." Her eyebrows arched quizzically, and she gave him a swift hug before vanishing into the crowd again.

Ivan stood looking after her, feeling a warm glow spread across his chest.

Anders had regained his annoying grin. "She likes you," he said.

"Shut up."

28

They left the warm circle of the fire and the car park and headed down the street. When they were almost at midtown, they ducked into an alleyway, and Ivan pulled out his phone.

"This is it," said Ivan.

Anders nodded, tense.

He took out Benioff's card from his pocket and dialled the number on it. It was picked up on the second ring.

"Benioff here."

"Detective Benioff," said Ivan. "This is Ivan."

"Ivan Luca?" Her voice sounded a little crackly.

"Yes. You said to call if I had information to pass on regarding Amelie's abduction."

"That's correct. I'm at the police station. You'll have to come here to talk to me."

"I have something different in mind," said Ivan.

He could feel the tension on the other side of the line.

"You see," he said, "the information I want to give you isn't hearsay or even a sworn statement. I want to show you who I think is responsible for Amelie's abduction and maybe some of the other disappearances too."

The silence stretched. "Continue," said Benioff. She sounded perfectly calm and level, except Ivan's mind painted him a picture of her that seemed too real to discount: a slim, elegant figure looking out of place in the worn 80s decor of the local police station break room. She was watched intently by some other detectives who were also from out of town, and they had all fallen still when Benioff answered a call from an unknown number.

"That's all for now," said Ivan. "I have to…put a few things in motion. I'll call you as soon as I can tell you where to meet."

"No, this isn't—"

Ivan hung up on her mid-sentence and nodded tensely at Anders.

Anders took his phone and called Amelie.

"Everything's ready," he said. "We'll meet you at Magnus's house in five." He hung up. "Game on."

Magnus's house was swallowed by the shadow of the mound behind it.

Amelie walked around the corner, and Ivan was relieved to see the dark shape of the Wolf trotting beside her. She didn't say anything as she reached them, and Anders gave her a quick hug. Her face was pale and tense.

"Ok, we stick to the plan," said Amelie. "Anders and I go in with the key. Ivan, you stay on guard. One of us will stay outside the secret room, so you can text us if anyone comes."

Ivan waited in the shadow of the hedge, the Wolf an inky shadow at his side. He ran his fingers lightly over its fur, and it leaned against him. *The weird shadow stuff I'm not sure about, but having a Wolf by my side is pretty damn awesome.*

One minute ticked by. Two minutes.

Ivan felt both chilled and sweaty at the same time. The tension built in him till he was shifting from one foot to the other, heart pounding from nervous energy.

Frantic footsteps sounded, running towards him. Ivan drew into the shadows, then stepped out as he recognised Amelie's figure. She slowed as she reached him, then looked behind her.

"Where's Anders?" said Ivan.

She gasped for breath. "They got him."

Ivan's breath caught in his throat. *No!*

Amelie carried on. "As we left, there were two guys, and they tackled him. They're more of them in the house, and they're coming. We have to go now!"

With a harsh cry, the Raven took flight from Ivan's shoulder, circling for height.

Ivan's heart gave a lurch as seven dark figures came out of Magnus's house and spread out across the road behind them. Ivan couldn't recognise them, but he knew the silhouettes of firearms and hunting bows.

"Shit." He tried to summon shadows to hide them, but his heart was pounding like a battering ram and the calmness he needed was a million miles away.

Amelie was tugging at his arm. Ivan glanced at the men behind him. The street had lights at intervals along it and walls on both sides for at least fifty meters. *Even we run in zig-zags, we'll get hit.* With that many men firing on them, it was certain. *We're screwed.*

"We need to—" Ivan felt the warm presence of the Wolf leave his side.

The men shouted as the Wolf launched itself at them, the deep growl from its chest echoing across the street.

There was a sharp 'crack!' of a gunshot. Then another. And another.

"Ivan!" Amelie pulled on his arm so hard it wrenched him round, and then they were sprinting full tilt down the street, away from the men. Away from the Wolf.

Just as they reached the corner, Ivan looked back.

The men were gathered around a dark mound. It was wolf-sized, and it was not moving.

There was a pain in Ivan's chest that went deeper and deeper. As he watched, one of the men prodded the still shape of the Wolf, and then they all stepped back. A dark cloud of smoke rose from it, and then the shape of the Wolf simply dissolved, like ink running on wet paper.

Above him, the Raven gave a raw cry. Ivan rubbed his chest, where an ache gnawed into him. He squeezed his eyes shut against the tears that threatened to overflow. Amelie tugged on his arm.

"Ivan, we need to *go*."

Their run ended as they ducked around the corner from *Henrik's* and down the alleyway. Ivan scrubbed tears angrily from his eyes. Then he rubbed at his chest, which still ached. *Why does it hurt so damn much? How could the Wolf be dead just like that?*

Amelie was dry-eyed, but her shoulders were whip tense.

"We have to get Anders back," she said.

"How?" said Ivan. His voice sounded choked. "What happened?"

"We went in when the men were in the front of the house, but they must have heard us. Or...there was a silent alarm we didn't know about. We had just opened the chest when they arrived."

"What was in the chest?"

Her shoulders slumped. She pulled a small pouch out of her pocket and shook its contents into her hand.

"Just a bracelet," she said, and this time her voice was thick with despair. "It's no good as evidence to get Magnus locked up. Here."

She put the bracelet back in its pouch and handed it to Ivan. He could feel the weight of it in his hands as he tucked it into his chest pocket, next to his heart. As it rested there, he felt a slight *shift*, as if something vast but invisible had moved imperceptibly into place.

He drew in a deep breath, then let it shakily out.

"So," he said. "We go to plan B."

"Yes," said Amelie. "With complications. I'm sorry about your Wolf, Ivan."

Ivan looked away for a long moment.

His jaw clenched. "Let's get these bastards."

Ivan took out his phone and dialled a number.

It rang a few times, and Ivan held himself perfectly still as his mind raced through plans C and D if the call wasn't picked up. At the third ring, someone did pick up.

"Yes?" the person was trying to make their voice sound deeper and more grown-up than it was.

"Karl," said Ivan. "Where is your father?"

There was a long silence on the other side.

"He's out with his friends," said Karl. "They're at the football club doing weird shit."

"Can you get a message to him? It's very important. He has something I want, and I have something he wants." He marvelled at how calm he sounded.

Almost thirty seconds went by, the longest of Ivan's life. All he could do was wait and hope.

"I didn't know what they were planning," said Karl. "In the forest. I tried to warn you."

"Yes, I know," said Ivan. "Can you get a message to your father?"

"I'll do it," said Karl.

Ivan silently let out the breath he'd been holding. "Tell him I'll meet him at the end of Blackburn lane in fifteen minutes. I'll be alone. Tell him to bring Anders unharmed, or there's no deal."

The silence was deafening. Then Karl said, "I will do that."

As Ivan hung up, his head ached where Magnus had hit him in the forest. *This feels like a terrible plan. It's just that all our options are bad ones right now.*

"Ok," he said to Amelie. "Let's go."

Ivan stopped three steps out of the alleyway as the Raven's caw sounded above him. Something was wrong.

He looked right and left, and then sirens blared as three police cars came full bore towards him.

"Amelie! Go!" he shouted. As the cars screeched to a halt, he made for the gap between them. *Draw their attention away from Amelie.* Policemen jumped out of the cars, and a moment later a grip like iron went around his arms. He clamped down on the desperate urge to fight his way free with everything he had.

"Officers," he smiled, "How may I assist you?"

They didn't smile back. One shoved him against the side of the police car, and the other patted him down to check for weapons.

The shorter one spoke into his radio. "Yes, confirmed, we have the suspect in custody. Bringing him in now."

∽

Ivan sat in the back seat of the police car, his wrists handcuffed in front of him. On either side of him were two extremely solid officers. He schooled his face to show nothing, though on the inside, he was screaming. *There's no time for this!* Magnus would be showing up in the alleyway any moment now.

They pulled into the back of the police station and hustled Ivan up the steps. He realised this was the entrance for criminals, rather than the respectable folk who came to enquire about missing cats. The thought gave him pause.

When exactly in the last week had he crossed the invisible line that separated law-abiding citizens from criminals? He didn't remember crossing it, but here he was. *Will it feel the same if I end up wearing an orange jumpsuit inside a high-security prison?*

Ivan followed the first burly officer down a corridor, with the second officer following close behind. The naked fluorescent light reflected off the dull grey linoleum. The first officer knocked on a door and then opened it. He stood aside as Ivan entered.

There was a one-way mirrored window on the wall, a table bolted to the floor, and two chairs. On one chair sat Detective Benioff. The other chair was empty. Slowly, Ivan sat down in the second chair. One of the officers took handcuffs attached to the middle of the table and snapped one on each of Ivan's wrists. He then removed the first pair, nodded to Benioff, and left, closing the door behind him.

Benioff looked like the cat who'd eaten the cream. She gave a small, prim smile.

"I believe it's your turn to answer my questions, Ivan Luca."

Ivan tore his gaze away from her and studied the small room. Chipped paint on the walls, lino on the floors, the light too bright for such a small space. Nowhere to hide.

Except...he closed his eyes and felt his heart pumping blood. Atoms of air moved in and out of his lungs as he breathed. The same air, breathed by both him and Benioff.

He opened his eyes.

"We have the same goal, detective," he said.

He could tell by the quickly controlled widening of her eyes that this was not the response she'd expected. She searched his face for the telltale signs of uncertainty kicking in. He looked back at her steadily.

"What you need to know is that I haven't committed any of the crimes you suspect me of, and I can help you convict the person who did."

"That isn't your job," she said. "Don't play at being a detective, Luca. You'll end up cuffed to a table in an interrogation room."

Ivan drew in a slow breath and let it out. "What would you like to know?"

She opened her mouth to tell him when Ivan's phone rang. They both started.

"Expecting a call?" said Benioff.

"Yes. Please!" Ivan tried to reach for his phone, but the handcuffs around his wrists were too short. "Please let me answer it. It's important!" he said.

Benioff regarded him a moment, then swiftly got out of her chair and reached into his pocket. She put the phone on the table between them and pushed the button to accept the phone call. She put it on speakerphone and sat back quietly in her chair.

"Hello Ivan," said a voice Ivan knew all too well.

"Who's this?" he asked, wanting to get an ID for Benioff.

"You know who it is," Magnus said. "I'm waiting for you at Blackburn Alley, and I have something rather important to you."

"What do you mean?" Ivan tried to keep his voice calm while his pulse hammered wildly in his neck.

"Let me see..." the voice sounded amused. "It begins with an A and rhymes with Flanders. I think you know who I mean."

Ivan drew in a deep breath. The whole room was closing in on him, going dark in the corners. He swallowed thickly.

"If I come alone, unarmed, will you promise not to hurt him?"

There was a chuckle on the other side of the phone. "We're long past that, Ivan. And unarmed? I think you know how little that means to someone with your...abilities. But yes, I can promise I won't harm him until you arrive. But when you're here, unless you give me what I want..." there was a pause, and then Ivan heard the sloshing of liquid and harsh breathing. "If you don't give me what I want, your best friend will end up as a living bonfire. I've just doused him in petrol; one spark is all it will take. Do we have an understanding?"

"Yes," said Ivan. "We do."

There was a short pause, and then the phone clicked off.

He met Benioff's shocked gaze. She remained frozen in place as Ivan jumped up, shoving the chair backwards.

"You have to let me go! I have to get there now!"

Benioff was also standing. She pulled a comms unit out of her pocket and spoke into it. "All units, calling all units, we have a hostage situation. Repeat: all units report now to the station."

"Benioff!" shouted Ivan. "You have to let me go there now! He'll kill Anders! Please!"

She stopped at the door, and he saw the pity in her eyes. "I'm sorry, Ivan. We'll do everything we can to save your friend. Right now, this is out of your hands." She opened the door and went through it.

"No! You have to let me go! Please!" screamed Ivan. Her quick footsteps echoed down the corridor, and the door swung shut again, leaving Ivan standing alone in the merciless glare of the fluorescent lights.

29

As the door closed, Ivan bucked backwards, hauling on the cuffs. They gave not a millimetre as the metal cut into his wrists.

He slumped back down in the chair, staring at the handcuff chains disappearing into a slot in the table.

Think! He shouted at himself furiously inside his head. He needed to get to Blackburn Alley now.

He knew Magnus. Benioff and her colleagues wouldn't be able to keep Anders safe. They'd think they were bargaining with a sane man, and Anders would end up... His mind blanked out the mental image. He couldn't let that happen.

This is my fault. I should never have tried to challenge Magnus. We should have run away.

Ivan's head sank until he was staring at his chest. The weight of his utter failure pressed down on him like a continent. All he wanted to do was close his eyes and never open them again. Inside him, an emptiness stretched out for a million miles.

I could die right now, and it wouldn't matter. I'd rather be dead.

Then Ivan's gaze snagged on something. His chest pocket, where Amelie had put the bracelet they'd stolen from Magnus on their ill-fated mission. It was still nestled there, like a kernel, waiting. *Why was this so valuable that Magnus kept it locked away at all times but never wore it himself?*

Ivan closed his eyes. He thought about the lightning that had struck the cave on that first night and how it had taken him outside of himself when it hit. He remembered the feel of it, crackling with energy, more alive than anything he'd ever seen. *Sometimes, an empty vessel is what you need.*

Drawing into himself, Ivan dove into the emptiness inside him until he reached the centre. Everything went utterly silent, and he felt the pulse of the world. This time, something *was* different.

He could feel it in his chest. The weight of the small object in the pouch centred him. Ivan leaned forward over to where his cuffs were attached to the table. He had just enough room to reach up and take the small pouch out of his pocket.

Holding it awkwardly in his left hand, he shook its contents into his right hand.

As the copper bracelet with its single dull black stone hit the palm of his hand, Ivan felt like a hammer had struck him in the chest. The whole world shifted around him. In the small ugly room, shadows streamed down the walls like he was inside a waterfall. There was a sense of vast distances within him, and that *other* place that had been miles away was now within an easy arm's length.

The emptiness inside him filled with a strange power. It took him to a place apart, a place where he could push reality just a little.

He almost laughed at how simple it all was. *It's been here all along—I just didn't know how to stretch out and take it.*

This time, when the shadow realm reached for him, Ivan reached back.

The real world tilted away as the shadows grew, sliding out from the corners of the room.

He heard distant singing, or maybe it was the sound of the blood rushing through his veins. Ivan leaned *into* the shadow realm and at the same time, kept a fingernail grip on reality.

And it was *easy*. The rushing sound in his ears grew as the shadow world flowed through him like a strong river.

Now.

Ivan reached out with his will, and shadows flowed around his handcuffs. He stepped backwards, and the cuffs were no longer around his wrists. They lay on the table, discarded.

Carefully, he took the small bracelet and fastened it around his left wrist. It locked into place with a snap.

His eyes lit on the pen lying on the tabletop. What was it the library book of Norse legends had said? *All ways are connected. All you need is a door.*

Ivan picked up the biro and pushed the button on top of it. The pen nib slid into place with a click.

He walked to the grey-painted wall and crouched down. In one smooth motion, he drew a straight line up from the floor to just higher than his head. Then across, then down again. Finally, around waist height, he scribed a small circle.

It was a little wobbly, but now there was a door drawn on the wall. Ivan stepped back and closed his eyes. *All ways connect.* He reached out, and shadows flowed from him to the wall. When he opened his eyes, a black door with an ebony handle was set into the wall in front of him.

There was an ache behind his eyes, a hint that using this power was going to take a toll on him. Concentrating, Ivan fixed his mind on Anders and where he needed to be.

I can channel shadows. A world of shadows. Right now, I can do whatever I want. The shadows surged around him. *It's time to go get that fucker Magnus.*

Ivan took the door handle. It turned smoothly and opened into blackness, dark as a forest pool.

He stepped through the doorway into shadow and out again onto the cobblestones of Blackburn lane.

The smell of petrol hit Ivan as he drew breath. At the dead-end of the lane, Anders was kneeling, his hands tied behind his back and a gag stuffed in his mouth. His blonde hair was wet with petrol, and his eyes were streaming. Anders's jaw was clenched hard, and Ivan thought it was to stop him from screaming.

Magnus and six other robed men stood behind Anders. Magnus had a cigarette lighter in his hand. He was flicking it, and each time he flicked it, a little spark jumped up.

Police cars blocked off the other end of the alleyway, and Detective Benioff stood alone, facing Magnus. She must have been sent in to talk Magnus down from whatever cliff they imagined he was on. *Good luck with that, detective.*

The calm centre within Ivan wavered when he looked towards his friend. He stilled his thoughts and stepped out of the shadows into the light of the streetlamp.

Ivan ignored Benioff's gasp of surprise. He focused on Magnus, who regarded him with a hungry gleam in his eyes.

"You came," said Magnus. "I knew you wouldn't abandon your friend. So, now we will reach an understanding. You don't know how to use your powers. We have killed your wolf and taken your friend hostage. I assume you don't want him to die screaming. So you will give me what I want."

"And what do you want?" said Ivan.

"Your blood," said Magnus simply. "All of it. Spilt out here, so I can harvest your power. You stole what was rightfully mine, and I am going to take it back."

"You're going to kill me?" asked Ivan, conscious of the recording cameras they'd set up earlier and the need to buy time. Inside him, power was building again, but it wasn't enough yet.

Magnus cocked his head at Ivan curiously as if he wasn't quite sure what he was seeing. Then he flicked the lighter, and a flame sprang up. His eyes reflected the gleam of the fire and his hand dipped down, ready to throw it.

'Do you remember what you said to me in the forest?' said Ivan, trying desperately to keep Magnus's attention while his power gathered. *One wrong move, and Anders goes up in flames.*

"I said you were soft. That you had no stomach for doing what is necessary to wield power. That your attachment to others will lead you to your death." Magnus sounded pleased. "And here you are, ready to prove me right."

At the corners of Ivan's vision, reality wavered like the reflection in a pool when a rock is thrown. Shadow power filled the space he held inside him. *Just a few more moments.*

"You were right. I was soft. And weak," said Ivan. "But you were wrong about my friends bringing me down. After all, look at the fine piece of jewellery they gave me."

It's now or never. Slowly, theatrically, Ivan drew up his sleeve. The stone in the bracelet glittered orange under the halogen street lights. Ivan took a moment to treasure the shock on Magnus's face.

"Brings out my eyes, don't you think?" said Ivan.

"That's mine," said Magnus, taking a step forward. "Give it back, you little shit. You're not worthy to even touch it."

For the first time, Ivan felt anger, hot and direct.

"I've had enough, Magnus. Enough of you, your little cult, and your delusions of power. Had. Enough." He lowered his voice. "I have the power now. And I'm going to take everything back from you."

The shadows slid around Ivan, cloaking him. Anders cried out in warning, but Ivan was already moving. Not his body. His *will*.

Fire to ice. As Ivan brought his hands together, shadows cold as black ice covered everything in the alleyway. He heard the crack as they coated the robed men. The firelighter in Magnus's hands went out.

He sent a surge of will towards Anders, and his friend heaved himself up, the frozen petrol crackling as he rose.

Anders staggered forwards. His hands were still bound, so Ivan snapped the cable tie with a draft of pure darkness. Ivan grabbed Anders's arm to steady him and pulled him to one side of the alleyway into the shadows.

"Stop!" Benioff had drawn her pistol and was pointing it straight at Magnus. "Put your hands in the air, Magnus. Do it now."

Ivan saw Magnus nod to someone behind Benioff.

Back at the parked police cars, a policeman stepped forward, reaching for his holster. He pulled out his pistol and aimed at Benioff.

Shit! Karl was right about there being a cult member in the police.

Ivan threw out a wing of shadow and pushed Benioff to the side just as the shot went off. He grabbed Anders around the shoulders.

"Come on!" Frozen petrol seeped through Ivan's shirt as he dove across the alleyway, pulling Anders towards where Benioff was lying.

She gasped in pain as Ivan hauled her up, and wetness seeped through the arm of her suit jacket. He gripped Anders's arm and clasped Benioff tightly around the waist, and then everything, the alleyway, his friends, Magnus, went distant as the roaring in his ears became a flood.

A wave of shadows rushed through him, lifting them all and carrying them along. Anders gave a muffled yell as the wash of darkness swept them out of the alley and up above the rooftops.

There was a flash of stars overhead, and they were flying, the dense cloud of shadow swirling around them. There were glimpses of other things in the shadow - a pack of wolves, a flock of ravens, and a huge shape that could have been a woolly mammoth.

Ivan's fingernail hold on reality was slipping, and he didn't know what would happen if it did. It should have worried him how relaxed and peaceful he felt, like you do just before falling asleep. *And in that sleep of death what dreams may come...*

Ivan's conscious thoughts were a distant shouting, telling him to get a grip. So he struck out for the one place he was sure of.

With a rush of air, they landed on soft grass. Ivan stumbled and sank to his knees. The night dew seeped into his trousers.

They were on Ivan's back lawn, just outside his living room.

30

Ivan took the spare key from its hiding place on top of the pergola and unlocked the French doors with unsteady hands. They stepped inside Ivan's living room, and Anders sank onto the floor, shaking. Ivan dropped down next to him, one arm around his friend's shoulder. *Get up, Ivan. We can't both fall to pieces now.*

He got to his feet and hauled Anders up next to him. He sat Anders down on a chair and helped Benioff inside. Her face was white, and she was cradling one arm in the other.

Ivan ran to the kitchen and pulled out the first aid kit. It was an unusually good one due to a safety-conscious mother and numerous childhood accidents.

He opened it on the couch next to Benioff.

She eyed him sardonically. "So you know first aid? I have a bullet hole in my upper arm."

Ivan blinked at her. "Maybe I'll pour you a whiskey instead and call an ambulance."

"Not an ambulance. Call my unit and—"

"I'll take you to A&E soon," said Ivan. "We just..." he gestured helplessly at Anders, pale and reeking of petrol.

Benioff lay back on the couch. She was breathing carefully in the way people do when they're in a lot of pain.

"Whiskey," said Ivan and dashed off to pour her a glass. Then he pulled out his phone and texted Amelie their location.

"I'd like to know what the hell –" Benioff interrupted herself, then grimaced as she swallowed a slug of whiskey. "Go get your friend cleaned up, Ivan. I'll deal with you next."

Ivan wondered how she managed to give orders with a bullet hole in her arm. Supporting Anders, he walked him to the large bathroom.

Inside, he turned on the shower, waiting for it to warm. He handed his friend a hand towel and a bottle of shampoo.

"C'mon,' said Ivan and pushed him gently into the tiled shower bay. "Wash the petrol off, and I'll get you some clean clothes." His friend continued to stare into space, wide-eyed. "Anders. It's ok. You're safe now."

Ivan knew he should be as freaked out as Anders, but he wasn't. The thrum of the shadow world still buzzed through him. He felt strong, invincible. *It's like I'm drunk on shadow power. I have no idea if I'm acting weird or not.*

"Anders," he said. "You need to get cleaned up." Anders stood there for a moment, then started mechanically stripping off his wet, petrol-soaked clothes.

Wordlessly, Ivan handed his friend the shower hose and headed upstairs to get him clean clothes.

When he came down, Anders was sitting on the sofa wrapped in a towel, trying to keep his hands from shaking. Ivan passed him the folded clothes. Anders barely acknowledged them.

The detective was leaning back in her chair, and some of the tension had gone out of her face. The glass of Greg's best whiskey was nearly empty. *Better get some whiskey into Anders as well. Not me. I'm already high.*

Ivan half filled another glass tumbler and set it down by Anders.

"Do you want to talk about it?" he said finally.

Anders nodded slowly. Then shook his head. Then he changed his mind and spoke in a husky voice, low and unsteady.

"I got tackled just as we left the secret room in Magnus's house. They were just...*there.* They kicked me around a bit, then cable-tied my wrists and called Magnus. They took me to the alley, and then Magnus arrived."

Anders shivered. "He's...changed. It's like he's gone crazy. He said you'd be coming. Then he took a can of petrol and poured it all over me." Anders's voice shook, and Ivan could see he was ashamed.

He touched his friend's shoulder. "You don't have to go on."

Anders didn't appear to hear him. He was staring blankly into space.

"He kept playing with the lighter." Anders's voice sunk into a whisper. "I was so frightened I wanted to die, just to stop being so frightened."

Ivan didn't know what to say. It was as if a huge void had opened up between them. He was on one side, and Anders was on the other, and there was no way to bridge between them. On the couch, Benioff's face was perfectly unreadable.

The tense silence stretched between them. Ivan cleared his throat and turned to Benioff.

"You do know you were shot by a policeman, right?"

Benioff frowned. "I felt the bullet hit me from the back. You say it was a policeman?"

"Karl said there was a policeman in the cult," said Anders, his voice husky. "Looks like he was right."

Ivan checked his watch. "It's just a couple of hours till moonrise. Magnus is going to make his move very soon. I have to go." He stood up, then stopped because he'd said 'I' rather than 'we.'

Anders didn't correct him. His friend just looked tired.

"Going to try and stop me?" Ivan said to Benioff.

"Above my paygrade right now," she said, waving a casual hand at her injured shoulder. "I'll see what I can do about the police situation," she said finally. "Although I really should be arresting you again."

Ivan stared at her, then flicked his gaze over to Anders.

"I'll look after him," said Benioff. "I promise."

"Thanks," said Ivan.

He hated seeing Anders's slumped shoulders and the defeated lines around his friend's mouth. Ivan pulled him into a quick hug and was surprised at how strongly Anders gripped him back.

Ivan gave Anders's shoulder a last encouraging squeeze, then turned away.

"Oh, and Ivan," said Benioff. He frowned, wondering what new warning she'd come up with. "Thanks for saving my life."

"Sure." A warm rush crept into Ivan's chest. He searched for the still place in his mind where anything was possible.

For a heart-stopping moment, he couldn't find it. Deliberately, Ivan relaxed.

There it is.

The shape of it was in his mind, a doorway that could open to anywhere. Ivan took hold of the bathroom door handle and turned it. It opened on blackness, and he stepped through it into somewhere quite different.

31

The Viking headquarters still smelled of cake, leather and coffee. Ivan stepped into the kitchen and was greeted by the cook, Raveka, who smiled over her shoulder at him.

"Hey, Raven Speaker guy," she said. "Where's your handsome friend?"

"He, uh," *freaked out because a maniac tried to burn him alive and is now in police custody,* "Had to do some family stuff," said Ivan.

"Ah, well."

"Has the night raid left yet?"

She smiled cheerily. "If you scoot out that door right now, you'll be just in time to jump on the longboat. They're using it to launch their attack on the Shadow Cult."

"Right...it's ok for me to join them?" *The Vikings have no idea what they're heading into. But—it's as good an opportunity as I'm going to get. At least Magnus will be distracted by their attack.*

"It's what we all came for, right?" She waved a spatula towards the door. "Go on, get out there and raise some merry hell."

That might be a little too close to the truth. The tingling pressure built inside Ivan when he directed his attention towards the football club. Magnus was gathering power there. *If the writing we translated is correct, this is going to be bad. Major league bad.*

Ivan pushed his hair back and squared his shoulders. He wished the Wolf was here by his side. And Anders. It wasn't like he knew what he was doing. *But there's no one else. I'm going to have to fight Magnus again. And this time, I'm going to win.*

Across the hall, Galen and Ida stood in a tightly drawn circle of other Vikings. There was a buzz in the air as they made last-minute preparations. They paused as Ivan entered the hall, and a welcome cheer went up.

Galen grinned. "Good to see you, Ivan! We're about to sortie, send the Shadow Cult back into the dark ages."

The Vikings' armour glinted, and Ivan could feel the excitement in the air. The Vikings looked badass, like the warriors from olden times who lined up to fight to the death with the names of their gods on their lips.

I really should be more worried. This whole thing is mad.

Instead, Ivan felt like there was a balloon inside him, pressure filling him up. *It's shadow power waiting to be let out.*

Ivan stepped out of the town hall. The longboat loomed above them, cloaked in shadow, its rigging vanishing into the night sky. There was a rush of wind, and talons gripped his shoulder as the Raven settled there.

I'm glad you're here, he thought. He could feel its grief and fierce intent. *Let's go get those bastards.*

Ivan climbed into the longship with the rest of the Vikings. The warriors held themselves in tense readiness, quite different from the fun feeling of their outing earlier in the day. Ivan retrieved his staff from the mast foot and went to the prow. With a harsh cry, the Raven spread its wings and took flight to circle the ship.

There was a 'sput sput' from the truck below, and the longboat shuddered as the engine roared into life. A muffled cheer, and they swung out onto the road to begin their slow progress up toward the football club.

The wind pushed past Ivan as he stood in the bow, and strange shadows and shapes whirled past. *Something has begun.* Ivan could feel that other world drifting closer as the shadows beneath the boat came to life.

Ivan texted Amelie.

> Going to join the Viking attack on cult. At Football Club.

Too late, he wondered if he was doing the right thing. *Maybe it's best I keep my friends away from all this.*

Galen and Ida joined him, one looking serious, the other excited.

"What's the plan once we get there?" he asked.

Galen shrugged. "Pitched battle, most likely. Although," he hesitated. "There is something strange going on. The communication with the cult hasn't been great. In fact, it's been downright rotten. They haven't replied to any of our messages. I've warned our bunch not to get too excited. But, things may escalate."

Ida grinned, her hair swept up in a spiky braid Ivan found dangerously attractive.

Galen sighed. "It'd be bad for the next annual meet-up if things get out of hand."

They're a death cult trying to summon an ancient power from the night realm, was what Ivan did *not* say. Although, in this company, they'd probably all nod and say, 'Yeah! Nice detail on the world-building.'

Slowly, grandly, the boat travelled up the quiet main road towards the football club. Even above the truck engine and chatting Vikings, Ivan could hear a thrumming bass sound and a chanting, stamping rhythm.

As they reached the football club and swung into the car park, everyone fell momentarily quiet.

The floodlights were on, casting multiple shadows of the cultists gathered there. They were gathered in a strange pattern, doing a swaying, stamping, dance, and chanting a harsh cry with every stamp. If anything, the bright halogen glare made the black-robed men look more menacing, not less.

With a chill, Ivan recognised one word repeated again and again.

"Tursas! Tursas!"

Even from fifty paces away, he could feel the pressure building. It was dark above the floodlights, but he sensed the menace gathering there. *Very soon, the moon will rise, and the old powers will rise as well.*

A man with a braided mohawk came up to them. "Jarl Galen, your orders?"

Galen looked briefly blank, and then he roared at the assembled Vikings.

"Vikings of the Raven Elag! The time has come to do battle! To honour your ancestors and our gods! Get ready for war!"

An answering yell leapt from every throat. Ivan didn't yell but listened to the change in the tempo around him. The Vikings beat swords and axes against their shields and armour in a rhythm that quickened Ivan's heart.

Below them, Dave revved the truck engine. The Vikings roared louder. The longboat was at the border of the football club now.

"Forward!" Galen yelled, pointing at the football field. And, forgetting everything about careful agreements with the local authorities, Dave drove the truck onto the football field.

From his view up on the bow, Ivan saw Magnus, his hood thrown back, with a tight circle of men around him. The gathering power centred on him.

When Ivan closed his eyes, he saw the power Magnus was summoning stretched up into the night sky, into the storm clouds, and back to the mountains.

"Vikings! Attack!" Galen brandished his axe and pointed it down at the field. The Vikings poured down from the float with a roar, surging towards the monks. Ivan slithered down the ladder behind a guy with a shaved head and tattooed skull. He tried not to catch his staff on anything.

"Break up the circle!" he shouted to Galen up ahead. How Galen was going to hear him above the shouts, chants and truck engine, he had no idea, except Ivan *wanted* him to hear. It was almost like his wishes took a physical form. *That kind of power* should *worry me.*

Galen led the Vikings in a V-shaped formation towards Magnus, the Vikings all shouting and brandishing various weapons.

"Tursas! Tursas!" The robed monks advanced to block their path, still chanting and stamping.

The pressure built like a toothache in Ivan's head. A white glow brightened the black outlines of the mountains. The moon was rising. *If we don't break this up soon, they're going to succeed.*

The shadows were building up in him again. When he pushed against the power centring around Magnus, Ivan could feel the other man's iron will pushing right back at him, like a solid bar. He clenched his fists on the smooth wood of his staff and gritted his teeth, setting his will against Magnus's.

Seeing the Vikings charging toward them in a fierce mob, the monks didn't scatter as Ivan had hoped they would. A tall monk at the centre of their line shouted something, and the monks in the forefront of the group swept aside their robes, revealing chain mail. Each monk had a sword at his side.

"Draw!" A metallic sound, unmistakable for anything else, echoed up and down the line as the monks drew their swords.

"Shields!" Galen roared, and the Vikings brought up their shields. With a huge shout and a crash of timber on steel, the Vikings rammed against the monks, shields held up like battering rams.

The monks staggered back, and then the two lines dissolved into chaos, monks and Vikings all trying to smash each other with sword, shield and axe.

A robed monk careened towards him, and Ivan whipped his staff out, hitting him on the forearm. The man staggered back, and a Viking to Ivan's left cracked the man on the side of his head with his shield, and he went down. *I guess the usual combat conventions got left behind at the town hall.* Ivan pushed forward, the Vikings on either side crowding with him.

The pressure of gathered power was a lancing pain through his head now, and a purple glow lit one side of his vision, like the start of a migraine.

Ivan pushed harder. There was a low and guttural shout from the monks, and a warning cry, high above, from the Raven. *They're almost there.*

On one side, Galen caught a monk with a blow to the chest with his axe. Blood was running down the side of Galen's face, but he didn't seem to notice. The monks had bunched together now, the sheer mass of them enough to halt the Vikings' charge. *We're going to be too late.*

A siren sounded, and from the other side of the park, a fire engine drove into sight, lights flashing. Anders was hanging off the side with Amelie and Karl, but Ivan couldn't see who was driving it.

The truck stopped with a squeal of tires and Amelie was already running with the hose to plug it into the fire hydrant. Karl and Anders dashed towards the monks with the fire hose nozzle. Anders stopped and squared himself before shouting back to Amelie.

"Now!"

A thick jet of water arrowed out of the hose, flinging aside the monks running to attack them.

It was beautiful. Ivan found himself whooping in delight as Anders mowed down another row of monks.

"Anders," he yelled. "Get Magnus!" He pointed towards where his enemy stood. Anders started pushing forward with Karl, sweeping the robed men away with the high-pressure jet.

"Forward!" bellowed Galen, and the Vikings around Ivan surged forward, driving the monks back across the pitch.

It was close, so close. Ivan could feel Magnus's grip on the gathered power slipping as his monks scattered in confusion.

From one side, Vikings drove forward in a scrum, shoving the monks aside. On the other side, his friends were gleefully mowing down the monks with the firehose, and...was that Benioff behind them? Exiting the fire truck with her arm in a sling?

It was glorious chaos, and Ivan yelled along with the Vikings in savage triumph.

But above them, something was sliding together, like a connection coming into place. Something was so, so close to finally lining up.

"Anders!" yelled Ivan. He barrelled forwards, hitting a monk in the midriff with his staff and shoulder barging another. Now he was only twenty feet from Magnus. "Hurry!"

Anders scrambled forward with the hose, Karl hauling it with him, Amelie frantically reeling it out from the fire truck.

But they were too late.

With a triumphant howl, Magnus thrust his arms up high, and a jet of green fire shot down from the whirling blackness above.

There was a moment of echoing silence, cancelling out all sound. A feeling of suffocating pressure. Then a shake of the ground sent everyone to their knees except Magnus.

He was transfixed, arms raised, pinioned by green lightning. Circling above them, the Raven gave out a warning cry. As he lowered his gaze to meet Ivan's, Ivan saw the triumph in Magnus's eyes.

An ice-cold wave of fear swept through him. *This was a trap, and I walked right into it. Shit.*

Magnus swung his arm out in a wide gesture.

Green fire curled out from Magnus's hand and whipped towards Ivan. He ducked and tried to back away, but the arm of fire swirled back around and struck him in the chest.

An instant later, it curled around him in a crushing grip. Ivan bucked, trying to free himself, but it held him tight.

Ivan heard someone screaming, then realised it was him. Deep inside him, something was burning and pulling loose. *My power. Magnus is sucking the shadow power out of me.*

It felt like a thornbush being dragged out through his mouth. He screamed again.

A dark mist started to pull out of Ivan's mouth and tendril back towards Magnus. He knew without a doubt that by the time it reached Magnus, he would be dead.

There has to be something I can do! Ivan thrashed around, looking for a way out, but all he could do was spasm in terrible pain as another branch of shadow ripped loose from inside him.

This is really it. The end.

"Father! No!" Out of the corner of his eye, Ivan saw Karl run towards his dad. Behind him, Benioff had drawn her gun and was pointing it at Magnus.

Ivan croaked, "No," but it came out in a harsh whisper. Benioff's eyes narrowed as she trained her gun on Magnus, but Karl was squarely in her line of fire.

Ivan screamed again as the pain lanced into his midriff, and then without warning, the crushing pressure eased. Ivan drew a deep breath and raised his head.

Magnus had let him go. He was backing away from the vortex above him, raising his arms to ward something off. The green fire that had encircled Ivan whipped back to its owner.

Ivan fell forward on his hands and knees, breath rasping in his throat. The shadows whooshed back into his mouth and soothed the deep pain of the raw places within him where they'd been pulled loose. A flood of cool darkness flowed through him, and he drew a shuddering breath in relief. *Not quite the end, then. What stopped Magnus from killing me this time?*

Ivan looked above Magnus and saw the answer. Something was forcing its way through the portal.

Magnus was chanting, his voice strained and desperate. The monks who hadn't been blasted off their feet by Anders had gathered behind him, joining him in the chant.

The fire hose hung loose in Anders's hands, the flow shut off as his friends stared wide-eyed at the blackness above Magnus.

The thing trying to force its way through was vast, the size of a truck. Its shape was indistinct, but Ivan's imagination supplied detail to the coiling mass of limbs.

The monster from the cave in the mountains. Eternal Tursas or whatever. That's what's been helping Magnus. Only now, it's busting through. Going to cut out the middleman, so to speak. Eat the middleman.

"Help me, Ivan!" shouted Magnus. His face strained as he tried to stop the creature from pushing through the vortex. "We can't let it enter this world!"

Slowly and painfully, Ivan got to his feet. He still felt fractured, like a glass bottle had smashed inside him. But he remembered the Wolf, fighting to save his life, and the crackling blue lightning, more alive than anything he'd ever seen. *Sometimes, you just have to keep fighting. Even when you don't think you can win. Especially then.*

Magnus was reversing the pull of his spell, trying to close the portal, and Ivan put the weight of his own power behind him. It was like trying to shut a door against a gale.

The malignance from the creature above sucked on the edges of his senses like a dark oil slick. He, Magnus, and the monks pushed and heaved, and inch by inch, the whirling vortex above them closed.

There was a moment when all the resistance vanished. Magnus's power stumbled forward, off-balance.

"Brace!" shouted Ivan. "It's not over!"

But it was too late. With a surge of whipcrack force, the thing blew the vortex wide open. There was a silent explosion as the portal burst, and a blast of wind knocked Ivan onto his back. The same explosion threw Magnus across the field to strike the side of Dave's truck with a hollow clang.

Ivan had no hope of shutting the portal now. There was something powerful holding it open, something with a will of iron. Its power gave Ivan a horrid feeling, like running barefoot along dry wood and getting splinters stuck in your skin.

Ivan got to his feet, stumbling away from the portal. Black mist billowed down, clouding the area. Through the fog, something moved with a dim glimmer, something dark and shiny.

Ivan reached out with his new awareness, and nausea churned his guts as he encountered something so strong his ears popped with the crushing pressure. He put both hands on his stomach, feeling acid in the back of his throat.

Stepping back, Ivan nearly tripped over a monk lying at his feet. The monk had his hands over his ears, making a high, thin sound as he jerked back and forth, trying to block out the sensation of the creature's power. Black liquid oozed out of the monk's ears, running over his fingers.

Ivan tried to pull the monk out of range, but his own hands were weak and numb, and he gave up, retreating twenty paces till the pressure died down enough for him to breathe.

"Back to the boat!" Ivan's voice sounded hoarse in his ears. "Everyone back to the boat! Now!"

The Vikings around him had frozen in numb horror, but now they started to back away, then run to the truck and longboat.

"Anders!" yelled Ivan. "Over here!"

Anders grabbed Amelie's arm, and he and Karl helped Benioff get across the field to the boat. Behind them, water shot skyward from the burst water mains.

The monk Ivan had stumbled over was trying to crawl away from the portal now, in slow, jerking movements. But something black was slowly inching up his feet, moving with a swallowing motion. The monk cried out, trying to haul himself away, and feeling sick, Ivan turned back to help him. It was too late. Fingers clawing the grass, the monk was pulled back into the darkness and disappeared.

Shit.

Ivan ran over to the side of Dave's truck. *We better get out of here, quick.*

Magnus was lying half on his back, crumpled. There was a big dent in the side of Dave's truck where he'd hit.

Ivan grabbed the front of Magnus's shirt and hauled him into a sitting position.

"Wake up, you bastard," he said. "You don't get to summon a monster from the abyss and then just go to sleep." He shook him hard.

Very slowly, Magnus's eyes drifted open. "I'm sorry, Ivan." His voice was a hoarse whisper. "I thought I was using the monster, but it was using me. You have to stop it now. Send it back. For all our sakes."

"How?"

"You'll figure it out." Magnus's breath rasped, but even with his face drawn tight with pain, his gaze was darkly amused. "You've done pretty well so far, right?"

His eyes drifted shut.

"For fuck's sake!" Ivan's grip tightened on Magnus's shirt. "Wake up! You have to tell me how!"

A heavy hand landed on Ivan's shoulder. He looked up to see Galen with his hair wild, blood dripping into his beard.

"Lad," he said. "He can't hear you."

Magnus's eyes were closed, but his pulse still beat weakly when Ivan put two fingers on the man's neck.

He let go of Magnus and rocked back on his heels. *Now I feel truly empty.* He glanced around the chaos of the football field.

"Galen. Help me get him onto the boat?"

Galen nodded. Behind them, black smoke cascaded down from the portal, swallowing the monks who hadn't yet run away.

"Best hurry, lad."

They heaved Magnus up and staggered to the ladder. Getting him onto the float reminded Ivan eerily of that time three, or was it four nights ago, when he and Anders had carried Amelie out of the cave. *Rescuing Magnus. Not how I imagined this night going.*

Back on deck, Ivan rushed to the side of the boat to see if the monster was coming for them. The black cloud was building, and Ivan could feel a surging, questing menace within it. *It's looking for something. Magnus? Me?*

"The football club committee is going to kill us." Galen slumped on the gunwale beside Ivan, his face covered in sweat. "If that thing doesn't kill us first. What the hell is going on?"

"Bad stuff," said Ivan. "Really bad."

"No shit," said Galen. "What are we going to do?"

Up in the boat's rigging, the Raven took flight, winging its way down towards the port. *When the battle has changed, change your ground.*

Ivan closed his eyes. *I need a vessel. Something to ride the river of night on. Something to fight from.*

He searched for that secret still space where he could give reality a shove and make things how he wanted them to be. Inside him, Ivan found that place and *pushed.*

32

ake it so.

Black fog spread out to fill the football field. It rose to lap around the hull of the boat like a midnight sea. *Just like the runes said. Shadows cover the earth. Or was it swallow the earth...* Ivan licked his lips and tried to calm his breathing.

The black tide rose higher until it seemed it would soon overrun the boat. But it didn't. Instead, the boat rose, floating on the fog.

"Oars!" commanded Ivan, and now there were oars and oar benches lined up along the gunwales of the ship. The cheap painted plywood of the float had vanished, and they were on a true Viking longboat, oak riveted with iron, and a high prow with a raven carved on the head of it.

"My truck!" cried Dave. "What's happened to my truck!" He hung over the side of the boat, peering down into the fog, trying to see if his truck was still underneath. Ivan was pretty sure it wasn't. *Maybe I can turn it all back? If we survive...* He didn't think either event was likely.

"We need to get out of here," said Ivan. "We'll sort out your truck later."

"You lot," Galen pointed at a random group of Vikings. "Get on those benches and row."

"But my truck!"

"Shut up, Dave," yelled Galen. "Shit just got real!"

"For real real," said Ida.

"All of you, start rowing now!" said Galen. "It's time to prove you're worthy of the Raven Elag."

Eyes wide, a dozen Vikings hurried to pull on the oars. The boat started to swing away from the football club. *At least they know how to row. Maybe they all went to a Viking longboat camp.*

They floated up on the rising sea of inky blackness over the car park and out onto the road, sliding between the football club and the next-door church. The menace of the creature faded as they left the portal behind them.

Anders, Karl, Amelie and Benioff had come up behind him. They were all off-kilter in different ways. Anders was grinning maniacally, a sword gripped in each hand. Benioff was tight-lipped, maybe from disapproval and probably from the pain of her wounded shoulder. Amelie's eyes were a little wild, but her face was focused. Karl...Karl was more unreadable than usual. *Well.*

Ivan stuck his hands in his pockets (he was glad he had pockets) and leaned against the boat's gunwale. The Raven's feathers touched his cheek as it landed on his shoulder.

I have no idea what we're going to do next. I should stop posing, at least. And I should be far more worried about the monster behind us...But we're on a real Viking boat! Floating down the main street! And it's because I wanted it to be so. A grin turned up the corners of his mouth.

"Welcome back," he said to Anders.

Anders flipped him off, and Amelie rolled her eyes. *My friends have no proper sense of occasion*, thought Ivan. But his smile stretched wider.

Benioff's mouth tightened as she took in the scene.

"How is this?" her voice trailed off, and she twirled a finger, indicating the general area of the floating longship, the sea of shadow, and the nexus of darkness behind them.

"It's magic," said Anders blithely.

She narrowed her eyes at him.

"Whose magic?" she asked.

"Ah, just general magic," said Anders unconvincingly.

"Ivan," said Amelie. The euphoria of their escape was fading, and she was starting to look tense again. "What the hell happened?"

Ivan nodded. "We were very close to stopping it, but...the thing that was helping Magnus got through. Something ancient and evil. It's here."

"What does it want?" asked Amelie.

A very sensible question. Ivan had no idea. He inclined his head towards the raven perched on his shoulder. It ruffled its feathers. Gradually, Ivan became still and *listened*.

It wants what all ancient, powerful, pre-human things want. It was like hearing thoughts inside his head, except they weren't his. They felt...raven-ish. Ivan hoped he wasn't going mad.

It wants to rule again, to feed on the strong, prey on the weak, and gather power to itself. It desires your death too, of course. And if we don't close that portal soon, it will cause a Shadowstorm.

A Shadowstorm?

The Shadow World will merge with this one. It will flood this world with darkness. You really don't want that.

"Ah," said Ivan aloud. Everyone looked at him. It had grown eerily quiet on the boat as they rowed down the main street, passing shops and power lines.

"It wants," he said, "to kill things. It's...not good. Also, if we don't stop it and close the portal soon, it'll destroy the world."

Anders cleared his throat. "So, not a friendly monster."

Ivan shook his head. "It's going to come after us. So we have to choose our ground."

Benioff raised an eyebrow. "Which ground?"

"The island," said Ivan.

"Of course," groaned Anders. "Coming full circle, and all that. Also, Ivan, how come you're all Mr Magic Pants now?" he gestured at the boat floating through town. "This would've been real helpful earlier."

"It was that amulet," said Ivan. "The one you stole from Magnus's chest. It's like a focus or something. Makes it easy to do stuff."

"No wonder Magnus was pissed when you got all the juju," said Anders. One corner of his mouth tilted up in a smile. "This is cool, bro."

Ivan grinned.

"You're all forgetting one small detail," said Amelie. "Monster? Portal flooding darkness? End of the world?"

"Haven't forgotten," said Ivan. He headed to the stern, where Galen stood steering the boat, and Ida kept watch behind them.

"Jarl Galen, we're headed towards the sea. There's an island out there, about a mile offshore. It's a place of power and our best chance if we're going to face the monster."

Galen tightened his hand on the stout oak rudder.

"Ivan."

"Yes?"

"You do have some idea of what you're doing, right?"

"You mean as in I've done something like this before?"

Galen shrugged helplessly. "I find that hard to picture."

Ivan blew out a breath. "No. I haven't done anything like this before. But, and I don't know if this helps, we have to do this. Because otherwise, everyone is probably going to die."

"End of the world stuff?" asked Galen, squaring his shoulders.

"You betcha."

"And to think I thought I'd signed up for one of the more relaxing Viking weekends," said Ida. "One with minimal dramas and a bit of downtime." She didn't sound upset, though.

There was a murmuring from the Vikings as their ship headed for the docks. It rose to a crescendo, then dropped down.

One voice could still be heard above the others.

"I was thinking maybe I could just hop off now?" said a man in a shaggy brown tunic. "I get low blood sugar if I don't eat regularly."

Behind him, Ivan heard Ida mutter, "Shut up, Stanley, you utter git."

Galen pulled himself up to his full height and addressed the knot of worried faces. "If any of you wants out, no one's stopping you," he said. "You can all see the ladder there; that's your exit. If you want to abandon the fight, your honour, and your clan, then go right ahead. You should know, though, that this is the Raven Clan's chance to save the world. This is what we've trained for. This is when we find out what we're made of."

There was a chorus of muttering from the Vikings.

"Alright, alright," said Stanley. "If it's to save the world and all. But—did anyone bring some snacks they could share to keep my blood sugar up?"

Galen harrumphed into his beard and set the tiller, taking the last corner before the docks.

Ivan closed his eyes. He sent his senses out into the night, further than he would have believed possible. Beneath the boat, the black mist swirled, both ephemeral and solid enough to float a ship on. It had covered the town and was starting to spread out across the sea.

Good. Without the mist, taking the ship across to the island would be much harder. Ivan sensed the black mist wasn't from the monstrous creature. It was something else, a wild thing, let into the world when the old powers were awakened, and the portal opened. He wondered briefly if the creature from the mountains even planned for it to be released when it forced its way through into their world.

Somewhere down in the darkness, he knew the monster was there, seeking living things to devour as it woke up and grew stronger. *Soon, it will be seeking you—a bright spark of power amongst the frail mortals.*

They left the last lights of the town and rowed out over the docks. Ahead, the dark mist was spilling across the ocean towards the squat shadow of the island. The moon hid behind a cloud, and only the bright stars relieved the inky black of the sky.

Someone nudged him, and Ivan opened his eyes.

"What are we doing at this island?" asked Benioff.

Ivan sighed inwardly. *Of course, she wants to know we have a plan. Which we don't, really.*

"I think it would be a good place to face...that thing," he said. "It's where this all began. Unless, of course, you have something in your standard policing manual that could help?"

He knew he was being snarky, but he didn't have the bandwidth to argue with Benioff right now. *Also, I'm still sore about being locked up while bad guys poured petrol on my best friend.*

When Benioff didn't reply, Ivan relented. "I'm sorry, this is all a bit...crazy. Thanks for helping us with the fire engine, by the way. How did Anders get you to come?"

"It was Amelie," said Benioff. She sounded tired. "She was peculiarly convincing. Said there was a riot that needed breaking up and that she knew you'd be there. I was alone in the police station by then, after getting my shoulder patched up. Everyone else was out searching for you and Magnus."

"Huh," said Ivan. He rubbed his jaw. "You still want to arrest me?"

"Maybe," said Benioff. "Though I'm less and less sure what to charge you with. How is this all working? Anders seems to think you have some sort of...thing going on. With the wolf and the crow and all that."

"Raven," corrected Ivan automatically, "and the Wolf's gone. Magnus's men killed it." It hurt saying that. He leaned against the gunwale to stare out over the black sea. "And the thing I have going on is...I don't know. It's new to me. We just need to stop the monster that Magnus summoned. And close the portal." He realised he was rambling, talking out of anxiousness rather than thought.

"You have a monster gun on this boat?"

"Not as such...do you?"

Benioff said, "Hmmmm," and awkwardly stretched her injured shoulder.

"I'll take that as a no, then." Ivan squinted back into the darkness, searching for the monster. "Detective?"

"Yes?"

"Who was the girl?"

"Which girl?"

"The one with the red coat. In the library."

Benioff narrowed her eyes at him. "You saw her. In the library."

"Yes."

Benioff looked at him with narrowed eyes, then slowly relaxed. Now she just looked sad. "She was my neighbour's kid. She disappeared wearing that coat when I was about your age. No one ever found out what happened to her. That's when I decided to become a police officer."

"I'm sorry," said Ivan. "I...I don't know anything about her. I just...saw her. I thought she was really there."

Benioff's jaw clenched briefly, and then she gave him a nod. "It's okay, Ivan. I can see you're one of the good guys. You're just weird as shit. But not a criminal. That is," she revised, looking around the boat, "I don't think anyone's specifically written rules against flying Viking boats, so you're not breaking any laws right now."

"I'll take that as a vote of confidence."

"I wouldn't go that far."

Ivan decided to let that one pass. Benioff left to talk to Galen, and Ivan's phone gave a quiet 'ping.'

> Darling, we've just got back from a day exploring the Vatican. The Sistine Chapel was magnificent! Been thinking of you quite a bit lately. Is everything alright?

Ivan looked around the black shape of the longboat. The Vikings' weapons shone blue in the starlight as they tracked across the dark ocean.

> That's great mum! Yes, everything's fine here. I've met some new friends.

> Darling, that's wonderful! Looking forward to seeing you soon XXX

Ivan grimaced and put his phone back in his pocket. *Here's hoping this works out, then.*

The boat glided out towards the island, and Ivan willed it to go faster. Behind them, the smog swirled and corkscrewed in their wake. Somewhere in the darkness, the monster was gaining on them, a single point of hunger and malevolence.

We'll need more than medieval weapons to win this fight. Even with berserker Vikings on our side. Ivan rather hoped none of this lot was berserkers.

Up ahead, the island seemed to loom taller than it had in the past. Ivan remembered the cave, how the rain, the sky, the forked tree, and the lightning all seemed so alive. *I've learned a bit since then. Maybe this place can help me?*

The boat slowed as they approached the shoreline. Black mist lapped up high on the island, close to the lighting-struck tree. Ivan could feel the power gathered there, like a reservoir waiting to be tapped. *This is the birthplace of my power, where it was first awakened. Surely, this is my place.*

Ivan reached out and the island shivered like a wild creature, both ready to flee and wanting to be tamed. Slowly, he touched the centre of it, and the island's power eased, then surged, coming to life within him. *It knows me!*

Ivan's senses expanded, flooding out in all directions. *And not a moment too soon...* Behind them was a ripple in the black fog. The monster was coming straight towards them — fast.

Galen had seen it too. "About turn to starboard!" he shouted, and the oarsmen on one side heaved to swing the boat around. "Ready your weapons!"

Vikings drew swords and axes with a sinister scrape of metal on leather. Half a dozen archers, Ida among them, positioned themselves at the bow.

Ivan nodded to Galen. The big man nodded back. His face was grim, but his eyes glinted. *I hope he's not about to go berserk.*

"Forward!" roared Galen. "Row for your lives! And victory!"

A savage cheer greeted this, and the boat shot forward, straight toward the V-shaped ripple making a beeline for them. Out of the corner of his eye, Ivan saw Benioff give a slow exhale and flex her shoulders forward, then backward. She flicked the safety off her pistol.

Ivan had a moment to think: *maybe we should be dodging and weaving,* and then the monster was upon them.

It surged out of the black mist, a storm of tentacles writhing around an open maw of needle-sharp teeth. The Vikings roared, half in anger, half in terror, and a hail of arrows struck the beast.

Tentacles shot towards the boat, grasping at men and women. Ivan saw it take one Viking around the shoulders. The Viking screamed, and Anders hacked at the tentacle as it tried to heave the man off the boat. Anders's sword narrowly missed hitting the trapped Viking in the head, but the creature let go, and Anders hauled him to safety.

Benioff braced herself on the gunwale, firing into the curling mass of tentacles, trying to hit the monster in the eyes. Karl was knocked clean off his feet by a flailing limb and nearly went overboard. Ivan started forward, but Amelie was already there, dragging him back from the railing.

Then the monster vanished.

It was suddenly, eerily silent. The Vikings panted puffs of steam into the air, and their surge of battle frenzy halted. A dark liquid was splashed on the deck, and for a moment, Ivan couldn't figure out what it was. One Viking was lying on the deck, his leg twisted at an awkward angle, and another lay unconscious by a shattered shield.

At this rate, I don't know how long we'll last.

There was a muffled groan from the man with the twisted leg.

"We can't fight something that big," said Dave. His axe was embedded in the deck next to a stray bit of tentacle, and he tugged at it, trying unsuccessfully to pull it out. "We're all going to die out here."

Galen dashed sweat from his eyes and rolled his shoulders. He straightened with a grimace and raised his voice so all the Vikings could hear.

"No one signs up for something like this, Dave," he said. "This is a once-in-a-lifetime deal. It's up to us. All this time, we've been fighting mock battles, practising being brave. And now, for the first time, it really counts. You want to run away? Let evil into our world without a fight?"

"Oh, come on, Galen," Dave muttered. "You don't have to be so...fine. Let's do this." He held his finally freed axe over his head. "Raven Clan Victorious!"

There was a ragged cheer.

"Good," said Galen. "Rowers, about turn, and everyone look sharp."

"That was as good as Aragorn before the last battle," said Amelie approvingly. "How's my Viking warrior going, my love?"

Anders grinned and hefted his swords.

"Bring it," he said.

With a whisper, the Raven landed on Ivan's shoulder, brushing against his ear. *The next attack will come from below. The beast will try to crush the longship in two. Then it can easily pluck you out of the water and feed.*

The boat swung around. Ivan ran up to the bow and peered into the dark swirls of smoke.

The mist doesn't belong to the creature. He remembered the picture in Magnus's house of the two worlds and the figure joining them. *The mist has to be part of the shadow world. It came through the gate between worlds. It's neutral or maybe even an ally —if treated with respect.*

Up ahead, Ivan saw a swirl of mist. *There.* The monster was waiting for them to pass over it, and then it would strike.

"To the right!" he called back to Galen. "Now!"

"Pull right!" roared Galen.

The boat swung right, and the monster erupted on their left side. It gave a curious screeching cry and flung tentacles over the bow of the boat. The boat rocked alarmingly, and Ivan had a vision of it tipping over, men and women spilling into the cold ocean.

Anders swung his swords and chopped at a black tentacle, and the other Vikings followed his example. The creature shied back, but as it did, it pulled at the boat again. The whole boat skidded sideways, and the deck angled steeply. Ivan caught the gunwale with one hand to stop himself from sliding off the boat.

The boat tilted back upright, creating a huge wave of black mist as the monster let go. *One more like that, and we'll be over.*

The creature disappeared into the darkness below them. There was silence, except for harsh breathing. The Vikings were afraid. Ivan could see it in their eyes, in their ragged breaths. *They know they can't win this fight. The monster is playing with us. We've hardly touched it, and it has all night.*

"Forward!" yelled Galen. "To the island!"

Men and women leapt to obey. Ivan understood - the island meant safety.

Except...

Ivan cocked his head, listening to something off in the distance. *The black tide we're riding on. It's alive, and it can feel my presence.* An idea of what to do next formed in Ivan's mind. He could feel the shape of it, having seen its twin half an hour ago on the football field.

I stand at the bridge between worlds. And I can make a passage. Ivan blew out a breath from his suddenly tight chest. *It's now or never, dammit. Time to go loud or go home.* From somewhere deep within him came a small, quiet voice. *You can do this.*

Before he could think twice about it, Ivan climbed onto the longboat railing. On the bow, the Raven blinked at him with its black eyes. Ivan took a deep breath, steadied himself, and stepped down onto the dark mist.

The first step sunk him knee-deep in blackness. Ivan concentrated and slowly rose till he floated on the mist, just his feet sinking into the inky blackness.

It was a mental effort to do so, like holding a song in your head when some other music is playing. Ivan took three steps away from the boat, then three more, before anyone noticed him.

"Ivan!" shouted Anders. "Where are you going?"

Not 'what the hell are you doing' or 'how are you doing that?'

He half-turned. "I don't think you can follow me. Please don't try." He walked away from the longboat into the darkness.

The mist was rising around him now, inky clouds billowing higher than his head. Ivan reached out with his mind, and a tunnel started to form in front of him.

Ivan held the two places in his mind: here and now, the ocean, the island, the boat, the monster below...and the other place. The other place was further away than he could ever imagine, and at the same time, it lived behind every breath, between each moment. *The thickness of a shadow away.*

He searched for the portal back in the town where the mist was still pouring in and concentrated on closing it, like a faucet, and opening it here, where he was.

The fog swirled around him, and a tunnel began to appear ahead, a shifting circle with the core bending darker and darker.

Ivan's heart thudded as he focused, giving the tunnel weight and solidity. He stepped forward, and now he felt the pull of it, the same way you can feel the pull of water draining down a plughole.

Gently now. Timing is everything.

The longboat was moving away from him, towards the island, the rowers straining against the pull of the vortex he'd created. But Ivan knew the monster would follow him, sensing his power.

There, below in the black mist. A swirl. The monster was nearly underneath him.

Two tentacles shot up, one almost catching his ankle. Ivan stumbled and dodged down into the tunnel. The monster heaved itself up out of the mist and entered the tunnel. Ivan glanced back and all he saw were glistening tentacles and dark rolling flesh as it slithered towards him.

He ran, and as he did, the pull of the vortex bore down on him. The pressure squeezed his chest, and he knew soon it would become unbearable.

Behind him, the monster seemed to realise the trap. It tried to stop itself, tried to brace against the tunnel walls and crawl back into the world it had left, but it was too late.

The vortex had them both in its grip now, and they were sliding into it, the monster coming towards Ivan in a horrible black slithery mess. Ivan let go, and the vortex sucked him into infinity.

33

Ivan was falling past stars, solar systems, galaxies. Reality thinned in swirling layers as he passed between the worlds.

And then he landed, not onto the black mist, but sand. Level ground stretched away as far as he could see. Black sand drifted beneath a sky as dark and starless as the ocean depths.

Ivan stumbled away as the monster exited the tunnel. His staff dropped from numb fingers. Feeling like a man letting go of the last thing that kept him from falling into an abyss, he released the connection to his home, the island, the Vikings. His world.

The portal closed, and as it did, the black tunnel of mist vanished.

The monster screamed, its tentacles flailing, and advanced murderously towards him.

It was only then that Ivan discovered that all the power, all the strange ability he possessed in his world, was gone. It had shut off like a light as he crossed over into this starless place.

Ivan's heart sank, and cold fear flooded his veins. *There's no way to win this fight and no way home.*

The monster Tursas heaved towards him, a nightmare of black sucking tentacles and shiny dark teeth.

Ivan turned and ran.

In the depths of the strange night country, Ivan despaired. He'd been running for what seemed an age. His side started to cramp, and his breath burned in his chest. *How the hell does a slithery tentacle monster move so fast?*

It was out of its element, the black sand clinging to its slimy black flesh as it groped towards him. But it was relentless.

I'm going to have to do something before it eats me. Sick dread filled him. *I got nothing.*

He risked a look over his shoulder. The monster was not exactly gaining on him. Not yet. But he had the feeling it would keep going forever while he could not.

I am NOT going to get eaten by a slimy tentacle monster, Ivan told himself, and stumbled up a dune. *Come on, think!* He yelled inside his head. *What can I use? I made a portal here, why not make one back?*

In his mind, Ivan reached out for shadow power, for a portal. It was *almost* there but still out of reach. *I had better find it quickly. Before...well. Bad things happen.*

The monster was at the bottom of the rise. Two huge eyes stared out from among its tentacles. They were a dead grey colour, like week-old fish, and they blinked and then fixed on Ivan. The creature was enraged but in a cold way. He knew it would never stop until it had devoured him.

Ivan thought about weapons. Why hadn't he thought of that before? *Because it's bloody huge and has tentacles. Long ones.*

His staff was back where he'd dropped it as they came out of the portal.

It was a long shot, but probably his only chance. The monster started towards him, its tentacles reaching out and pulling it up the slope.

Ivan ducked down the back of the dune and circled around, out of sight of the creature. He hoped it wouldn't guess his route and ambush him.

When he finished his loop back and dashed towards his spear, the monster was just cresting the dune. Its tentacles whipped around angrily, and the sand behind it slimed a faint green.

Ivan picked up his staff. It was sleek, and heavy, and the pointy end of it was reasonably sharp. It was elegant, the simplest version of what a staff could be. *Or a spear.*

The shape of the portal hovered above him. It was fading, flowing out of existence, but slowly, like honey going back into a jar when it's cold.

Looking into the blackness above him, Ivan gasped. What he'd taken for a starless night sky wasn't that at all.

Huge shapes flowed above him. He made out the outlines of vast whales and manta rays, and there, on the edge of his perception, something familiar.

Sloping shoulders, shaggy fur. A giant wolf stretched above him, its paws resting on the horizon, its ears reaching almost to the dome of the sky.

Maybe I'm not entirely alone here. The thought comforted him.

A ghost of a plan formed in his mind. *I think I could open the portal again. But not for long. Hey,* he thought at the sky wolf. *I could use a little help here.*

It was too distant and too huge to tell if it had heard him. *Guess it's up to me, then.*

"Hey, ugly!" he shouted at the monster on the sand dune. "Even your mother thinks you stink!"

The creature turned, its malevolence directed at Ivan. Like him, it didn't have the power it had in his world, but that didn't matter. It was huge, with needle-sharp teeth and an endless appetite. This close, he got the shape of its thoughts, coming into his head not as words but as images. It sent him a picture of how he would die, drenched in acid in its stomach, mouthless and screaming.

Ivan felt slightly sick.

The creature advanced in a leisurely fashion. It sensed a trap, Ivan thought, and so planned to take things slowly, playing its advantage of long tentacles and vast size.

He backed a few steps, and now the trace of the portal was right above him.

Two tentacles whipped out towards him, and Ivan swept his staff in front of his body. The tentacles were both scored by the sharp end of it, green blood falling on the impossibly black sand.

An inhumanly high shriek tore out of the monster, and the tentacles whipped back. Now it was pissed.

'Ivan," Ivan whispered to himself. "If that monster comes one step closer, you're going to shove this staff right into its eye."

The edges of the portal above him glowed in his mind. It was nearly closed now. *If I die here, no one will know what happened to me.*

The thought should have devastated him, but instead, it freed him.

"Come on," he yelled at the monster. "You putrid sack of fish guts!"

He edged backwards to make the monster believe he would flee again. It was hard not to do exactly that.

The monster surged forward. Ivan backed away a few more paces, and then it was upon him.

A tentacle wrapped around his legs, and another snaked around his waist. Their grip was shockingly strong. The tentacle cinched his waist with a force that took his breath away. He smelt the oily, fishy smell of the monster's breath as it jerked him upwards.

The creature's maw opened below him, row upon row of razor-sharp teeth. Ivan caught the acrid whiff of its stomach. With his mind, he tried to open the portal to set the trap he'd planned, but the edges of it slipped from his grasp. Cold fear seeped into his chest. *This isn't going to work.*

Ivan still had hold of his spear, but the monster had his arms trapped tight against his side. *Shit.* Ivan fought to free himself, but all he could do was try and stop his ribs from being crushed.

Help! Ivan kicked his legs and struggled as the monster lowered him slowly towards its mouth.

It was toying with him, waiting for his terror to reach a fever pitch before it swallowed him. Behind the rows of teeth, he could see its dead grey mouth, folds of gelatinous flesh moist with juices to digest him.

A pitch-black shadow flashed down the dune towards them. It was wolf-shaped.

Ivan's heart hammered in sudden wild hope as the Wolf charged forward and bit deep into the monster's throat, worrying at it. Ivan heard the deep thrumming growl above the monster's high-pitched shriek.

The tentacle around his waist loosened. *Now!* Ivan fought his arm free, holding his staff tight. He drew his right arm back and sighted along it. As the monster moved to stuff him whole into its mouth, Ivan threw the staff with all his strength.

It flew straight and true. For a heart-stopping moment, Ivan thought the creature would flinch, and the staff would miss, and then it plunged straight into the monster's vast eye. With a terrible scream, it let him go, and Ivan, arms flailing, landed with his legs in its mouth.

There was a searing pain in his leg as Ivan scrabbled desperately to heave himself out of the monster's mouth. His hands found the shaft of his staff, and he hauled on it, pushing it further into the creature's eye.

The monster wailed, tentacles flurrying desperately, but Ivan was not letting go. He swung his legs clear just before the creature slammed its jaws closed. Grimly, he pushed the staff further and further into its brain. At last, the monster gave a huge shiver and was still.

Hands shaking, Ivan slid down the creature's side to the sand, its slime leaving a stinking trail on his jeans. He staggered away and collapsed onto his knees.

The world was spinning around him, faster and faster. Ivan rolled over onto his back. The huge shadow shapes swam across the sky above him, and the moment seemed to stretch out forever.

An even darker shape angled across his vision. Inky black, with sloping shoulders and a shaggy mane, the Wolf stood over him. Ivan reached up to touch its muzzle, and his fingers met thick fur. It lowered its head towards him, and its hot wolfish breath mixed with Ivan's as it licked him right on the mouth.

Ivan's face stretched in a smile as he hauled himself upright and wrapped both arms around the Wolf.

"Thank you," he whispered. "You saved my life again."

They sat there, the youth and the wolf, on black sand under a black sky, next to the wreck of an ancient monster, as giant shadow creatures wheeled overhead.

Ivan was at peace. He didn't feel the need to do anything ever again. But the Wolf stirred against him and then stood up.

"Time to go?"

The Wolf took a few steps, then looked back at him, its meaning clear.

Wearily, Ivan got to his feet. The cut on his leg burned, and his ribs ached from being squeezed by the monster's tentacles.

The Wolf led Ivan up to the fallen beast, then pointed its head to where his staff was, wedged almost entirely into its eye.

"Seriously?" said Ivan. "I gotta go back up there?"

The Wolf sat back on its haunches and waited.

"If I really have to," said Ivan. "Yrrrch."

Very gingerly, he approached the monster. Even in death, it was menacing, and Ivan found himself worried that, in the way of horror movies, it would suddenly come back to life and try to eat him again.

Cautiously, he climbed up one tentacle to stand on its vast cheek. Its skin was a rubbery bluish grey, mottled and patterned. It was, Ivan thought, almost beautiful when it wasn't trying to kill him and destroy the world.

The staff was embedded so deep in the monster's eye Ivan had just enough space to fit two hands around the haft.

He paused, ready to pull it out when something caught his attention.

The monster's eye was pallid and cloudy, but there was something reflected in it. It was a galaxy, whirling. He bent closer, trying to make sense of what he was seeing, and the galaxy came closer. Ivan lent away, and now he could see his outline and within it, the swirling stars of his world.

I guess I am an empty vessel, after all. Is this how I appear when I'm in the Shadow World?

Ivan gripped the heavy wood of the staff and pulled. It came up surprisingly smoothly, and he almost staggered back off the creature's head.

With a shlupping sound, Ivan yanked the staff free and slid back down to the sand.

"This," he brandished the staff at the Wolf, "is disgusting. Now what?"

The Wolf led him behind the creature to the spot where the portal had first opened.

Ivan gripped the staff with both hands, trying to ignore the fishy gel coating it. *Monster eye jelly. My favourite.*

The Wolf looked seriously from Ivan to the portal above. Ivan ran his fingers over the dark hardwood grain of the staff. *This came from my home. Maybe it wants to return there.*

Feeling like an utter fool, Ivan raised the staff in what he imagined was the accepted Viking spellcasting pose. The Wolf growled softly and shook itself from nose to tail.

Ivan closed his eyes and tried to feel for that still centre where he could hold two worlds in balance. He gripped the staff and concentrated on where it had come from. *This staff was once part of a tree that grew in my home world. It sent its roots down into the soil and gathered energy from our sun.*

A tug in his sternum and in his mind's eye, the portal became more solid. He *reached* into the feeling, and the doorway between the worlds cracked a little wider.

Focus. Ivan channelled all he had into the connection. Now the wood of the staff was pulling against his hands, tugging him upwards as the vortex opened. Black sand streamed past him, and his feet left the ground as the staff lifted him towards the portal.

As the vortex pulled him towards it, Ivan looked down at the Wolf, suddenly stricken.

"You're coming too, right? Please!"

The Wolf settled back on its haunches, its gaze steady. Ivan closed his eyes to stop the tears. "It's too bad," he whispered. "I thought you were going to come with me."

The Wolf seemed to nod at that, but now everything was spinning around Ivan. He flew upwards into the vortex, and the shadow world vanished in the mist. Ivan couldn't tell which way was up or down. Around him, galaxies spun, and vast shapes that were maybe whales, or giant squid, or black holes.

Now he was rushing towards the end of the tunnel, and a small voice inside told him to take a deep breath and hold it. So he did.

Smack!

Ivan arrived home straight into deep, dark water. Panicked, he flailed around. There, very far above him, was a faint green glow. *I must be about a hundred feet underwater. Shit.*

The pressure was intense, hurting his ears and pressing on his bruised chest. Ivan forced himself to slow his racing heart and resist the urge to panic. Lungs burning, he gripped the staff in one hand and started swimming up towards the surface of the ocean. is arms were heavy as lead, and his jeans tugged at him every time he kicked.

The green glow came closer, achingly slowly. His diaphragm clenched, trying to get him to take a breath.

I'm going to drown after all this. What a letdown. Ivan tried not to laugh. *Euphoria. That's a bad sign.* He was starting to feel relaxed and floaty like everything was going to be fine. In the back of his head, alarm bells were ringing. *This is how people feel just before they black out.*

Ivan tried to focus on each kick, each pull towards the surface, but darkness was already narrowing the edges of his vision.

The surface was closer now, maybe just a few metres, but Ivan knew he wasn't going to make it. *I've reached the end of the line, at last.*

His vision blinked out as night came for him.

34

Ivan awoke to the sound of the ocean and the sensation of water lapping gently at his arms and legs. He felt like a visitor in his own body, not sure if he was going to stay. He opened his eyes to see pale dawn washing the sky a delicate pink.

Gradually, he came back to himself and noticed how very cold he was and the heavy weight of exhaustion weighing him down. There was also a band of pressure around his torso, which puzzled him.

Ivan turned his head to the left. He was lying on a half-submerged wooden pallet about half a mile from the island. He turned his head to the right and found the source of the pressure on his chest.

Ida was next to him, half sitting, and she had one arm hooked across his chest to keep him from slipping back into the water.

Ivan gazed at her, coming properly awake. Her curly blonde hair was spiky from the salt water, and she'd ditched her armour.

She was wearing a white cotton tunic, which had gone slightly see-through in the ocean. Ivan pulled his gaze up to her eyes, and she raised one dark eyebrow.

"You don't even know how many fantasies you're fulfilling at this moment," said Ivan, then froze. The words had popped out of his mouth before he'd thought them through.

Ida grinned, her dark eyes laughing at him. "Just be grateful this isn't a reenactment of the final Titanic scene," she said. "As you can see, there's room for both of us on this pallet."

Ivan smiled and propped himself up on his elbows, and unfortunately, she let go of him.

"Is this pallet from the longboat float?"

"The very same. Our ship turned back into a plywood float when you disappeared."

"And Dave's truck?"

"Your guess is as good as mine."

"My guess is the bottom of the ocean."

"Probably."

Body aching, Ivan hauled himself up to a half-sitting position. And immediately dropped back down again as the pallet lurched and tried to tip them both off. His staff rolled away from him, and Ivan grabbed it before it slipped into the ocean.

"Thank you for rescuing me," he said gravely.

"You seemed to need it," she said equally gravely.

Ivan watched the waters ripple around them for a while. Words were too big an effort.

"We'd all given up on ever seeing you again," said Ida. She paused, considering. "Anders was quite upset."

Ivan noticed she didn't say how *she* felt.

"Imagine my surprise when you floated up from the depths, clutching a staff. You weren't breathing. You're lucky I keep up to date with my first aid."

"That is a good thing," said Ivan. "Did you do mouth to mouth?"

Her eyes sparkled, but she declined to answer.

Ivan spent a long moment studying the shoreline. "You're not going to demand an explanation for what happened?"

"Can you explain what happened?"

"Maybe... " said Ivan.

"Well..." Ida frowned and stared into the distance. "I don't think I want an explanation quite yet. Not yours anyway." But she said it kindly.

I'm not sure how good an explanation I could give. The exhaustion was back with a vengeance now, seeping into his bones.

Ivan realised the force that had been flowing through him since he put on Magnus's bracelet had shut off. He hadn't realised how much it had been propping him up until it was suddenly gone. *Damn.* Ivan tried to reach out for the power again, but it was like trying to grab smoke. *I don't think I've felt this tired before, ever.*

Ivan surprised himself by leaning back against Ida's shoulder.

She gave a faint snort of amusement. "Now you're just taking advantage."

"I think you have the advantage of me," said Ivan dreamily. The sky above was blurring, and a vast weight, big as the ocean, tall as the sky, was settling onto him.

I think I did find out how to hold eternity in an hour. By being scared to death, and then being so tired, I could sleep through to the end of the world. Ivan smiled at the sunrise. *This is as good as it gets. This moment, right here, right now. This is it.*

The sea lapped gently around them as Ivan gathered his thoughts together.

"Anders and Amelie are ok? And the Vikings?"

"Everyone made it out alright," said Ida. "They're on the island."

"Do we have to power kick this pallet all the way to shore? Is this kind of thing covered in the Viking manual?"

Ida laughed.

"Ivan, there is nothing even close to this covered in the Viking manual. We are so far off-manual you couldn't see it if you had a big telescope. You broke the manual."

"I see." Ivan considered. "How good is your power kicking?"

"It's pretty good, but we're not going to need it. Because I think that nice man over there is going to give us a lift."

Ivan looked at where she was pointing. It was Henrik in a small red motorboat, and he was grinning.

35

It took a while for the rescue boats to pick up all the Vikings.

Henrik dropped Ivan and Ida at the wharf, and the two of them watched him turn the boat around and head back to the island. A small crowd gathered, and Ivan saw police cars behind them.

"Do you mind if I just...slip away?" he asked Ida. "I don't want to end up in police custody again."

She looked at him. Ivan could feel her measuring him up, weighing all the options, assessing *him*.

"You may," she said finally. "I'm not done with you yet, Ivan Luca. Galen can give you my number. Call me."

"Yes, ma'am," said Ivan, then left quickly before the police could arrest him again.

As he walked through town, Ivan was surprised to find the thought of calling Ida didn't stress him out as much as these things usually would. *Maybe fighting monsters in other worlds does change a person.*

Ivan hesitated by his front door. Slowly, he unlocked and opened it. He was afraid of what he'd find - an utterly empty and silent house.

Ivan let out a deep breath and leaned his head against the doorpost. *It's empty. No Wolf.*

Feeling a hundred years old, Ivan went through into the kitchen. Gently, he opened the pantry. Inside on the floor was the faint scattering of white flour, cat biscuits, and a huge paw print. *I guess it was too much to hope the Wolf would come back.*

He reached for the place within him that formed the fulcrum between worlds and pushed. It was like trying to push a building. There was nothing there.

The morning light came through the open pantry doors and illuminated the bracelet on Ivan's wrist. The copper links glowed, but the onyx stone in the centre was cracked right through. He took off the bracelet, the cracked stone rattling in its casing as he put it on the kitchen bench.

Ivan climbed the stairs to his room to change into dry clothes. There was a tapping on his window, and he crossed to open it.

With a beat of its wings, the Raven landed on his shoulder.

"It's good to see you, too," said Ivan.

Its eyes were impenetrably black, and Ivan glimpsed a star hidden right in their depths. *I am surrounded by wonders. And I need dry clothes and coffee. Right now.*

A few minutes later, Ivan found himself sitting on the couch, staring into space. He wasn't just drained. He was *empty*.

All the strange awareness, the ability to push reality, seemed to have dried up and gone. Ivan wasn't sure how he felt about this.

Maybe it was all Magnus's doing after all. He summoned the old powers, but I was the one who could channel them. Ivan shivered. There was no way he would follow Magnus and try to gain power down *that* particular path of sacrifice and murder.

I guess that's it, then. Ivan lay back on the couch and sunk into a fitful sleep, full of restless dreams of shadow and starless skies.

Ivan woke to his phone buzzing in his pocket.

"Hello, Karl," he said.

Karl's voice was quiet on the other end. "I heard you made it back."

"How are you?" asked Ivan.

A long silence, then: "Ok, I guess. I'm at home with mum."

"Has um...has Magnus woken up yet?" said Ivan.

"Not yet," said Karl. "Police took him away in an ambulance. They say he's in a coma. They don't know if he's going to wake up."

"I think," said Ivan, "That it wouldn't have ended well either way. With Magnus. He told me he'd made a bargain after the cave fell in, and that's how the monster escaped."

There was a gusty sigh on the other end of the phone. "Yeah, I figured that too."

"I'm sorry," said Ivan.

"What for? My father chose his path. He was a real bastard to live with too."

"Will you be ok?" said Ivan. "And your mother?" *And Owen...*

"We will be," said Karl. "I'll make sure of it."

"Let me know if there's anything you need," said Ivan. It was a trite, formulaic statement, but he tried to invest it with sincerity. "I mean it."

"I know," said Karl and hung up.

Ivan got up, stretched, and went into the kitchen. He heard the click of the front gate closing and peered out the kitchen window to see a small delegation coming down the path: Anders, Ida, Amelie and Galen.

Half an hour later, Ivan was on his third coffee, and the rest of his friends were on their second. None of his friends had asked Ivan what had happened after he disappeared. *Maybe they don't clearly remember last night.*

He wasn't sure how this made him feel—relieved, maybe. Lonely, yes. But he felt a huge reluctance to bring up his part in the night's events. Maybe later, with just Anders. *Though if Anders doesn't remember what happened, that might be worse.*

"How did you go down at the police station?" he asked.

"They weren't very happy with us," said Ida. "We spent an age being 'processed.' That means tons of paperwork. Galen had to do a lot of apologising. Luckily the property damage wasn't as bad as we'd thought, and it was only over at the football club."

"Magnus still hadn't woken up by the time we left," said Anders. "The robed guys were being proper tossers, and that made us look good in comparison. Then Benioff shows up, and suddenly Magnus and the robed guys are being taken away by some serious police, and we're being shown the door. I was well pleased to get out of there."

"What did you tell them?" asked Ivan.

"Police expect you to lie, so why disappoint them," said Ida.

"I said there was a gas leak, and everything went kind of hazy after that," said Anders.

"Boring, yet effective," said Ida. "It was Benioff who got us out, though. We'd still be getting quizzed or sitting in a holding cell if she hadn't pulled some strings. I have the feeling she's been given a rather sudden promotion. "

"Proper X-files stuff," said Anders, sipping his coffee. "Nothing more to see here, folks."

When Ivan returned with his fourth coffee, they were all teasing Galen about how this was the best Vikon event ever and too bad the town would never have them back.

Galen looked pained. "The clan board back home are going to grill me even worse than the police. And Dave's still sore about his truck," he said.

Ida shrugged. "We'll make it up to him, somehow. A Viking longboat, perhaps?"

Then they all turned to Ivan.

"Umm..." he said.

The silence dragged on.

Ida rescued him. She lowered her fierce eyebrows at him, then smiled. "If you don't want to talk about it, that's ok, Ivan. Just know we're here when you're ready. Just checking, though—the tentacle monster isn't going to show up any time soon?"

"God, I hope not," muttered Galen.

Ivan shook his head. "It's dead." Anders was gathering himself to launch a barrage of questions until Amelie shot him a look. Ivan relaxed. His friends remembered everything, they were just giving him space to tell them in his own time. A warmth bloomed in the general area of his chest.

"I..." he said. He tried again. "There's this place. I don't know where. Another world, maybe. The sand glows black, and there are no stars in the sky. I ran away from the monster for a while, then waited for it where the portal was. I let it catch me, and," he swallowed, "it was going to eat me. Then the Wolf appeared. That world is where it's from, I think. It distracted the monster, and I got my arms free and javelined my staff right into its eye."

Amelie made a face. Ida grinned.

"Savage..." breathed Anders.

"But," and this bit was hard. "I don't think I can do *things* anymore." He waggled his fingers in the air, ignoring Amelie's smirk. "It's gone. It must have been all to do with Magnus and his mad rituals after all. Plus, the bracelet broke."

Anders made a disappointed face. "That's a downer. I thought we were going to have magical adventures from now on."

Ida looked at Ivan, her head cocked to one side. "I wouldn't be too sure about it being gone. Maybe you just don't understand how it all works."

"Yeah, well," Ivan shrugged uncomfortably. "That's true, I guess. It feels gone, though."

"You're a real Viking now, Ivan," said Galen. "And our clan proved themselves in battle. With a bit of encouragement."

"You mean you shouted at them a lot," said Ida.

"What happened to your Raven?" said Amelie. "It flew off after you disappeared."

"It's roosting over there in the kitchen," said Ivan. "On top of the fridge."

"Ravens don't roost," said Ida. "That's owls."

"I think any birds can roost," said Amelie.

"Only at night," said Ida.

Galen sighed. "I don't think I'll be able to enjoy Viking gatherings in quite the same way after this."

"Maybe you should get more serious about your axe fighting technique," suggested Ida. Galen just sighed again.

"We'd better get going," said Ida. "In fact," she checked at her watch, "my ride will be leaving soon." She stood, pulling Galen up after her. "Back to London we go." She looked down at Ivan. "You better call me, Raven boy."

Ida left with a cheery wave, and Galen trailed after her, grumbling about board meetings.

Anders gave Ivan a sidelong look. "London, eh?"

"I saw a university application on your table," said Amelie. "One you haven't sent in yet. An application for Regents University." She stretched her arms out in front of her, cracking her knuckles. "You're in luck, Ivan. I will help you."

"You can relax now, bro. Amelie aces these things," said Anders. "She got me into a course that was already full. It's her superpower." He leaned back on the couch and gazed into the future. "We'll all get a flat in London."

"One that takes Ravens," said Ivan. The Raven opened one eye and blinked at them.

"And remember," said Anders, "Ida's in London."

He's not going to let that one go in a hurry.

"That sounds good," said Ivan. And it really did.

There's just one other person who will want to debrief me. Sure enough, there was a knock at the door.

The response from the others was immediate. Anders stiffened, looking for exits, and Amelie's hand twitched towards her concealed gun.

But Ivan took his cue from the Raven, who cocked its head, listened, and then shut its eyes again.

"I'll go get it," he said.

Ivan walked down the hall to the front door.

Through the dimpled glass was the shape of a single figure. Taking a deep breath, Ivan turned the handle and swung the door open.

Detective Benioff stood outside.

"Hello Ivan," she said.

"Would you like to come in?"

"I'm not a vampire, Ivan. I don't need your invitation. If I wanted to come in, I would. Possibly with a warrant card and backup."

He settled back on his heels. "Have you come across vampires before?"

Feathers brushed his neck as the Raven swooped in to land on his shoulder. Benioff's eyes brightened at that. *She likes Ravens. That's a good sign.*

She studied him intently for some sort of clue—he wasn't sure what.

"What were you doing earlier?"

"Sleeping on the couch," said Ivan. He suddenly felt that's what he would like to do again despite four cups of coffee. "Seriously though, would you like to come in and have a coffee?"

Benioff relaxed against the door frame, and her police-ness slowly evaporated. Now she looked like he felt: drained but still buzzing slightly.

"Thanks, Ivan, but I've already downed three cups of police coffee, a substance so vile it's criminal. I also have enormous amounts of paperwork to do. It doesn't help that the principal in the case, Magnus, is still in a coma. It's slightly more helpful that his close associates are willing to swear he was injured in an 'occult accident' possibly involving a gas explosion and an evil entity from another dimension. They're denouncing him for everything up to and including human sacrifice while somehow still believing they can avoid jail time themselves." She shrugged one shoulder a little stiffly. "It's almost heartening, their belief in the stupidity of the police."

"Did you get the guy who shot you?"

"In custody, and he's being very cooperative. Unlike some witnesses, I might mention." She raised one perfectly manicured eyebrow at him.

Ivan said nothing. Warning bells were ringing in the back of his head. *Just because she helped you fight an eldritch monster doesn't mean she won't arrest you now.*

"It would make my job much easier if everything after the part where a monster appeared from the sky, and we all took off on a magical Viking boat remained..." She searched for the right words.

"Off the record," said Ivan.

"Exactly," said Benioff. "My career is already on shaky ground. I don't want to add mass hallucinations and dissolving under pressure to the laundry list of issues."

"Will your career be alright?" he asked.

She looked pensive, and then her mouth curved up in a smile that made her look sixteen. "Oddly enough, I think it will. Someone high up seems keen to keep this under wraps, and even stranger, doesn't want to sweep me under the carpet as well."

Ivan wanted to ask whether this meant he was off the hook but decided to keep his mouth shut.

"And?" he said instead.

"And I am due some vacation days, so I'm going to take a nice trip to the seaside. NOT this seaside. Somewhere hot and sunny. With no tentacled monsters. Maybe Ibiza."

"That sounds good."

She turned to go, then paused for a moment.

"Ivan?" she said, and he waited, wondering what she was going to say.

"It's been fun." Benioff stepped forward and gently patted his cheek. It felt like a promise, and it made his face buzz like he'd been given an electric shock.

Ivan didn't even try to maintain composure. He just stared wide-eyed at her as she walked jauntily back up the path, waving him a languid salute without turning round. The gate clicked as it closed, and she was gone.

"Well," said Ivan.

The Raven looked at him, and as usual, gazing into its pure black eyes, he had no idea what it was thinking.

"Well," said Ivan again. "I think that just about wraps it up." The Raven's eye twinkled, a tiny star shining bright in its depths. Ivan grinned back.

It was going to be a good summer.

...AND THEN WHAT HAPPENED?

For a free short story about what the Raven did in London that summer, go to:

www.ShadowKingdomBooks.com

Printed in Great Britain
by Amazon